Last Letter
from
Istanbul

Lucy Foley divides her time between the UK and the Middle East – much of this novel was written in a garden in Tehran – and she also spends the year travelling around the world for research and inspiration. Lucy studied English Literature at Durham and UCL universities and then worked for several years as a fiction editor in the publishing industry, during which time she also wrote her debut novel, *The Book of Lost and Found*. Lucy now writes full-time and is currently working on her next book.

Also by Lucy Foley

The Book of Lost and Found
The Invitation

Last Letter *from* Istanbul

LUCY FOLEY

HarperCollins*Publishers*

HarperCollins*Publishers* Ltd
1 London Bridge Street,
London SE1 9GF

www.harpercollins.co.uk

First published by HarperCollins*Publishers* 2018
1

A catalogue record for this book is available from the British Library

ISBN: 978-0-00-816907-7 (HB)
ISBN: 978-0-00-819595-3 (TPB)

MIX
Paper from
responsible sources
FSC
www.fsc.org   FSC C007454

This book is produced from independently certified FSC™ paper
to ensure responsible forest management.
For more information visit: www.harpercollins.co.uk/green

To Al, always my first reader.
I love you.

VICTORIOUS ALLIES IN CONSTANTINOPLE!

Today, November 13, 1918, the Occupation of Constantinople began. The vanquished Ottoman Empire, which ill-advisedly threw its lot in with the German campaign, must now yield to a victorious Allied force.

British ships entered the famed Golden Horn, having travelled through the Dardanelles on Tuesday – passing right by the fateful beaches of the infamous battle of Gallipoli three years ago. A disaster for Allied forces, perhaps, but also for the then victorious Ottoman army. It was upon these same beaches that it spent the flower of its youth, a loss from which it would never recover.

Reaching the famous Golden Horn, forces numbering nearly 3,000 British, some 500 French, and 500 Italian soldiers landed immediately and occupied military barracks, hotels, houses, Italian and French schools, and hospitals. There these men will remain until the Allied administrative machine can be set up and the requisitioning of private homes begins, and order can be restored to this war-beleaguered city. These men will not return to their families like the vast majority of their soldierly compatriots. Instead they will remain thousands of miles from home in execution of this noble endeavour.

THE ENEMY ENTERS STAMBOUL

Today, November 13, 1918, enemy ships arrived in our great city, flower of our Empire. This move by the so-called Allies is in express contradiction to promises that they would not seek an occupation of Ottoman lands. Fortunately the Ottoman people have long ago learned to doubt the word of our Western European counterparts.

Men, women and children observed the advancing ships from the banks of our beloved Golden Horn, sorrow in their hearts. Some of those men had fought a valiant battle in 1915 against the 'Allies' on the shores of Gallipoli, losing many comrades in the process but emerging from the conflagration with victory and great honour. To see their vanquished enemy follow them here, ready to lay claim to their city and requisition their homes if the fancy should take them, is the greatest imaginable indignity.

PART ONE

CONSTANTINOPLE

1921

THREE YEARS OF ALLIED OCCUPATION

Nur

Early morning. In a room above the dockyards of the Bosphorus, a woman sleeps. Her hair, a long black skein of it, has tangled itself about her in the rough seas of the night. She forgot to tie it back as she usually does. Too tired. Above her head an arm is flung in a bodily abandon never shown by day. Her fingers splay, her palm open as though in supplication.

Quiet, save for the self-important ticking of a clock: a dark wood, rather brutish affair. MADE IN ENGLAND. It is conspicuous, perhaps, because there is so little furniture in the room beside it and the low divan with its sleeping human cargo. There *was* furniture: one can still see the darker impressions upon the floor which the sunlight has not yet been able to fade. Of rugs, too, far finer than the rather workaday affair that remains. *Kilim* from Anatolia, s*oumak* from Persia.

The sun is coming. It crests over the sward of green on the opposite bank of the Bosphorus, and smooths itself across the water like so much spread butter. Now it touches Europe. In the space of a few minutes it has spanned two continents; a daily miracle. It gilds the ugly mechanical detritus of the docks. It reaches the room with its sleeper. In the fetid air another small miracle occurs: the suspended layer of dust becomes a dancing mass of fine gold particles.

No matter how frequently this apartment is cleaned, the dust remains. It may be to do with the age of the building, or the fact that it is entirely made from wood that over the years has weathered days of rain, broiling heat, frost and snow. Has shrunk and grown and warped and breathed, active as the living thing it once was.

Now the light has slunk up onto the bedclothes, finds sleeping toes beneath a funnel of material. A pattern of embroidered pomegranate, inexpertly but vividly done. The colours are almost a match for the real fruits that will ripen on the trees in a garden across the water. The red seeds of the split fruits become a pattern, marching along the border of the quilt; gold thread forms the fibrous strands between them.

Now the light reaches the tangled strands of hair. In the shade they appeared black – now they reveal themselves as various shades of brown, caught in places as bright as that gold thread. The light gathers itself for the final occupation: advancing up the neck, the fine bones of the jaw, the slightly open mouth, the prow of the nose, the eyelids . . .

Nur wakes. Pink light. She opens her eyes. White. She sits up, groggy, wipes her mouth. A restless night's sleep. What woke her, in the small hours? A bad dream. She cannot recall the details now. The more she grasps at them the faster they sink, like creatures burrowing into sand. She is left only with the feeling of it, a lingering unease. More unsettling, this not-knowing. She rises, looks at the day. Across the flat rooftops she can just make out the water, a coruscation of light. She will shake this feeling from her by breakfast, she is certain. For what can there be to upset one on a morning like this?

Oh. A pause. *Something is missing*. Now it happens to her, as it does every morning. The remembering of all that has changed. She feels the knowledge resettle itself upon her shoulders – familiar, almost reassuringly so. For at least now she has found it again, knows the weight of it. It is far worse than the invention of any mere bad dream.

In the next room, someone is making coffee. The scent of it is like the day itself; intimations of warmth and comfort. She can hear the particular musical note of the copper pot as it strikes the stove. She thrusts her feet into her worn *babouches*, shuffles out into the corridor. Leaning up, chin just clearing the top of the stove where the pot exhales a dangerous plume of steam, is a small figure. The boy. He looks up at her, caught between pride and guilt. Then he smiles.

She cannot quite bring herself to be angry with him. The boy is like a different child from that of two years ago. Often, in that time, she would find him in the mornings lying upon his back with his eyes open, and wonder if they had ever closed, or if he had merely spent the night watching a projection of horrors upon the ceiling. He began to eat, at least. But there was something mechanical in it, the way he took the food and chewed, and swallowed, and opened his mouth for the next bite. It was a keeping alive, the pure instinct of an organism.

For a long while there had been no glimmer of the boy he had been. She wondered if that child had sunk completely from view – never to return. There were things that could change a person absolutely. And in childhood one was more malleable, more impressionable; the change might be all the more devastating.

She takes her cup up onto the flat roof of the building. This is her secret place; she does not think any of the other inhabitants of the apartment block know of it. Here the day cannot touch her yet. She is mistress of it. The morning is clear, still cool. But there is the promise of heat. The water is eloquent. There is a shimmer of warmth on the horizon, too, the clouds massing above are saffron-coloured.

She takes a sip of coffee. He has made it well, far better than her grandmother, who thinks herself above the making of coffee and always burns it.

The day is still as a painting. It is hard to imagine that down there is movement, chaos. But she can hear it: the waking sounds of the streets, the call of the milk seller, the faraway shouts of stevedores on the quay, the fishermen beginning to hawk the catch of the day. From a short distance away the rattle and whine of a tram. From the nearby district of Pera, some two hundred yards to the west, there comes the thin wail of a violin – relic of a night's revelries.

Before, she never considered this area, Tophane, as somewhere one might live. It was a nowhere – an afterthought, clinging to the coattails of the great city, a place where the different neighbourhoods inevitably met up with one another, their great streets coming together like so many loose ends of string.

She looks beyond the quays, to the great sweep of the Bosphorus, spotted with warships. From up here they seem miniature, as though she might sweep them back out to sea with the flat of her hand. Below are represented three of the four languages she has in her possession. A dimly imagined peacetime future of tranquil pursuits – of Paris, London, Rome; the reading of European Literature.

The beginning of the occupation. The storm of their boots against the cobblestones. A hundred eyes observing from behind shutters in what might seem to the uninitiated like an empty street: old women, young women, hating them, fearing them. The gun turrets of the huge ugly ships in the Golden Horn swivelling toward the city's ancient glories – the Aya Sofia, Süleymaniye, Sultanahmet. A threat unspoken, yet deafening.

Those first nights like a held breath.

And they said *there would not be an occupation*. They had promised it. The British, the French, the Italians – at the Armistice that ended the Great War. Even those who have never read a newspaper, even those who cannot read *at all*, know this. Know, now, not to trust them in anything.

The new indignities, stinging like a slap: men ordered to remove the red fezzes they had worn for as long as they could remember. Women leered at, somehow all the more so if they were wearing the veil.

Up here, on the roof, this was where she had sat, hidden from view, as soldiers of the British army marched through the streets below. Snatches of speech floated up:

'Living like animals . . .'

and

'Their women little better than whores, really . . .'

and

'A man here can take as many wives as he likes . . .'

and

'You might be in luck, Clarkson, if the ladies don't have a say in it . . .'

and

'Just look at the state of this place. No wonder they lost.'

Would they have been so loud, if they had known that they were being listened to and understood? She suspected – and this was the most insulting probability – that they would not have cared. The city was theirs for the taking. They even have their own name for it: *Constantinople*. This other name is from the realm of officialdom, of mapmakers. İstanbul: that is what people call it. That is how she has always known it, that is the place in which she grew up, familiar, beloved. But the rules are made by others now.

As those men had continued with their insults she had crawled to the edge of the rooftop, making sure to stay hidden from view. She had tilted the cup of coffee she held in her hand, and allowed a few hot drops to fall. The whim of a moment; but they fell as though she had planned her target perfectly. A fat lieutenant, removing his cap for a few seconds to scratch his bald pate. The almost perceptible sizzle as the scalding liquid made contact with the sensitive skin. His howl shrill as one of the street cats.

But those were more courageous days. Murmurings of resistance. Brave words, rebel words: they would undermine them at every turn; they would set fire to their storehouses, they would defy the curfew, they would spit in their faces. But then the indignity became commonplace. A numbness, setting in. The business of living got in the way, that was it. By silent agreement, all seemed to decide that the best form of resistance was not with outward mutiny but to continue as though absolutely nothing had happened. They would defy their enemy by ignoring the presence of khaki in the streets, the armada in the Golden Horn. With the exception of a few, that is, who work in the shadows plotting real destruction and death for the invaders.

Now she looks beyond the Bosphorus, to the opposite

shore, to the dark green hillside of another continent. Asia. The few dwellings visible amidst the trees are as intricate and delicate as paper cut-outs. Among them is a white house, more beautiful than all the rest.

She is filled with longing. Familiar, but condensed this morning, as strong as she has ever felt it. Something occurs to her. Why not, she thinks? What possible harm can come of it?

She calls down to the boy, 'I have to drop some embroideries off with Kemal Bey.'

'I could come with you?'

'No.' She has a second destination in mind for the morning, now, and she must go there alone.

'But I love it at the bazaar.'

'Yes, I know you do. But you're like a cat following a scent there. Last time you wandered as far as the Spice Market before I realised you had disappeared.' The memory of that moment brings with it a reverberation of the panic she had felt. She shrugs it away. He is here, he is safe, she will not let it happen again. 'Besides,' she says, 'you have some reading to do, I think?'

He casts a longing look through the window at the sunlit streets. 'It's so warm outside.'

'You can read outside, then, in the sun.'

He opens his mouth, meets her gaze, closes it. She is many different things to him now. But at such times, first and foremost, she is his schoolteacher.

Almost a lifetime later

The Traveller

Early morning. November. Cold so that the breath steams, blue-cold like a veil drawn over everything. This is one of the first trains out of the station. The place is thronged with people despite the hour. There is already a small queue for newspapers and cigarettes at the *tabac* kiosk. The platform is already crowded. Good, I like watching people. Above me soar ribs of iron, the vaulted skeleton of some industrial age monster. A lofty, echoing space: temple to speed and efficiency.

There was another station, like this. A long while ago.

There are businessmen in uniform grey, bound for Lausanne, perhaps. At a glance they all appear mould-made, hatted and shod from the same outfitters. Many are reading papers. The latest news: nuclear tests, Russian spy rings, anti-Vietnam demonstrations. All of it the story of the now. I wonder what use they make of me, an oldish man with an even older suitcase. Or what they would make of the pages I hold, so many decades out of date. The two articles, the British and Turkish, are clipped together. I have read them many times; certain phrases are known by rote. *Noble endeavour. Greatest imaginable indignity.* Somewhere between them, these few terse paragraphs, is the beginning of the story. The key by which a whole life might be understood.

Funny how similar they are, these clippings: though I am sure their writers would have been appalled to know it. Two halves of a whole? The face and its reflection in the mirror – every detail reversed but essentially the same. Or the two poles of a magnet: fated to forever repel.

Us — Them.

East — West.

Somewhere in the middle: me.

Now I watch an elegant couple a few feet away. He is a few years older than she. She wears a powder pink coat, a pale shock against the grey of the businessmen and the day itself. He is in dark blue, as though his outfit is intended to provide a foil to hers, to allow it to take centre stage. They might be newlyweds, I think, off for a honeymoon in the mountains. Or they might be having a liaison; running away. There is something about the way they look at each other that suggests the latter. Snatched and hungry. A memory comes. Not crisp and whole, sharp-focused, to be replayed in the mind like a scene from a film, but consisting mainly of sensation, atmosphere.

I must be staring: the man glances straight at me, and I am caught out. I have seen something that was not meant for me – not meant for anyone other than two co-conspirators.

I prop my suitcase on the bench beside me: the leather worn into paleness at the corners.

I open it, to return the newspaper clippings to their place within. As I do I block the contents from the view of the crowd with my body; a protective instinct. Some of the baggage within, you see, is rather unorthodox. Inside my suitcase alongside my toothbrush, my change of clothes, my shaving accoutrements, I carry fragments of the past. If one of my fellow passengers has caught a glimpse of the contents they might think I am an odd sort of travelling salesman, specialising in antique curios. They might wonder exactly who I would think might have any interest in buying such items. They have no value in and of themselves. Their value as relics, as evidence, however, is infinite. They are clues as to how a brief interlude in the past shaped an entire future. So it seemed only right that I should bring them with me, these talismans, upon this journey.

The train is pulling into the station now. There is the inevitable panicked surge, as if my fellow passengers fear there won't be space for them, though they hold tickets stamped with seat numbers. I find I am momentarily transfixed. For the first time, I realise what it is that I am doing. I have always been this way, I suppose: acting immediately, considering – regretting – at leisure. But suddenly, now, I am fearful. If I get on that train I sense that my life will change again in a way I cannot anticipate.

A reframing of the story, the same one that was broken off so many years ago, never permitted its proper conclusion. I am suddenly unsure.

The platform around me is emptying. A horn sounds, ominously. I have perhaps thirty seconds.

A hiss of releasing brakes. And then I am hurtling myself

toward the train, case rattling behind, before the gaping passengers.

In through the door that the conductor is just pulling closed, into the warm car.

The Boy

From the window he watches Nur *hanım* leave, rounding the end of the alleyway onto the larger thoroughfare with its thronging crowd. Funny, she always seems to him such a powerful person. But now he sees that compared to other adults she is not large at all. In fact she is dwarfed by many of them, and by the great bag of embroideries at her hip that causes her to stagger slightly beneath its weight. In some complicated way this worries him. He watches her now as though his gaze were a cloak that might keep her from harm, until she is lost to sight.

He knows exactly what he will do now, and it does not involve reading his schoolbooks.

* * *

He is hungry all the time. When the war came the city forgot how to feed the people that lived in it. Once food was everywhere. A different smell around every street corner: the sweet yeast of *simits*, piled high and studded with seeds, the brine of stuffed mussels cooked on a brazier, of fried mackerel stuffed into rolls of bread, the aroma of burned sugar drifting from the open door of a *pastane*, even the savoury, insubordinate tang of boiled sheep's heads.

Sometimes it was enough to merely breathe in these scents, so powerful that if one came close enough it was almost like tasting them. Sometimes one found it necessary to part with a few emergency *piastres* – only to be used in the case of *direst need* – and share a warm *simit* with one's friends on the way to school.

The pride with which the sellers displayed their wares: fresh-shelled almonds arranged by the *bademci* – the almond seller – upon a shimmering cake of ice; the sour green plums, that one could only eat for twenty days of the year, carefully arranged in small paper bags. A towering pyramid of plump tomatoes, smelling and tasting of the sun itself.

When the war came, these vanished. Not at once. In the first weeks there was just a little less. The street food went first, fading from the city like the detail from an old painting. Then the bakeries. In the beginning the bread was a day old. Then a week, then two weeks. Then it disappeared altogether.

In the burned place he did not eat for three days. He stayed in the dark, and waited for it to take him. When she found him he could not have walked out of there on his own – he hadn't the energy to lift his head from the floor. Now it is like the hunger has found its way deep inside him, has put down roots. Even now, when there is more to eat, even now it remains. Even after he has eaten it is there, gnawing at his insides. He thinks about food constantly; he dreams of it.

The other women are in the other room: the old one, and the one who never speaks. From beneath the door comes the scent of tobacco. It smells of burned things. It speaks of the time before. He will not think of that. The important thing is that they are busy. This leaves him free to explore the kitchen.

These searches are never particularly rewarding. An old onion, perhaps, aged to softness. Eaten like an apple. The memory of it in the mouth had the exact odour of a man's sweat. Or perhaps a heel of bread, with a white-green bloom of mould. Cobwebs, too, if it has fallen into some hard-to-reach place from which only an arm as thin as his can extract it.

But now, reaching further into the dark recess than ever before, his fingers brush a new object. He draws it out, mildly curious. A book. This is not of any particular interest; it cannot be eaten. Books are school, and difficulty. In its favour, though, is the fact that it had been discovered by him alone.

'Hello,' he says.

There is mystery attached to it. He takes it into the patch of light spilling from the street lamp to look at it. It is home-made, not printed, written in a hand somehow familiar to him. No pictures – this is a disappointment. He has little time for words. He knows that he is clever, but words can outwit him, can shift before his very eyes.

He stares at it for a few minutes, hardly bothering to puzzle it out, ready to give it up as a bad job. Then a word makes itself familiar to him, as though the light itself has drawn its meaning up out of the page. *Chicken*. His mouth floods with saliva. He goes to the next word. *Walnuts*. It is already, thanks to these two words, the most interesting book he has ever come across.

Concentrating intently, frustrated by his own slowness, he puzzles out the rest of it. *Paprika* – he knows that, the bright

19

powder made from peppers. The words, he begins to realise, describe a larger whole. A dish. *Chicken with Walnuts and Paprika.* He can imagine it, yes. He closes his eyes and summons the flavours with a great effort of imagination. The tender flesh of the meat, the bitter of the nuts, the sweet smoke of the spice.

The idea of the dish in his head is a kind of pleasurable agony. It is almost as good as eating it. Of course, one does not have the fullness in the belly afterward. But he hardly ever has that anyway, cannot remember a time when he has felt fully sated by what he has been given to eat.

Now the magic of this imagined meal is used up.

He turns the page, to discover the next delight. *Chicken* – easy, he had the shape of the word in his mind now. *Chicken with . . .* he squints at the word. *Figs.* That is the best time of the year, when the tree in the schoolyard yields its fruit. In the time of worst hunger they had been everything to him. Less filling than bread, but more so than the aubergine skins he had scavenged from the bins. There are two kinds: white and purple. The latter are bigger but the white are finer-flavoured. Tiny, fragrant morsels. They are his favourite. Unfortunately they are the birds' favourite too. He was almost tearful with frustration, upon leaving lessons, to discover that they had got to so many of them before him. And they were so wasteful. They would eat part of a fruit, and leave the rest hanging upon the branch to dry out or rot. They would scatter half of what they stole upon the ground. He would eat these remains, or collect them in his pockets.

He reads on, his mouth wet with longing, his stomach protesting, his mind filling with impossible fantasies.

Nur

There are difficult negotiations with the linen buyer. 'Every week I have another woman coming to me with a story like yours, *hanım*. Great families who have lost everything, fallen on poor times. And all their work is beautiful.'

'But I came to you first – that must count for something?'

He seems not to have heard. 'The Russians! They come to me straight from the ships laden with great bundles on their backs: silks from Paris, the finest cashmere shawls. They are such poor wretches now: no homeland, no future. You must count yourself lucky. There are others who are far more unfortunate. We have all lost a great deal.'

It is true. Every day new inhabitants arrive, fleeing the ongoing consequences of the Great War, the revolution in Russia. Dispossessed, desperate. Regular flurries of chaos at the quays: vast carriers arriving with human cargo. Some filtered into the system of Allied camps. Others absorbed by the city, disappearing with little trace. But she hopes that he sees the long look she gives his stall, occupying four times the space it once did; the smartly refurbished sign with its gilt lettering, the beautiful new silver samovar from which he has declined to offer her any tea.

As she leaves the bazaar she sees the Allied soldiers, buying trinkets. It is not enough for them to have occupied this place; they want to take a piece of it back with them. A souvenir. A war trophy. Exotic, but harmless, like a muzzled dancing bear. Her linens will be stowed in trunks, will make the long journey back across the breadth of Europe to decorate sideboards and tables in houses in London and Paris. She likes, in more optimistic moments, to think of this as a colonisation of her own.

Their uniforms are clean but she sees them drenched in blood. How many men have you killed, she asks, silently, of some sunburned boy as he holds a fake lump of amber up to the light with an unconvincingly expert air. And you? – of the fat officer fingering women's sequinned *babouches* – did you slaughter my husband, at Gallipoli? My brother, in the unknown wasteland in which we lost him?

She thinks of Kerem, her lost brother, every day. There are reminders of him, everywhere – particularly in the schoolroom where it should be he who stands in front of the pupils, not her. But it is more visceral than that: it exists in her as a deep, specific ache, as though she has lost some invisible but vital part of herself.

With the loss of her husband, it is different. She can go whole days without thinking of Ahmet – and then remember with a guilty start. It is not that she does not care, she has to remind herself. It is that all of it – him, herself as a bride and then briefly as a wife, the night that followed – all seem abstract, intangible as a dream. Once she found herself rooting through the chest of clothes in the apartment, desperate to find her wedding outfit. She thought the sight of it might make her feel the grief she was supposed to feel. Because she grieves him only as she might the loss of a stranger. But then that was what he had been – even in those two weeks as husband and wife before he left for the front. When she thinks of Ahmet she thinks, with genuine sadness: how terrible for his mother. What a waste of young life. She does not think of it, not at first, in relation to herself. What sort of a widow does that make her?

On the ferry back she stays on past the stop at Tophane where she would normally disembark for home. As they cross the great channel of the Bosphorus she watches the shore of Asia approach and feels her skin prickle like someone about to commit a crime. Upon the opposite bank, growing visible now, is the white house.

She should not do this. She knows no good can come of it. A destructive thing. This instinct of hers, however, has overwhelmed reason.

The worst thing was that they took it, and did not use it. The final insult, to leave it gathering dust, like the skeleton of one denied the burial rites.

Her father – in his whimsical way – once described the house as a woman who had lain down beside the water for a rest that had become endless slumber. This idea, as with certain things heard in childhood, ignited in her mind. Even now she cannot help but see the sleeper, the cluster of trees that form her wild dark hair, the small jetty her hand trailing through the water. Nur feels, looking at her, a sense of betrayal. What luxury might it have been, to have slept through all of this without the least concern? She feels the same way about the stray cats she feeds. When she sees the tortoiseshell tom stretch himself out on the sun-kindled tiles of the roof opposite she knows that she is witnessing a contentment that for any human, especially one living here, would be impossible to obtain.

Her eyes never leave the house. As the ferry shudders its way toward the dock of the station she is certain that she catches a movement in one of the downstairs windows. This is impossible, of course – it must have been a reflection. It has remained empty, useless, all this time. Still, the animal part of her mind has been worried by it, and she finds herself watching for more movement. She thinks it was in the *haremlik*, the women's quarters, the domain over which her grandmother presided like a queen. Well. There are so many memories confined in there that perhaps she really did see some flicker of the past.

As she alights, she feels exposed on the quay, imagining how she might appear to someone who knows her, what they would guess of her mission. That they might pity her – that is the worst of it. Far worse, certainly, than the censure they had shown previously. Her dead father's innocence has been all but proven by the fact that the occupiers have done nothing to recognise or reward the family. What more did they have to lose to prove their support for the cause? A son lost, a daughter widowed . . . what more had to be sacrificed before they were considered free of suspicion?

For the first time in a long while she rather longs for her veil, for the shield of it. She keeps her head lowered, and at the same time detests her own cowardice. There is nothing shameful in what she is doing, only a little sad.

The path to the house, the private one through the trees and bushes immediately beside the water, has been exposed. Nur would have thought the thicket would have closed itself around it by now in an impenetrable tangle. In fact, had some self-preserving part of her hoped that she would be forced to turn back at this point? Now she must continue with the thing, see it through.

Here, too, are unexpected assaults of memory: scents of

wild fig, olive, blue mint, bracken, mingling with the brine of the water. A pressure in her chest, a knot of tears that will not be shed, that cannot be relieved.

There is less magic in it up close than viewed from the water. Now visible are the places where the white paint is beginning to peel from the old grey wood beneath, how the elderly balconies sag with the weight of more than a century, that in the eaves of the roof are the fragile remains of birds' nests from years gone by. Yet these flaws, for Nur, are as tenderly observed as those in the face of a loved one.

She is close enough now that she can hear the effect of the water in the boathouse, the strange echoes: the gargle and slap. The accompaniment to hours sitting on the little jetty reading a book, casting a line out to catch fish as her father had taught her – she was better at it than her brother. When she did land one, however small and spiny, Fatima would take great care to serve it at the next meal, transformed with lemon and parsley and tender cooking over fragrant wood. As a child she had sat on that platform with her ankles and feet submerged in the water, instantly cooling on a hot day. She is caught by the idea of it, it grows inside her. There is no one here to see. She makes her way down the stone steps, onto the wood of the platform, lowers herself until she is sitting, slips off her shoes and extends her bared feet into the water.

Sometimes, now, the old life seems as remote as one read about in a book. But this afternoon it seems very close at hand, an assault of memory. If she refuses to look at the great grey warships marshalled further downstream she can almost persuade herself that she is sitting here suspended in her past.

How old is she? She thinks. She is in control of this fantasy, she can choose. Twelve. The time before anything became complicated. Before talk of marriage, or propriety, before illness and death. She has just climbed a tree . . . it has left her hands and feet sticky with sap. She will wash them, here, in the waters of the Bosphorus before she casts out her fishing line.

The older women will be sitting in the women's quarters, the *haremlik*, after a lunch of several courses. Perhaps they have friends visiting them from the city, in Parisian gowns that sit oddly with their veils. Or perhaps they have come from further afield, from Anatolia, traditional in loose silks, their fingernails stained with red dye. By now they will be deep in gossip. Or perhaps they have summoned a female *miradju* to entertain them all with tall tales. Most of these professional storytellers rely upon a carefully honed set of stories, most known fairly well to their listeners, yet still pleasing because of the unique style and flourishes of the teller. But the very best of them can invent narrative upon the spot, conjuring people and places straight from the imagination.

Once Nur told her mother that her greatest ambition was to become one of these women – and received a lecture on the importance of knowing one's class. These women were still salespeople – no better than the *simit* sellers or the rag women – even if their currency was words.

Footsteps, behind her. Her father, come to join her in her fishing. Or perhaps he has brought with him the backgammon set, inlaid with ebony, ivory and mother-of-pearl. She turns.

Behind her, at the top of the steps, stands a man in a white robe, a pipe dangling precariously from his open mouth. A lit match burns unattended in his hand, forgotten in his surprise.

'By Jove,' he says, stepping quickly backward. And then, as the flame from the match climbs high enough to lick his fingers, 'Ouch!'

An Englishman, half-dressed, here on the Asian side of the water. None of this makes any sense to Nur: she thought, hoped, that they were confined to Pera. He stares, she stares back. They are like two street cats, she thinks, watching one another warily.

'By Jove,' he says again, under his breath, as though the important thing is to say something – that by doing so he will wrest some control over the situation. Nur is standing, attempting to retrieve her slippers with furtive movements of her feet. She risks another quick glance. She has never seen an Englishman – indeed any man – dressed in such an outfit. It is a longish, very loose, very *thin* white shirt; if she were to allow herself to look properly she would realise that it does not quite preserve his modesty.

'Well,' he says fiercely, 'what the devil are you doing here?' He has made his pitch for the upper hand, she realises. 'You don't understand me, do you?' His pride has marshalled itself. 'This is private land. Private. Be gone with you . . .' He raises an arm, imperious, points in the direction of the path. 'Shoo!'

'I suppose I might ask you the same question.'

He takes a step back.

She has learned this, especially in that time since the occupation began: to wield language, her command of it, as an instrument of power.

He shifts onto his other foot – and for a moment he seems to teeter. The surprise seems to have taken all the force out of him. He looks rather pale, she thinks, even for a pallid Englishman – there is a frailty that she had failed to see before, distracted by his odd attire and her surprise.

Now another figure is approaching, from the house. He is properly dressed, in British army khaki. Her stomach clenches. It is now that she becomes aware that she is effectively trapped on the jetty: these men on one side of her, the water on the other. She will stand her ground; she has done nothing wrong, after all.

There is something familiar about him, this other man. He, too, seems to be experiencing some struggle of recognition. He frowns. His eyes travel from her face to her bare feet, and back again. 'It's you. The woman with the books.'

Yes, she does recognise him. Not the face so much as the voice. But she will not give him the satisfaction of admitting it; in refusing she will retain the upper hand. 'I do not know what you refer to.'

He frowns. 'You don't remember? Just two weeks ago . . . past the Galata bridge. I'm sure it was you. You dropped . . .' a pause, then, in triumph, 'a red notebook!'

A week ago. She was late, on her way to the school. There were painful negotiations with the linen buyer, who tried to convince her that the trade had reached saturation, and he could only offer a third of the usual price. She had to go through the whole charade; to turn on her heel and march away from him before he called her back. This had wasted a good quarter of an hour that she did not have spare.

She could imagine chaos in the classroom already – it seems to unfold even when her back has been turned for a minute, even now there are so few of them. Nur rather loves them for it. But now dread visions appeared before her: desks overturned, ink spilled.

She could not go fast enough. The cobblestones in that part of town are lethal, especially if one is in a hurry. Every third step seemed to be an awkward one, sending her pitching forward as though she might fall. She had felt a building irritation. There was nothing to direct it at other than the men who had laid these uneven stones at some unknown time in the past. But it grew, to a low-level anger at this city in general. Where everything and everyone seemed suddenly world-weary, broken. There was too much history here, too many lives and ages layered one over the top of another. How could one ever hope to grow, to move forward, with this ever-present, melancholy, hot-breathed closeness of the past?

She heard footsteps behind her.

'Excuse me?' In English.

Nur kept her gaze down, hurried her pace. Another misstep; her ankle turned on itself, an arrow of pain lancing up.

'*Bakar mısınız?*'

She hesitated, surprised by the Turkish, clumsy though it was. In her moment of hesitation, he had caught up with her.

'You dropped this.'

She turned. She saw, on looking up, a khaki form, the vague oval of a face. This was all her glance allowed time for; she could not have said with absolute certainty that there had also been eyes, a nose, a mouth. Because the thing about the foreign soldiers is that one does everything one can to avoid looking at them. Not to pretend that they don't exist; that would be impossible. After three years of occupation they have come to seem as much a part of the city as the thousands of stray dogs that roam its streets. Just like those dogs they have made it their own; taken possession, taken liberties. But one avoids looking at them to avoid trouble. From a man a too-long glance might seem a threat; many have been thrown into Allied prisons on smaller pretexts. From a woman, it might seem an invitation.

She took the thing he was holding out to her, though to

do so seemed in itself like a weakness. His fingers brushed hers, an accident, and she snatched her hand. It was her red notebook, the one in which she plans out her lessons. She pushed it beneath her arm with the others, turned, walked away.

She realised after ten more steps that she had not thanked him. Well, she thought. One small act of defiance for the vanquished.

'It was you, wasn't it?'

'Yes,' she says. 'It was me.' If he is expecting her to thank him, he will have a long wait.

He smiles. She thinks how much she would like to hit him, or spit at his feet. 'How is your ankle?' he asks.

'There is nothing wrong with my ankle.' She hears the edge in her voice. Careful, must not push it too far. He is smiling, but these invaders can turn in an instant. And yet she refuses to show that she is afraid of him, especially here, in this place. 'Why are you here?' she asks.

'This is a hospital,' he says. 'I am the doctor here. This man, Lieutenant Rawlings, is one of my patients.' Then, almost to himself, 'Who should not be out here, in fact.' He turns to the robed figure. 'Why are you out, Rawlings?'

'I came here to smoke my pipe. Can't have the damn thing inside – Sister Agnes complains about it.'

'Well, I would return post haste if I were you, or you will have to answer to her. I think she will find this a worse crime.'

The man seems about to retort, then thinks better of it. Flushing, he extinguishes the pipe and begins an unsteady retreat toward the property. But she sees that he does not enter – he remains on the edge of vision as a silent audience.

'I'm sorry for the lack of courtesy.' The doctor's voice

is gentler. 'We don't have many visitors here, as you see.'

She knows that this is British dissemble. Some sort of explanation is still required, he is waiting for her to make it. She would not know how to do it even if she felt he deserved one. Instead, she asks, 'This is a hospital?'

'Yes. It was a house, originally, the owners have since left.' Something occurs to him. 'Perhaps you knew them?'

'No.' He is still waiting, she knows, for her explanation. There is nothing threatening in his voice or manner, but then the threat is sewn into the very uniform he wears.

'I have family,' she says, 'a little further down this shore. I knew of the path, I thought I would come this way, along the water.'

He frowns. She is fairly sure he is not convinced. And yet she suspects that his courtesy will not allow him to call her out in the lie.

'Do you know why this house was abandoned? What happened to the owners? I only ask because it feels as though they did not leave long ago.'

'I never knew them.' She draws herself together. 'If you will excuse me . . .' She steps toward him. It is the closest she has ever been to one of them, and she feels the clench of fear again in her stomach.

For the first time he seems to realise that he is blocking her path back to dry land. He steps aside.

She walks slowly back the way she came, not caring that he will think it odd; that if her tale were true she should be walking in the other direction, past the house, not back in the direction of the ferry terminal. Her hands are trembling; she clenches them into fists.

Behind her she hears: 'Well, that was all rather confounding—'

'What I'm more confounded by, Rawlings, is why you are still outside.'

It could be worse, she supposes. It could have been turned into a barracks, or a nightclub like those that have sprung up in Pera, the European district. A hospital is at least less shameful than that. But her home has been colonised. All of their memories, the intimate, private life of the family. She feels the loss of it a second time. And that smiling Englishman, with his quizzical politeness. Somehow it would have been better, almost less insulting, if he had spoken to her with the abrupt rudeness of the other man.

Her mind fills with fantasies. She sees herself lunging toward him as he moved aside for her on the jetty. Pushing out with both hands . . . him toppling backward into the Bosphorus. His imagined surprise is a delicious thing; the indignity of his fall.

She could have run back toward the ferry . . . before he or that invalid had time to act.

She catches herself. She knows that she could never have done it. Her mother and grandmother, the boy, the school: there is simply too much at stake. Still, it cannot hurt to imagine. The realm of fantasy, at least, is one that cannot be occupied.

George

Medical Officer George Monroe watches the woman leave, picking her way along the path – surprisingly sure-footed in her long skirts. She seems a melancholy figure, but this may be nothing more than the effect of the dark clothing, and the way she holds herself against the breeze from the water.

'Touched in the head,' Rawlings says, authoritatively, 'if you ask me. Found her looking as though she were about to throw herself into the Bosphorus.'

This seems a little rich coming from the man who, in the grip of a fever, asked George to bring him 'a glass of the tawny '05. Generously poured. And tell Smythson I'd like my usual spot by the fire.'

George feels that, actually, she had seemed as sane as any of them. With the Allied officers all gone a little wild from the heat and new freedoms and too long spent away from home, the locals sometimes seem the only ones with some connection to reality; getting on with the business of their lives.

But what on earth was she doing here?

He was not convinced by her explanation; he suspects that she is not someone used to lying. He entertains briefly, and dismisses, the idea of sabotage or espionage. A less threatening figure – a woman bathing her feet, for goodness' sake – he cannot imagine.

A week ago. He had just been to the barber, making his way back through the streets toward the bridge. One of the figures coming toward him had been moving faster than the rest; his eye had followed it instinctively. And then, as he saw her clearly, with curiosity. There are far fewer women than men on the streets, for one thing, and this one was running. Attempting to, at least – hampered by long skirts, the cobblestones, a teetering pile of books. He watched, half-amused, half-intrigued and also with a wincing certainty that calamity was about to follow.

He had seen something fall.

When he had handed her the book she had looked at him with something close to hatred. Despite himself, he had rather respected her for it.

How odd to see the same woman twice in the space of a week . . . in this vast city. Yet he is beginning to understand that there are recurring motifs within this place, encounters that, at times, can make it feel more like a village. Some of the faces within it are already familiar to him: the sellers of mackerel sandwiches along the quay, the men who man the ferries, a certain French officer who seems to have the same taste for Turkish coffee as he.

He is not a superstitious man – his only belief is in the essential chaos of things. And yet he feels oddly certain that he will see her again.

The new site for the British military hospital in Constantinople is not the most convenient, but it is a peaceful spot, and will prove useful if there is a need for quarantine. It is not really part of the city at all – the wild sprawl of trees and bush behind the grounds seem desperate to swallow it and reacquaint themselves with the water. It was a case of needs must, however. A large, well-ventilated space was required, and this house was what was available: requisitioned from the Turkish authorities. Besides, it is a vast improvement upon a tent in the desert: those months during the Mesapotamian campaign. Where new flies clustered in wounds even as you swept the old ones away. Where temperatures rose to unholy, unbearable levels, even beneath the canvas, and where with no warning a gust of sand might blow in to cover everything, riming the nostrils and open mouths of men too ill to be sensible of the indignity of the invasion.

All his initial reservations about the position of the house – not built for the purpose, too far from the centre to be practical – faded at the sight of it. It is the loveliest building he thinks he has seen on the Bosphorus. It is not the largest, nor is it the most ornate. But there is a matchless elegance in the situation, in the graceful white poise of it, the dark, melancholy cypresses rising about it as though shielding it.

He has wondered how it came to be vacant. On first setting foot inside he had the uneasy impression that the former occupant had only just left – that he might return at any instant for something forgotten. There was a fine dust over everything, a pall of it hanging in the air. Evidently, it had not been occupied for some time. But much seemed to have been left, in the careless manner of one who did not know he was departing for good. Here, everywhere, were tokens of a life lived in all its chaos and elegance. In lanterns sat the half-burned stumps of candles; a heavy painted vase contained the brown exoskeletons of hyacinth blossoms. An encircling garden in which the work of a human hand is still evident: jasmine trained along a painted trellis, just beginning to run wild, shrub roses in crescent-shaped borders, a vegetable garden where huge yellow squashes rot uselessly and monstrous asparagus ferns dance in the breeze. From the bough of one of the fig trees hangs a swing seat. And centre of it all, the monarch to the court, is a grand old pomegranate tree. Most of the fruits have been split open by the birds or by the sheer force of their open unplucked ripeness. A few remaining seeds glisten within, promising a late treasure.

On the first day, when he was overseeing the placement of the hospital beds, he was certain that he could detect the sound of an infant crying outside: a thin wail, rising and falling. Unnerved by the sound, he followed it into the garden and discovered the seat creaking mournfully back and forth on its hinges in the wind. Almost as though – an uncanny thought – someone had only just vacated it.

George is a pragmatist, an atheist. Yet he found himself unable to quash the idea of spirits left behind.

The ward has been set up in the largest room: painted pistachio-green and hung with still life scenes: dusky grapes spilling from a platter; fat peaches with the delicate fur gorgeously rendered. They make the mouth water. There were times in the Mesapotamian desert when he would dream of fresh things like these – though his dreams were perhaps more humble. A head of lettuce. Taking the whole thing in his hands, biting into it as one might an apple and feeling it cold and wet on his tongue: the antithesis of all the desert was. If he could have this one experience, he felt, he could put up with any number of deprivations.

This room has a feminine feel to it: the colours, maybe. He knows little about Ottoman life, but has learned this one thing: that in many houses, grand or meagre, there is often an area reserved exclusively for the use of the women. A sense of trespass. He knows that if he were able to vocalise this sensation he would be laughed at. This is the way of things, how it has been since the dawn of man. There is no such thing as trespass for the victorious. All before them, conquered, has become their own. To say otherwise would be almost a form of treason.

In the streets his attire makes him indistinguishable from the rest, for better or worse. He has seen how the people here react to the different uniforms, that they respond worst of all to British khaki. There are liberties taken. But some soldiers, many, regard this as only their right.

Is it not the worst sort of shame, to be ashamed of one's own people?

A knock on the door of the study. It is a young sub-lieutenant, Hatton. Even after four years of war and nearly three of occupation, he still looks like a boy. The fair smudge of moustache is perhaps intended to bely this; it does not. He is rather red in the face. Fleetingly George wonders if this is the problem; sunburn. He saw terrible cases on the desert marches, shade several hours away, the skin blistering and peeling away in layers.

'Good day, Hatton. How may I help?'

There is no answer at first. But as the sub-lieutenant stands before George the colour seems to intensify. He shifts his weight between his feet. Ah. George has a sudden premonition of the complaint.

Hatton fastens his trousers.

'We cannot cure it, I'm afraid,' George explains, 'but we can manage it.'

'But if I were to have,' the patient takes a breath, 'relations with the same partner . . .'

'Unless she is being treated too, then no, it will not help matters.'

'She says it cannot be from her. But she's the only one . . .' He coughs. The next words are strangled by embarrassment. 'She's the only one . . . ever.'

'I think in that case,' George says, 'you best desist.'

'But I love her. And she – says – she loves me.'

And how many others has she promised the same to? He doesn't say it. This poor dupe has been punished enough.

'What is her name?'

'She was a Russian princess, before the Reds came!'

'Was she, indeed? Goodness.' And yet being an ex-Russian princess, it seems, is no immunisation against the herpes virus.

The patient leaves, clutching his prescription. George is amused by his insistence upon the former rank of the woman, as though this might make his unfortunate circumstances seem somehow less sordid.

Then he remembers that he is in no position to judge. The familiar shame visits him. The smile leaves his face.

The Boy

He sits in a patch of sun on the stone steps of the apartment building, playing with the stray cat he has befriended. It has beautiful eyes, large and palest green, ringed with black as though it were wearing kohl eye makeup. On occasions he has seen it angry and frightened, doubled to twice its size, eyes staring, breath hissing. For something so small it makes a rather impressive display. But when it is very happy, as now, it treads the air with its paws like a baker kneading bread, and flaunts its white stomach as though it hadn't a care in the world. Its favourite thing is for him to stroke the soft triangle of its chin, its sensitive whiskery cheeks.

He is so intent upon it that he does not hear Nur *hanım* return. As she passes him he starts guiltily. He should be reading one of his schoolbooks, not the book of food, which is open before him. When she does not say anything about this he knows that something is wrong. He looks up at her. It is not that she has been crying. He would be more likely to see this whole city topple into the Bosphorus than he

39

would to see Nur *hanım* weep. But her face frightens him all the same because it is like a mask.

'Nur *hanım*,' he asks, quietly. 'Are you all right?'

She looks down at him, but he has the strange impression that she is not actually seeing him. 'Yes,' she says, rather crossly. 'Of course.'

When she steps inside she pulls the door shut with such ferocity that it jumps back open again with a clang. The cat springs to its feet in fright, lets out a warning hiss. He thinks how much easier animals are to understand, how much more eloquent and truthful they are with mere actions than humans with all their words.

Five years earlier

The Prisoner

The Russian front. The edges of the Empire; a place of ice and snow. The snow was like a living thing, or many living things; a swarm. It sought the mouth, the eyes – any opening in which it could take up residence. The flakes were the size and weight of feathers. If he stood still his feet were covered in seconds.

It muffled sound. It stole the senses. It knew something that they did not. They spoke in whispers; they felt that they were being watched by someone immune to it, who laughed at their struggles as if from behind a pane of glass. They spooked at shadows, recoiling from the forms of their own men emerging through the curtain of white.

When he looked up there was only a vortex of the same, and he saw that it did not come straight down but in a vast spiral. For a few moments he was not looking up but hanging above – dangling by his ankles above an abyss. He stumbled, and almost fell.

It might have been beautiful, except for the fact that it was terrifying.

He at least had seen snow, even if it had been nothing like this. What he had thought was winter, the occasional dusting of white over Constantinople, the cold wind that blew in from the Black Sea, seemed to him now as nothing more than an artist's impression of the season. But there were men here from the southernmost parts of the Empire who had never seen it at all, to whom it had been a thing of myth.

They had lost a man to the snow: it had swallowed him whole. One moment he had been there, bringing up the rear, the next he had disappeared. He was an Armenian, recruited from a nearby village. He of all of them should have known the conditions, the lie of the land. But it had clearly proved too much even for him.

Some of the men had not liked him much; you couldn't trust the Armenians, they liked to say, they weren't true Ottomans. Still they searched the snowdrifts, digging in packed, freezing depths. You wouldn't wish such an end on anyone. And then to be discovered, pitiful, when the snow finally melted. But new drifts formed even as they dug. They were forced to move on, tramping through the fresh fallen white and each trying not to think of the man buried beneath it somewhere. If a man like that had succumbed, what chance did they have?

The idea came to him that they had been sent here to die.

It was said their enemy, the Russians, had fur-lined boots, thick greatcoats, astrakhan caps. Some of his fellow men, soldiers of the Mighty Ottoman Army, wore sandals. Some wore nothing at all: exposed flesh was dying, turning black. He was lucky to have kept his, thin-soled city shoes that they were.

To keep his mind off the cold he thought of home. He would summon to himself the memory of spring days beside the Bosphorus, light glancing from the water, the loud celebrations of the birds. The new warmth upon his face, the scent of things growing; the precise scent of the colour green. Then the drone of summer, a lazy spell cast by the heat, the city hazed with gold. He tried to remember the feeling of this. It was impossible to believe that there could have been such a thing as *too hot*: though he remembered his mother saying it, often, spending her days sheltered in the shaded cool of the *sofa*, emerging only with the respite of dusk. Colour, too, seemed an outlandish idea. Here was only the white of the snow and the grey of men's faces and the black of their hair and occasionally the bluish tinge they got around their mouths and fingertips when things were bad with them. He remembered: the purple of a fig, split open. The rust-red sheet of his mother's hair.

He had to believe he would return home, to that place of colour and warmth. There he had done the thing he had always felt himself born to do: to teach. The small satisfactions of his day: the walk to the school through the cobbled streets, his bag of books heavy on his arm. As he walked he would plan the day, the lessons, anticipate anything that might arrive; the miniature crises that occurred in a classroom populated by the very poor, by children who hardly spoke the language. The pleasure of knowing that something had been learned, despite all the odds.

How naive he had been to assume that his life would always be like this, that he would do the same thing until he grew old. A life in which he had never known fear, the particular taste of it in his throat. The joke of a man like him pretending to be a soldier.

There seemed to have been no consideration of how they

might feed themselves properly – it seemed they were expected to live entirely on *bazlama* bread. Before the war it had been delicious; eaten with honey and butter, washed down with a cup of strong black coffee. He had not known how little taste it had on its own. Baked on sheets of iron in the villages, it was stuffed into sacks, loaded onto donkeys and brought to the front. By the time it reached them it had frozen. To warm it you had to put it beneath your jacket, against the skin, under the arms. You saw men shaking it from their sleeves, scrabbling on the ground for lost morsels. The colder they became, the more difficult it was to unfreeze the stuff.

'If I could warm it between the thighs of a beautiful woman,' Babek said. 'That would be better than the finest honey.' The other men had jostled him, groaned in mingled disgust and appreciation, and felt warmed by their shared laughter. Babek grinned; he enjoyed a crowd. 'But a man's unwashed armpit – even if it is my own unwashed armpit . . . that has to be the worst seasoning imaginable.'

Babek was his friend. They met in the enlistment centre at the beginning of the war. None there were soldiers by training. Just ordinary men selected by the bad luck of their birth dates, ready to be forged into heroes. Babek had turned to him as they waited in line. As a barber, he said, all his experience had been about how not to injure someone, how not to spill their blood, and here he was about to learn how to kill a man. It wasn't a very funny joke. But he heard the tremor of fear in the barber's voice, fear that matched his own, and knew the bravery it took to make it at such a time.

They were opposites – Babek was the clown while he knew he was seen by others as too serious. He was nineteen, Babek was thirty, and seemed older. As though he had seen the world and everything in it and had not been particularly impressed by any of it: though found enough humour in it to get by. But he knew that there was greater depth to Babek. He might seem foolish, happy-go-lucky, but there was that bravery, too.

Once, when they were being taught how to fire the ancient rifles the army had provided, Babek had been caught in the shoulder by a glancing bullet, knocked to the ground with a huff of surprise, nothing more. All of them stood mute, watching as the wound bloomed with red. It was the first sign of blood any of them had seen. Perhaps it was just the shock that had kept him from crying out. But after that day, everyone who had been there had a new veneration for him, the thin, awkward man who managed to escape ridicule simply by being the first to laugh at himself.

Babek had a wife. For all his ribaldry about other women, it was she he talked of constantly – though not to the other men, in case they thought him soft. And children: two little boys and a baby on the way when he left. If it was a girl, they had decided, they would call her Perihan – a name like a flower, or a princess from the old days. His wife had the most beautiful hands, he said, she moved them like white birds when she talked. Even before he lifted the veil to look at her face for the first time he saw those eloquent hands and he knew.

They had come to see him off at the sidings of the railway track – his wife invisible beneath a *charshaf* and veil, the boys dressed like miniature men in their best clothes and fezzes. They waved handkerchiefs. They had looked particularly small and helpless down there beneath the bank, seen through a cloud of steam from the train, dwarfed by the great machine as it thundered above them on its way to war. Perhaps Babek had felt this too, because he had suddenly looked uncharacteristically sombre and his eyes had gleamed wetly.

'I wish they had not come,' Babek said, as though to himself. 'It would have been better if they had not come.'

Once upon a time, in another world, he himself had been a schoolteacher. He had imagined a small life for himself. Not the one his parents had hoped for him: he was not made for the world of government, or medicine. But perhaps this life could be great in its own way, even heroic. What better gift than that of knowledge? For the rich learning was just an embellishment, another asset among many others. For the poor, it could represent the promise of a different life.

But that was another life, as remote as if it had happened to another man. He had once known the children in his class so well that he understood each of their idiosyncrasies as well as he did his own. How Kemal began to swing one leg before he was tired, how Arianna looked at a stain on the ceiling when asked a question, as though she would read the answer there, how Enver spent most of every class looking out of the window, which was infuriating, but if challenged could recite the whole lesson word-for-word. Now he could hardly remember what any of them looked like. They were slipping from him, he was untethered from that life. His world had shrunk to this white void, driven only by hunger and fear, the animal instinct to survive. And this was what they said it meant to be a hero.

Within this blindness of snow one became very aware of the internal world. Of the rhythm of the heart in the chest. The beat of blood in the ears. But the extremities no longer seemed his own. His numbed feet felt . . . not like feet, but something else, two thin jeweller's razors upon which the full weight of his body could not possibly balance. They did not want to obey him. Beneath the snow was compacted into ice, and with every few yards gained he seemed to slip back several more. The fury of the snow. It felt a personal fury, vindictive. It whipped the cheeks like a lash and he began to long for the time when his face, too, would cease to feel.

A few days into the offensive Babek had begun to look unwell. He had always been thin, no matter how much he ate, and there had been so little food at the front. All of them had lost weight, but he had had none to lose in the first place. His lips had begun to turn bluish, the nail-beds of his bare hands. His breath rattled when he talked or even breathed, as though something had come loose inside his chest.

When he made his jokes now they did not always make sense . . . the words were disordered as though something in his mind was not connecting properly. He would never say this to Babek, though, because he did not want to frighten him, and because he did not want to give a voice to his own fear. So when Babek finished one of his nonsensical jokes, and waited with that expectant look – this at least was familiar – he laughed just as hard as he ever had. Harder, probably. If Babek suspected any fakery in this he did not mention it.

One man in the company – a southerner – had lost his genitalia to frostbite after relieving himself against a tree. He had died some short while later. A mercy, some said. But what message to bring back to his mother? The standard, of course: *He died with a smile upon his face, in proud service of the Empire.*

Some of the men were huge brutes, farmers and fishermen with skin like leather and corded muscles in their arms. They towered over him. And they were already half-broken. When he stood next to them in his mind's eye he saw not a man, but a small boy, gripping his bayonet with hands too small to reach, emerging from a uniform ten sizes too big to fit.

Suddenly a new sound, a hiss of air. At first he believed it was some new intensification of the snow. Then the man beside him fell, a little yelp of surprise. He looked down. The peculiar beauty of the colour in the white, spreading fast like ink upon tissue. Such a very true red, almost the red of the Ottoman flag itself. He envied the man his expression of absolute peace. By the time he had understood that he should call for help, and could summon the words with which to do it – he had not spoken for hours, days it seemed – it was far too late. The enemy had come for them.

The Traveller

As we leave the shelter of the station the rain begins, as
though it has been waiting for us. Some say rain spoils
everything. I say it depends on the position of the beholder.
Now, as water spreads itself in filmy sheets against the glass,
the austere train carriage is transformed into a hallowed
space; sanctuary from the onslaught without. The light seems
to change in defiance of the bleakness, to kindle; the winter-
pallid faces about me gain new colour. Beyond the glass the
drear suburbs and the formidable distant shadows of the
banlieues – the backstage of Paris – acquire the romance of
a watercolour.

I prop the suitcase on the couchette next to me. From the
cushioning of a scarf I unwrap a photograph in a tin frame.
I have looked at it so many times through the years, trying
to understand the sequence of events that changed everything,
that changed my life.

A building, surrounded by dark trees. It is slightly out of
focus, lending the house a blurred, provisional appearance
so that it does not appear made of wood and stone but

something evanescent, a structure of vapour and light. It looks more like the idea of a house, a phantasm that has alighted on the bank and is making up its mind as to whether it should stay. But I recall tangible things. Painted tiles, a stone fountain, fine objects, white linen, voices echoing in high-ceilinged rooms. Hard to believe . . . that for a short span of time it was something like a home to me.

I bring the photograph so close to my face that my breath steams the shielding pane of glass, hoping to catch some evidence of life within. For the merest fraction of a moment I think I have seen something in the lower row of windows: a small face, looking out at me. But it must have been merely the creation of a hopeful imagination. When I look again the windows are blank-eyed and dark, withholding their secrets.

Nur

Morning. She feels renewed, the humiliations of the day before have lost their sting. The streets are still empty enough at this hour that they can stride through them quickly. She enjoys the pull and stretch of her muscles, the sound of her shoes ringing upon the cobblestones. The lesser note of the boy's feet as he follows behind: two steps to her every one, and even then he struggles to keep up. He is still so small. But he is also, she knows, distracted by the scents that reach them from the bakeries and cafes they pass, his nose aloft in that feline way.

She is aware of the looks. In these narrow streets they pass near enough to see the glimmer of eyes through lattice-work screens and one woman pulls her shutters closed with an ostentatiously violent clatter. Odd, that it should be the women that seem most outraged by her bared face, by her presence in the street. The older ones are worst of all, understandably. She still feels the sting of their glances. At first they were almost enough to send her running back to the apartment for her veil. Now she steels herself against her own sense of shame. Because for all that the war took from her – and it was more than she ever thought she would have to give – there is this one thing that it gifted her. Her city. And she is not ready to give it up. The liberation of walking these streets that have always been her home and yet for so long have been beyond the limits of her knowledge.

She is not alone; much of a generation has joined her. Barriers shifted, dissolved entirely. Young women who had remained hidden indoors behind filigree screens ventured out into the streets. They appeared bare-faced. They took on the work of men – her grandmother is still outraged by the appearance of trouser-clad female street sweepers.

The boy is dawdling.

'Come on, hurry up – we're going to be late.'

She sees what has caught his attention; the same sight that she has been avoiding looking at. A group of French officers, in their blue uniforms, smoking their cigarettes and lounging against an old tree that has forced its way out of the cobble-stones.

Children, she has noticed, are disloyally fascinated by the soldiers. Now, with building horror, she sees one of the men drop his cigarette, stub it out with a smartly polished boot, and come toward them.

'Hello,' he says, to the boy, in French. From the crowds passing them Nur feels a low hum of disapproval, levelled as much at her as at the man, as though they assume she must have done something to encourage him. And with it there is a certain sense of shame, as though she really has.

'I have a little son like you, at home,' he says now. 'Do you know what he likes best?' He does not wait to see if the boy has understood. 'Caramels! Would you like one?' He fishes a gold-wrapped sweet from his pocket.

'No, thank you—' But Nur is too late, the boy has already taken one.

'I hope,' the man's eyes go to Nur's uncovered face now, and remain there, 'that you tell your mother how beautiful she is every day.'

She seizes the boy's hand, and marches him away from the officers as fast as she can, without a backward glance. Ribald laughter follows them.

When they have put a little distance between themselves and the officers she puts out her hand. 'Spit it out.'

'But—'

'Do it, please.' She knows what a cruelty it is to take food from a child like him. But the French officers are still watching, and this is a point of principle.

With an expression of profoundest agony, the boy does as she says. She throws it down, and within seconds a street cat has emerged from somewhere to sniff at it.

Now she feels as though a layer of skin has been removed, not merely a thin gauze of material. The city now seems to thwart her at every turn: the cobblestones turn her ankles, the crowds press against her. She has become clumsy and conspicuous.

She understands that she is an object of curiosity for such men, who have come expecting veiled forms. She knows that they see her – her hair covered but her face exposed, wandering about the city as she chooses – and make suppositions. She tries to remind herself that it must not matter. To wait until a day when one might not be reminded with every step of one's difference might mean waiting for a hundred years. More.

The Boy

He can still taste the buttered sugar of the sweet, shards of
it hidden in the small crevices between his teeth. Lucky that
he managed to swallow half of it before she made him spit
out the rest. He still hurts from the loss. He knew that he
had no choice, though. There had been a dangerous look in
her eye. She had already changed into her schoolteacher self.

Nur *hanım* is different at school. She seems to grow by
about a foot. She transforms into a new, more powerful
version of herself, like a very subtle shape-shifting *djinn*. He
can nearly forget the version of her that burns almost every
meal she cooks, and sometimes sings out of tune while she
cleans the apartment. Who sometimes, rather like Enver,
spends a rare free hour staring out of the window toward
the Bosphorus, silent, insensible to anything around her. He
can almost forget, too, that they live in the same apartment
together. That sometimes at home, as though she can't help
herself, she reaches down and strokes a hand through his
hair, or bends and enfolds him in a tight embrace. She does
not give him preferential treatment in the classroom. Often

he thinks that it is the opposite, that she makes a point of telling him off for talking or daydreaming much more than she does the other children. He would never dare say this to her, though.

Sometimes, when the chaos in the classroom reaches its highest pitch, he sees Nur *hanım* rub her forehead hard with the heel of her hand. Only he knows that this is something she does when she is particularly exasperated. When the old woman, for example, is complaining about how terrible their life is now . . . how wonderful everything was in the old days. Then she rolls her shoulders back (she does this with the old woman, too), and faces up to the challenge like a street cat readying for a fight. When she next speaks, the children fall silent. Even if she has not raised her voice, which she hardly ever does, and even if they don't quite understand the words. They know the tone.

Nur

'Who can tell me what word this is?' A pause. 'Enver, I do not believe you will find the answer out of the window.' The child in question jumps in his seat as though someone has pinched him.

'Wossis, *hanım*?'

This from one of the new girls, who wears the same dirty clothes every day.

'That, Ayla, is a pen.'

'Oh. Worrus it do?'

'You write words with it, Ayla. Like this word, here.'

A chasm of ignorance now stretches out in front of her. She puts down the card she has been holding up. 'We will return to the characters of the alphabet, this morning, instead.'

Perhaps she should not be surprised: the girl comes from one of the poorest neighbourhoods, where to educate a child, and especially a female, is not the norm. But then *all* of them come from the poorest neighbourhoods.

Some are newly arrived in the city; they have the half-stunned look of recently awakened sleepwalkers. There are

Russians from the boats that traversed the Black Sea disgorging human cargo without a backward glance. Girls and boys with the names of queens and kings, speaking exquisite, fluent French, at odds with their street urchin appearance. There are Turks who do not speak Turkish, who have seen the places they had called home dissolved into some new formulation, found themselves foreigners in their own land. There are the local children, like Ayla, who speak in such rough approximations of Turkish, the dialects of their particular neighbourhood, that they might as well be speaking a foreign tongue.

She is not convinced any of them are learning anything: except, perhaps, a kind of tribal order. Who speaks like them, looks like them, and who does not – ergo, who is friend, who is foe. When new pupils arrive she sees the interest of the room reach toward them. A rapid unspoken assessment takes place. Then one group will extend its invitation – swelling their ranks – others their hostility. It takes a brave child to step across these boundaries. It is a microcosm of the war. It unnerves her.

One odd thing: there used to be several Armenian children in the class. Now there is only one. There have been huge movements of people during and after the war, true – and the shifting numbers in her classroom reflect this. But it seems such a uniform disappearance that she cannot help wondering about it.

The school is one of the things that the war gave to Nur. But to celebrate this would be to celebrate Kerem's fate. She can be impatient with her pupils. The difficulty of it some-times amazes her.

But Kerem would have been patient.

Nur emphatically does not believe in ghosts. Yet sometimes it is as though she can feel him there in the classroom with her. A half smile, a watchfulness. She has turned, and thought if she only does it fast enough, she might catch him at it.

Her brother is the one that should be teaching now, not lying in an unmarked grave somewhere in the outer wastes of the Empire. A schoolteacher turned soldier – who could really have believed he would survive? Even his name was wrong for a soldier: Kerem – 'kind'.

'But there are so many good, respected Muslim schools,' her mother had said, when, at eighteen, he had told them all of his new role. 'Kerem. The boys' school at Galatasaray. Think of that! A man like you! They would welcome you with open arms.'

'Perhaps.' He had smiled, in his easy way. 'But I don't want to teach there.' He was a gentle man, that was the thing: but when he felt strongly about something that gentleness belied a surprising strength.

Her father had been rather quiet on the matter. Nur suspects that his ambition for his eldest son had been loftier. 'You must not neglect your science,' he had told a twelve-year-old Kerem. 'It is vital for medicine.'

As for herself? She does not think her father would have had the same reservations. This was one of the contradictions in him. He had sent her to the British school, which had a good standard of teaching. And at home, through his guidance, she had become as well read as her brother. He liked to joke about this, tell her that her intellect shamed them all. But at some point, it seemed, he was content to let her grandmother and mother's plans for her take over. Sometimes she feels that she has become a half-developed thing, a sort of freak. Too educated to be content with the usual lot of her sex, but not enough to do anything with it. At her most angry she decided that her education had been a pastime for her father, an amusement.

She had forgotten this anger. Too easy to let the dead become perfect, to forget their flaws. It was her father himself who had told her this. 'When we make the dead saints,' he had said, 'they become less real to us. We lose a truth. We lose something of who they were.'

The sound of the children's laughter. Every head is turned from her toward the back of the room: she sees quickly what has amused them.

'Enver!' – sharply. 'That is for writing with. Not for using upon your face.' The boy puts the pen down. The expression on his face wavers somewhere between guilt and pride. He has drawn what appear to be a cat's whiskers on each of his cheeks – with impressive precision, considering he cannot see his own work. She only wishes he approached his letter writing with such care.

The truth is that the interruption to her thoughts was a relief. An unexpected boon of this work – it leaves very little time for reflection.

George

He has the rest of the day to himself. Bill, his second-in-command, is in charge of things at the hospital. The afternoon spreads before him like the vista of the city as the ferry approaches, gleaming with promise.

The press of bodies at the Tophane quay is another world from the quiet Asian shore of the Bosphorus, though the two are only a few hundred metres apart. Out of the women's cabin pours forth a stream of veiled women, some clutching babies or leading children who stumble on their short legs down the gangplank. The crowd on the quay is so thick that it is hard to see how any of those alighting will be able to press their way through – and everyone appears to be intent on moving in a different direction. Somehow they all manage to thread a path through. On his way he is offered bread, coffee, fresh figs, lemonade from a gorgeously wrought brass urn that the seller carries upon his back. At first he feels helpless, jostled and henpecked, his ears ringing. Then he begins to enjoy it. The solitude of the Bosphorus is a fine thing, but there is also space for one's thoughts to grow too loud. Here they are drowned out by the volume of the business of living.

It is the most hectic place he has ever been in his life. Apart from the front, perhaps – but that was different, a no-place, and there it was a different sort of chaos.

But from afar, the city appears the opposite. A scene of perfect serenity. In the early morning light, viewed from the jetty of the hospital, it seems to be made entirely of white marble, gleaming expansively. The minarets rise above in their etiolated elegance, cloud-piercing. It appears a city sleeping beneath a spell.

He romanticises it, of course, like all those who have come before him with their dreams of the Orient. In doing so, though he is yet to learn exactly how, he does a disservice. He consigns it to some semi-mythical, unpopulated realm. And in doing so he discounts its current inhabitants, modern and war-wrung, trying to continue with the business of living. The woman in the garden, for example . . . what thought has he of her?

But that first sight of it, in 1918. Standing on the deck of the *Queen Elizabeth* as it muscled its way along the Golden Horn, with the great gun turret rotating toward shore in case some member of the watching crowd had 'any ideas'. All of them, even the rowdiest of his fellow soldiers, had been stunned before the wonder of it. It was suddenly inconceivable that they were arriving to occupy this great and beautiful place, more ancient than any of them could imagine. In that moment it had dwarfed them, taken possession of them. They were an inconsequential footnote in a tale begun millennia ago, in which armies far greater than they had come and conquered and been vanquished in their turn.

Now their numbers contribute to the chaos of the streets. To the black robes of Greek priests, the red fezzes of the

Ottomans, the silk-veiled women, the brown jackets of the street sellers, the long mustard habits of the toll collectors on the bridge at Galata, are added Italian, British, American khaki, French blue. In the first few weeks they appeared parade-ready, these soldiers. And some of them had paraded, about the whole of the city – up the steep hill of Galata and Pera, across the bridge to Scutari. Impressive formations before the Byzantine splendour of the Aya Sofia, the eternal grace of the Blue Mosque. This was an attempt to display strength, dominion. Silent crowds of the vanquished had gathered to watch. But had there not, he wondered, been something slightly ludicrous in it?

He takes the tram to Galata, walks over the bridge to the part of the city they call Stamboul. Here the majority of the Muslim population lives. Here are all the choicest wonders of architecture, glories of the ancient world. There sits the jewel of Byzantium, the Aya Sofia, towering above the surrounding streets, rust-red in the morning light. Facing it, challenging its beauty: Sultanahmet, pride of the conquering Ottomans with its gorgeous array of gilt-tipped domes. A short distance away is the Topkapi palace: home to four centuries of sultans. It appears innocuous from this distance, veiled by tall, old trees . . . but at one time this was the nucleus of great love stories, of empire-threatening feuds, scandals that supplanted dynasties. And few places can be so shrouded in myth as the imperial harem, where once scores of women lived out their lives in blue-tiled rooms. If there is such a thing as the spirit of a city, it might reside there.

This is the realm of the French occupation, pale blue uniforms weave among the crowds. In British-held Pera the streets have a European feel: a blocky stone grandeur, wrought-iron, modern boulevards that might almost have been designed by Paris' Haussmann. A municipal grandeur. This might be another city entirely. Here everything is built on a more delicate scale: houses of filigree wood, and the spires of mosques rising from the rooftops like lace-spindles. This is the city of which great men – and the occasional woman – have written, with which they have fallen in love. Here the streets seem to follow little logic, and look so alike that it can take several minutes before he realises that he is not quite where he thought he was. He has now a flimsy idea of the territory immediately beside the waterfront, based upon particular coffee shops and certain architectural features – green shutters, a building painted the unlikely pink of a sunset, a balcony of exquisitely detailed wrought-iron leaves.

He has discovered a barber here, in the shadow of the Blue Mosque, who will have one parade-smart for a song. He has a small assistant, eight years old, perhaps – or a malnourished ten – who brings coffee on a clattering tray. George usually tries to slip him a few *piastres* too.

He sits in the chair now, breathing the distinctive atmosphere of coffee, cologne, sweat. As he watches his jaw appears from beneath the shadow of bristles, starkly denuded, pale where the sun has not reached the skin. The moustache, too, with what seems like a single flick of the man's wrist. It is something of a shock to see his old face appear; an unexpected reunion with a once-dear acquaintance. As he looks at this old version of himself he feels something within him list sideways. He takes a sip of the coffee, scalds his mouth, chews through the fine sediment of grounds, and feels himself restored to equilibrium.

He has learned to like the coffee here. It is served treacle-thick, heavily sweetened. At the bottom of the cup sits a sediment of fine grounds. The first couple of times he ordered it he chewed his way manfully through them, assuming this was an important, if unpleasant, part of the process. Eventually, the elderly man at the next table took pity upon him and explained, in a performance of gestures, that one stopped as soon as the tongue touched them.

Now he drinks several cups of the stuff a day, accompanied sometimes by one of the small sweetmeats: fine pastry dripping with honey that you have to eat quickly before it trickles down your sleeve.

Sometimes in the cafes he frequents he catches a glimpse of fellow khaki, or French blue. But this is rare – few other soldiers seem to be interested in trying the stuff. When it happens, though, he moves on to the next coffeehouse: a magnet repelled by its like. It is his private ritual, almost a secret one.

He feels . . . difficult to explain exactly, closest at this time to his real self. Not his wartime or professional self. Merely a man taking a simple pleasure.

Leaving the barber's, he finds himself in the grand thoroughfare before the Aya Sofia, Baedeker in his hand. He found the book at a market stall, a strange relic of a time recent and yet so far off for everyone in this city, soldiers and civilians aside. He looks up in wonder at the gilded domes and then down at the page, only to see a rush of movement before him. He leaps back on instinct before he can properly understand what has just happened. Unseen until the last second, a little boy has run into his path and spat on the ground at his feet. He looks down, absolutely stunned, at the small gobbet of saliva where it seems to foam in the dust, and then at the boy. The child is tiny, with that pinched look that so many of the youth have here. He is caught as though frozen in the act of running away, almost equally surprised by his own act of defiance. For a moment they stare at one another, both wondering what George is going to do. And then a woman launches herself at the child, shielding him with her arms. 'Please,' she cries, looking up at George. 'Please, forgive.'

There is much George would like to say to her. After the initial affront of the act, it suddenly seems rather amusing. The boy is so small, after all, his bravery quite astonishing. He would like to explain that no harm has been done, that if he had been in the boy's position, he would hope he would have done the same. In this moment he feels all the frustration, the impotence, of the language barrier between them. 'It's all right,' he says, putting up a hand. 'It's all right.'

Nur

Through the open windows come faint strains of music with a foreign flavour: Russian and American imports. It is a relief not to be out on the streets; for the time being this cramped apartment is a place of sanctuary.

One November evening, a couple of years ago, she and the boy had stayed late at the school: she planning the next day's lessons, he reading at one of the desks. They were travelling home when a series of huge explosions rattled the windows of the tram. All of the passengers crouched low in their seats, bracing against the onslaught. Perhaps some, like she had, had been at Mahmut Paşa the day the English planes came . . . or had heard stories of it from others, stories steeped in gore.

Then someone had pointed to the sky and they saw it ablaze with coloured light; green, red, gold. It took her a while to recognise that these were fireworks, like those she had seen at Eid Mubarak a lifetime ago. It was some display by the Allies, no doubt – no one else in this city had anything to celebrate. The boy had asked if they could go and watch.

Together they had climbed the cobbled streets of Pera to get a better look, past the doors of *meyhanes* and restaurants. The boy lingered outside these, caught by the faint sounds of revelry within – she tugged him on.

From here it seemed the colours were everywhere, the Golden Horn lighting up with reflected fire. The boy gave a shriek of delight. She had been thrilled at this unexpected show of emotion, this sign, perhaps, of a brief respite from the things that haunted him. She had actually worried that they might remind him of that terrible night. After this re-assurance, she had begun to enjoy the fireworks too.

How democratic they were, for anyone who chose to watch them – though she doubted this had been the intention. They seemed to be lost on their intended audience, in fact, who seemed too absorbed by their business inside the *meyhanes*. Then without any warning one of the doors had opened and a chaos of khaki-clad bodies had been disgorged into the street in front of them, some clutching spilling glasses of beer.

Nur had pushed the boy behind her, but had not had time to prevent one of the men stumbling into her, catching her hard on the shoulder. Involuntarily she had shoved back with both hands, merely trying to keep him from knocking her down. He had toppled and briefly tried to right himself before his momentum had got the better of him, sending him crashing backward to the ground. She had stood there stunned by the act, by her sudden, unexpected power. His fellow soldiers had been beside themselves with glee – laughing and pointing, slurring insults at him where he sat in the pool of his spilled beer. Then the fallen one had looked up, and she had seen that the shock had sobered him; that his expression was pure menace. She had humiliated him, she understood this look to mean, and she would pay.

She had turned to the boy. 'Run.'

They had fled back down the way they had come, through the cobbled streets. The men had pursued them for a while, alternately laughing and shouting orders. But the men were drunk, and she knew the streets better – knew a secret shortcut through a series of interconnecting alleyways that would take them back to the tram stop.

They had escaped, but she still has a queasy fear of one of them recognising her in the street one day and demanding retribution. If she were arrested, what would become of them all . . . the boy, her mother, her grandmother? She looks at them all now, and decides it is not worth thinking about.

As the sky beyond the windows loses the last of its light, she heats a basin of water on the stove and begins to wash her mother's hair. She has a bar of soap scented with Damascene rose that she keeps for this purpose. The aroma is famed for its ability to soothe and heal. It reminds her of her mother, too. The woman she used to be – who would ask the girls to crush the petals into her skin and hair before her bath, who wore pure attar oil dabbed behind her ears. Who wore gowns of pink silk and read French novels.

From the corner, her grandmother speaks. 'You won't get anything out of her. Worse than an infant today.'

'She has suffered so much, *Büyükanne*.'

'So have we all, girl.'

Her mother stopped speaking on the day they had word from the front: *Missing, presumed lost*. They knew as well as anyone that the notice meant dead. Her brother survived only within the bureaucratic chaos that meant the exact circumstances of his death were not yet clear. Sometimes, in the early days, Nur had allowed herself to believe that he was alive. There were rumours of Ottoman men being taken as prisoners of war. If she did not *feel* his death, might it not be real?

Now she sees that this was just a fiction she had created to delay pain. She did not feel his death because they had been denied the absolute certainty of it: that was the cruellest thing of all.

From somewhere beneath them comes the eerie, distorted wail of an infant. The walls might be made of thick card, not stone. Above and below can be heard, with peculiar domestic intimacy, the sounds of other lives. Most of the time the voices are indistinct, as though they are travelling through water.

Her mother's eyes have closed. If one were to look briefly she might appear to be in a state of bliss. But her breath comes too quickly. Beneath the purplish lids there is restless movement, as though projected there is a play of images that only she can see. Nur has some inkling of what those scenes may be. They are the same that wake her mother at night, from which even in her sleep she is not safe.

She is trying not to think about how much more hair there used to be. Her fingers discover absences, patches of bare scalp where whole sections seem to have vanished. She sluices warm water, creates a silky white lather. She inhales, exhales, hears the hitch of her breath and tries to smooth it. She understands the importance of remaining calm. Knows how powerfully the fingertips, those tiny repositories of sensation, can convey emotion. She tries instead to convey only her tenderness, her love.

She fills another cup of water to rinse away the foam. The colour has changed, too. It used to be a magnificent colour: somewhere between brown and red. A great sweep of it, with the shine of metal. Depending upon the quality of the light it would gleam bronze or copper. Now it does not reflect anything at all. This, of course, may be merely to do with age. A cruelty, yes, but a natural one that comes to all. And yet it happened so quickly – in less than a year.

She tips the water. There is a small sound as the water drenches her mother's scalp, which could be a sigh of pleasure or pain.

'Is it all right for you, *Anne*?' But there is only silence.

The Prisoner

Their enemy, at the very entrance to their camp. The Russians had come for them, through the snow. Silently, cloaked in whiteness. Then they were everywhere, and death came all at once. Death came in pellets of metal that could travel the whole way through a body, and break it all up inside. Men were killed opening their mouths to speak, or scratching themselves, or putting both hands inside their jackets to warm them, or bending to fasten a shoe, or squatting to defecate against a tree. Some died even before they had time to shout, some of them with screams that outlived them. And some were dying slowly, with whimpers of fear and pain. They fell and the snow covered them. He had not known that death in the name of a noble cause, in the name of everything one stood for, could still be so ugly. So small, so pitiful.

He shouted to Babek to fall, to pretend to be hit. He lay down, and waited for the snow to cover him as they made their advance. He felt the cold enter him like a sword. He realised it might have been better to have been shot, because now he would merely freeze to death – and it would be slow.

He lay for an hour; perhaps several. But time had frozen too.

Beside him, on either side, stretched a phalanx of corpses. Bodies that would soon be hardly recognisable as such, skin turned hard as stone. The Russians had brought dogs, and some of them had begun to feast. He could hear them, a little way off, fighting over the spoils. There was more than enough to go around.

Babek lay somewhere close by. He thought that he could still hear the rattle of his breathing, but it was difficult to be certain.

The enemy came now, following the dogs. He could hear voices, the creak of the snow beneath their boots. Their boots lined with fur. This was the Russians' element. They were men of ice and snow.

He felt the weight of the dead man beside him disappear as the corpse was hoisted into the air and carried to some unknown place. Then they came for him, prodded at him with a rifle. He felt the sting of the bayonet's blade against his skin, but he did not cry out.

He could hear them talking; but he could not understand the words. He supposed they were gloating over their victory. And then he heard; unmistakable, a voice speaking in a language he understood. A heavy Russian accent, but the words were clear enough.

'You've done well. You will be rewarded for this.'

Another voice, accented, but not Russian. 'Thank you.'

He opened one eye. And he saw, he was sure that he saw, the same Armenian who they had thought lost to the snow.

* * *

When the Russians had finally left he dragged Babek into the shelter of one of the tents. They would wait here for the reinforcements to find them. He had to believe that they would come; and come soon – he wasn't sure that either of them had long left.

Every so often, Babek would let out a low moan. It wasn't a human sound. And he lay where he had been dragged; his limbs at odd angles.

He was not sure whether Babek could hear him, but it seemed important to keep talking. He could feel sleep pressing in, promising a respite from the cold which had found its way into him, deeper than it ever had before. He was lucid enough to know what this meant. It did not matter that he had somehow escaped being wounded – the cold would kill him with just as little mercy as the flesh-rupturing path of a bullet. So he talked: of home, of their return. It would not do to dwell on the things both of them had seen: the feasting dogs; the indignity of the bodies left out without a proper burial – when a Muslim man should be interred as quickly as possible. Even if he had the energy and strength left to do it he could not have buried them all. He would not think, either, of the treachery of the Armenian, the man who had been in their midst, and eaten with them, and drunk tea with them, and promised to help them. And for whose body they had searched in the snow, mourning the loss of one of their own. So instead he talked of the city they both loved; the orange blossom in spring, the first tiny bright green leaves on the fig trees, the smell of freshly brewed coffee and warm baked bread.

He tried to remember what it was to be warm. He talked to Babek of a summer's trip to the Princes' Islands. A secret beach he knew where the water was so clear that you could still see the bottom even when it was as deep as a house was tall. And then the feeling of the hot sand beneath your back, the sun drying the damp from your skin with the tenderness of a lover's caress. Sand with tiny pieces of broken shell, pink as a fingernail, the inside of your lip. He was so cold now that it was difficult to form each word – each had to be forced out on a little huff of breath, so that he almost felt he could see the letters in the freezing cloud as it left his mouth – but he thought he did the job well enough. If only he could *feel* the meaning of the words, though. *Please*, he thought, *if this is really how it ends for me . . . let me feel that tender warmth one last time.*

He tried now to think of his sister and his mother and grandmother. He had thought that if it came to it, if he found himself on a precipice, all he would need to do would be to think of them, and he would be able to keep himself going. He had not realised how difficult it would be not to die.

His friend's moans had ceased now. It was some relief. Perhaps the pain had lessened, slightly.

'Your wife, Babek. Think of how proud she'll be to have a war hero for a husband.'

Would his own family be proud? They would be relieved, certainly, to see him home. He tried to summon their faces to him but found that he could not do it. The cold seemed to have worked its way inside his head.

'They'll come for us soon. It cannot be too long. We'll be taken home.'

That word. It seemed to encapsulate everything that was good; everything that was the opposite of this place. His cheeks stung; the tears freezing upon the skin.

Time had become fluid, elusive. It seemed that they had been here for many days, many nights. But when it began to grow dark he realised that it could only have been a few hours. The loss of the light made him feel more alone. He reminded himself that Babek was with him. He looked over at his friend. Babek was sleeping now, his chin upon his chest. He looked almost comical, like a broken doll, his limbs splayed. He wondered how long he had been talking to himself, taking comfort from the mere idea of a conversation. He saw that the jacket that he had lent to Babek – because he needed it far more – had fallen open. Feeling rather like his mother – how she had fussed over them when they were little – he leant down and pulled the lapels up so it covered him properly.

He continued to talk to Babek, even though his friend slept, because it was a way of keeping awake himself, and one of them had to be conscious in case reinforcements came for them – or the Russians came back.

A little while later, as it was growing dark, something occurred to him. It was too horrible to contemplate properly, so he shunted the idea away. But it clung to him, to the edges of thought. And finally he looked over at his friend, looked properly this time, and saw that he was dead.

George

This evening he, Bill, his fellow medical officer, and Calvert, an officer they met in Baku, are having dinner in a new Pera restaurant. Russian: all the new restaurants seem to be, set up by the more fortunate of the refugees who have fled across the Black Sea from Lenin's Revolution.

At night the city becomes more than ever a place of two distinct halves. Stamboul slumbers early while the lights of Pera, just across the Golden Horn, seem to burn brightest in the smallest, darkest hours of the morning. Here the *meyhanes* and jazz clubs fill with Allied soldiers and naval officers. And there are also those other establishments which choose not to outwardly proclaim the sort of entertainment offered. They do not need to; their renown is spread quickly, secretly, among those who have a taste for such things.

Inside the restaurant is a fug of smoke and steam, a clamour of voices and crockery. Beneath it all, not loud enough to do anything other than add to the racket, comes the thin wail of a violin. The man playing it has one of the most tragic faces George has ever seen, and he wonders whether he was chosen specifically for this, rather than his indifferent skill with the instrument. The *maître d'hôtel* meets them, sweeps them to their table in the other corner of the room.

Calvert is not impressed. 'The French always get the best seats,' he says, darkly, indicating a table several rows across where three blue-uniformed figures sit smoking and laughing. There exists among the so-called Allied forces an atmosphere of mutual distrust.

'What's so special about that table?' Bill asks.

Calvert raises one fair eyebrow. He points to the place beyond the table. There, George sees now, sits a rudimentary wooden structure with a platform a few feet from the ground. 'It's closer to the stage. They'll be able to see right up the skirts.'

He looks round for the *maître d'hôtel*.

'Do you know,' George says to Bill, 'I completely forgot to tell you. The strangest thing happened yesterday.' He describes the woman on the jetty. Already the idea of her is like something not quite real, a fragment of a dream.

Bill frowns. 'You should report that.'

'Why?'

'Could be espionage. There are resistance groups, you know. The Teşkilât-i Mahsusa, the Karakol. You heard about the fire at the French barracks at Rami?'

'Yes, of course.'

'Well, all of the Algerian soldiers escaped miraculously unharmed. It's thought that they were in cahoots with the Turkish resistance.'

'I thought of all that – briefly. But I don't believe it was for a second. A solitary woman, for goodness' sake, washing her feet.'

'Still, you should make a formal note of it. She'd be the

perfect choice to scope it, because we wouldn't suspect her. At the very least it's British property. She trespassed.'

'Mmm.' He is rather wishing he hadn't said anything. He knows already that he will make no such report. He wonders whether, given the opportunity, Bill would also tell him to turn in the little boy who spat on his shoes.

They are brought chilled glasses of that Russian spirit, which tastes to George like a distillation of nothingness, a void. But it goes well with the food. Particularly caviar, which he ate for the first time in that godforsaken place on the shores of the Caspian Sea, bubbles of salt bursting upon the tongue, a concentration of the sea itself, at once delicious and slightly repellent. But isn't that the same, he thinks, for all tastes deemed refined? The sourness of champagne, the bitter of coffee, the fleshy gobbet of the oyster. Does one enjoy them as much for their taste as for one's ability to overcome this brief repulsion, even fear?

Calvert sucks back an oyster, drains his glass of vodka, and turns to him.

'What are you still doing here, Monroe?'

'What do you mean? This restaurant? Do you know, I'm really not sure . . .'

Calvert draws back his lips in an approximation of a smile. 'No, that isn't what I meant. I understood that you got offered home, some time ago.'

'I did.'

'Well, why . . .'

'I suppose I felt that I could be more useful here.'

'Your sense of duty, was it?'

George looks at him, sharply, but can find no obvious trace of sarcasm. 'Yes. Something to that effect.'

He does not like Calvert. He realises this with a sudden clarity. Even his face is somehow unlikeable. It has a peculiar fineness of feature: the nose small and neat, the chin delicately carved, the lips full as a girl's, with a sharp cupid bow. It is these lips, perhaps, that tilt the whole effect into a prettiness that doesn't quite work. And yet he prides himself upon them, George knows. One might even say that he wields them. It is a face that one cannot quite trust.

Now Calvert leans across the table and says in a conspirator's murmur, 'They have the best girls here. All bonafide White Russians – nothing lower than a countess, I assure you. Running from the Red Bolshevik devils.' His breath is tainted metallic by the spirit.

George casts an eye about the room, at the waitresses in question. They are all pretty, youngish, simpering. Not especially remarkable in any way . . . or so it seems to him. Perhaps one requires the fine gown and jewels to appear really aristocratic. But then what, exactly, is the difference between these and any other women? If the last few years have shown him anything, it is the mutability of all things. If entire cities – countries – can be denatured in so short a space of time, the odds of any human remaining essentially unchanged seem poor.

But clearly Calvert finds something fascinating in them, he watches them like a fox. Perhaps it is the fall itself that interests him. That he, the scion of shopkeepers – albeit extremely successful ones, as he is wont to remind them – might bed a destitute princess of Russia. The waitress comes over to them, ready for their next order. And George sees, with a small frisson of horror, that in the second before she switches on her smile – an electric flash – her eyes are expressionless as a corpse's.

He thinks again of the woman on the jetty. There had been nothing blank in the look she had given him. It had been a glance to singe the nostril hairs.

'Penny for them?' Bill is peering into his face. 'You're smiling like a loon.'

'Pardon? Oh – nothing in particular.'

'Well. Better get back here quickly; the show is about to start.'

A man has stepped up onto the platform, the compère. He wears an outfit that might once have been rather grand: a frock coat, pale blue, gold-trimmed, matching trousers. Now it is several decades out of date, too large, frayed at the cuffs and collar in a soft fuzz of thread.

'Where on earth do you think he found such an article?' Bill murmurs. 'You'd think they could do a little better, with this place being so popular.'

Calvert seems irritated, as though a slight on the club is one upon his taste; it was he who suggested the place. 'It's called The Turgenev,' he says, waspishly, 'it is meant to be old-fashioned. A glimpse of Old Russia – the Russia that saw off Napoleon.'

'Ah.' Bill seems unconvinced.

Fortunately they are all distracted by the announcement of the first performer. The song she breaks into is shrill as the violin, foreign to the ear as vodka on the palate. It is just an entrée, this musical interlude, for the courses to follow: the white thighs beneath silk petticoats.

'I'm going home with her. No, no – her.'

George looks over at him. 'I thought you had a wife, Calvert.'

Calvert's skin is so fair that the flush is instant. Difficult to tell, though, whether he is more embarrassed or angry. 'What exactly is that supposed to mean?'

George isn't exactly sure why he said it. There is hardly much novelty in Calvert's attitude. And who is George to cast judgement? Best to smooth the situation quickly. 'Sorry old chap, didn't mean to offend.'

Calvert nods, curtly. He doesn't speak for the rest of the act. Bill tries to catch George's eye, but he avoids him. The truth is, he is tired. He remembers poor Hatton and his herpes. He thinks he may have seen as much near-nudity in the months of being in this city as he has in his whole medical career, and as much adultery as an East End madame.

If this gives the impression that he is absolutely above it, it is misleading.

He has not always been immune to such intoxications.

Soft skin, perfume, a warm body against his. Being made to feel one was the most interesting man in the room.

No, he was not immune at all.

Nur

When Nur sees the boy reading a book, she almost doubts her own eyesight. All of her efforts to interest him in learning thus far have been thwarted, she has given up any hope. Now this small miracle. He is so engrossed in it he does not even hear her approach.

'What is that?'

He starts in surprise, looks about, furtively. 'I – found it.'

She peers at it more closely and recognises it: the book of recipes, long forgotten. Now she understands the furtiveness. 'You found it in the kitchen, I think.' She has discovered him there, foraging, on a number of occasions. She has not yet had the heart to chastise him for it. 'I haven't seen that for a very long time. May I look?'

He parts with it with some reluctance.

It is the book of recipes that Fatima had her transcribe, when Nur told her they would have to let her go. Her hand almost aches with the memory of the task. She has not opened it since. At a time when bread had been hard to come by, let alone anything else, what would have been the point?

The paper has yellowed, lending it the appearance of something far older. It is like a relic from another age. Not altogether untrue; those days seem long ago.

'I don't understand,' she says. 'I've never seen you so interested in a book. And this is just recipes, lists of ingredients.' But then she recalls his preoccupation with food, the way he never quite seems to be full, and thinks that perhaps, after all, she does understand.

'Which is your favourite?'

The boy takes the book from her, leafs through the pages with a practised air. He finds the one, taps the page. She reads. *Circassian chicken with honey and figs.* There is a pull of feeling associated with this particular recipe, but she cannot understand it at first. The memory eludes her.

She puts the book down. He grasps for it, immediately.

In the first years of war those with their own chickens did rather well for themselves. As fresh meat disappeared from the butchers', vast sums were exchanged for the birds, sometimes fine linens, furniture, jewellery. They were literally worth their weight in gold. Then came the days when no one would part with them for any sum, however outrageous. They had become priceless. And then fresh meat became something that belonged to the past. Perhaps one bird would be kept – and jealously guarded – for its eggs. By then, to eat it would have been a terrible extravagance.

She leaves the boy to his reading, goes back into the apartment. As she crosses the threshold she has it. She last ate the dish on the evening the drums of war had started. The memory hits her full-force.

She is peeling a white fig. They have just eaten the fruits cooked too, with chicken. In the middle of the table is a great platter of them, the room filled with the scent of the leaves. The sky beyond the windows is the dark blue of a late summer night.

They are sedated by the big meal they have just eaten, sitting back in their chairs, drowsy in the candlelight and warmth. It is three weeks before her wedding. She is trying to fix the moment in her mind, because she knows it will be one of the last evenings like this. How many suppers have there been like this? Hundreds? Thousands? The ease of not having to make conversation – though soon her grandmother will light a cigarette and perhaps begin the gossip with which she likes to round off an evening. Or her father, flush from the wine that his religion and his mother frown upon, may decide to make a little speech. He has been particularly affectionate this evening: several times the candlelight has caught the gleam of tears in his eyes. He has talked this evening of love and family, of how special she is to him – of his only daughter, his little rose. Nur thinks she understands . . . he fears the change as much as she does. She does not know the full truth yet. That this morning he evaluated his symptoms, as objectively as he was able, and realised that he would probably not live to see his daughter wed.

She eats a morsel of fig, savours the rich sweet juice. The first fruits of the season are always a revelation of flavour.

Beneath the murmur of voices around the table comes a sound, faint at first, carried across to them from the other side of the water like strange thunder. And then growing, seeming to swell in the silence as a fire feeds upon air. Whatever it is, it is loud. Few sounds reach them from the city here. Here they are protected. Even before they have understood what the sound is there is an ominousness in its insistence. It has silenced all talk. They are hardly breathing, so intently are they listening.

They come for the new recruits with drums too. A marching

band, the flag held high. It is – yes – rather exciting. Her grandmother, always an aficionado of pomp and circumstance, is delighted. They watch Kerem leave with this grand train, blushing at all the fuss being made for him. A schoolteacher turned soldier: such a strange idea! The crowd sings the old song. For the first time Nur hears the words properly: 'Oh wounded ones I am coming to take your place and my heart is crying because I am leaving my beloved ones . . .'

She goes to see him the next day as the recruits leave the building in Sirkeci for a temporary camp on the Black Sea. He has the eyes of a sleepwalker. He smiles at her, but he hardly seems to see her. She wonders if it all feels as unreal to him as it does to her.

'You'll come home soon,' she tells him. 'They have said it will be over quickly.' This is true. But then there had been a time, too, when they thought that he would not be called up at all. They came for the older age groups first – many of them veteran soldiers, battle hardened. The same drums of war. The *Bekçi Baba* – the warden – calling out his summons in the streets: 'Men born between 1880 and 1885 must report to the recruitment centre within a day. Who fails to do so will suffer the consequences of the law.'

Now they have come for those of her brother's age – the youngest group. But it will not be a proper war, everyone says.

'They say,' she tells Kerem, 'that it will be over by Eid al-Adha, in the autumn.'

'Yes,' he says, 'I know. I'll come home with some stories to tell. I suppose I have always wanted to travel a little.'

There is an unreality to it all, at first, that makes it feel rather exciting, almost romantic. Brave Young Men will go to war and return transformed: Heroes of the Empire.

So when her grandmother asks, later: 'Did he look

handsome in his uniform?' it seems only right to nod and say that he had looked very smart indeed. 'And his boots,' her mother adds, 'did they look up to much?' 'Oh yes,' Nur says. 'Excellent quality.' She has always hated lying – she is bad at it. The truth is that he had been wearing his own clothes, his own insubstantial city shoes. The only thing that was correct in the description she gave them was that he had been carrying his bag, stitched by her mother and filled with food, woollen socks and gloves, clean underthings.

When she imagines him at the very end – which she cannot stop herself doing – she sees him wearing these pitifully inadequate clothes, those thin-soled shoes. The shoes of a schoolteacher. A gentle, genteel man in a world utterly hostile to him.

The Prisoner

When they found him he had been cradling Babek as though he were his own dead child. The officer in charge had informed him, graciously, that he would not write this up in his official report: it was not quite seemly. What he would write was that Babek had: 'died in proud service of his country, a hero of the Empire'. There: that would be something for his wife and children.

On that train south he had caught sight of himself in the glass and seen how the cold had disfigured him into someone he did not recognise. He had grown so thin that his skull seemed to be only loosely covered by a thin layer of skin: his near-death writ large upon his body. But there was more than this: his eyes had changed. Perhaps it was just the reflection, but he thought he saw in them a new absence, something that the place had taken from him and might not give back. It frightened him, the sense of distance he felt looking at this stranger. Where was the man he had been? The cold seemed to have killed some invisible part of him as efficiently as it had destroyed visible flesh: the ends of his toes, the pads of his fingers, the scabrous patches on his face, and even the tip of his nose – black as a mark of punctuation, the cold's little joke. That young schoolteacher, who seemed now like a person he might once have briefly met.

The Red Crescent medical officer who treated him had seen worse cases, though.

'Worse how?'

'Oh. Well – the ones who have lost whole limbs, of course. And then there are the ones who die. You'll be all right.'

He wondered what this meant, exactly. He got his answer quickly enough: it meant that he was whole enough to join a new regiment in the south, below Lake Van. Here, their principal enemy was no longer the Russians.

It was quite simple, his new commanding officer explained. The Armenians had betrayed them. Now they had to leave Ottoman lands. There were two options. They had to be encouraged to go, leaving their villages after collecting the possessions and food they would need for the journey eastwards, toward Mesopotamia, or they had to be forced.

'All of the Armenians?' he asked the officer. 'Have they all turned against us?'

There had been children in his class who were Armenian – one of his favourite pupils, a small boy – had been Armenian. Then he thought of the man who had betrayed them. He thought of Babek. But these were simple people, weren't they? Their villages were sleepy, unremarkable places: the bleat of a goat, the wail of an infant, the constant low drone of the heat. Where the most dramatic things that happened was a wild dog running amok in the chicken coop, the occasional modest wedding, the death of an old man. They had lived like this for hundreds – perhaps even thousands – of years. These people, surely, knew nothing of grand deceptions.

It was unclear whether they even knew much about the war until these men of the Ottoman army had descended into their midst and ordered them to begin packing their bags.

'To remove the cancer,' the officer told him. 'We must remove everything. You think these people wear a uniform, to tell us, helpfully, that they're the ones to look out for? They're a little more clever than that. They work in the shadows. That's what makes them so deadly. But we have the element of surprise now. They have no idea what's coming for them.'

This was certainly true. The villagers had simply stared at them as they gave them their orders – even after they had been translated into the local dialect. When they had eventually assembled at the muster points – after threats both shouted and administered with the butt of a rifle – many had come empty-handed, without the possessions they had been ordered to collect. It was as though they did not believe any of this could be quite real.

'But most of these people,' he said to the commanding officer, 'the ones we're actually moving . . . they seem to be all women, old men, children. Surely we should be looking for young men?'

'Look – what's your name? These orders come from the very top. Oh. And you do know the penalty for disobeying a direct order, don't you?'

He thought of the dogs, feasting on the flesh of men who he had laughed with, and eaten bread with, and who had become almost like the brothers he had never had. That had been because of an Armenian. He thought of Babek's family dwarfed by the huge war train, the boys dressed up like little men, waiting for their father to return to them: a hero.

They were to take the Armenians further east, to the very edges of the Ottoman Empire, toward the border with Persia.

These were their orders; from the highest echelons of the War Office in Constantinople. A 'rehoming': this was the term used, apparently. But the area to which they would be moved was known only for its hostility to life: a desert place, a no-place. No one could be expected to make a life there. Yet he could not summon the indignation that he expected to feel, that he might once have felt. It was as though the cold had got deep inside him and frozen any repository of emotion. There was a barrier beyond which he could not go; a numbness.

Besides, Babek had not been given the chance to live. And his old life had been taken from him. He had witnessed events that had changed him, irrevocably. So perhaps it was no unexpected thing that he could not find the empathy he might once have felt. At least these people would be given an opportunity to make a new life, slim though it was. Wasn't that more than he and Babek and all those other frozen corpses had been allotted?

So he no longer complained, no longer questioned, when they marched into the desert with the elderly and very young, the sick, the unfit, the pregnant mothers and newborn babies.

The Boy

'I have something for you. Follow me.'

He stands, resenting the loss of the sun and his book, but curious.

Nur *hanım* leads him into the kitchen. There, on the stone counter a plucked chicken sits, nude and stippled. Beside it, a bowl of plump green figs. The figs on the tree here are over; she must have got them elsewhere. There is more. Excitement quickens in him. A jar half-full of honey, another – he reaches for it, waits for her to stop him. When she doesn't, he sniffs it. Oil. Onions, firm and glossy gold. Several branches of some fragrant herb.

'Thyme,' she says, 'the recipe asks for it.'

'Thank you.'

'No,' she says, 'I think I should be thanking you. I thought you would cook it for us.' Her eyes go to the stove, where – not being tall enough to reach – he recently upset a pot of coffee. 'We will cook it together.'

* * *

Nur *hanım*, who does everything so quickly, is the same with cooking. Though he has never done it before he knows it cannot be rushed. Such a thing requires reverence, patience . . . even a kind of love. He knows the method as well now as he knows his own name, as one might memorise poetry. Here is the onion to cut into delicate slices, the shape and slenderness of the new moon. He passes it to her and watches how she hacks into it with the knife, as though it has done her some personal injury. When she isn't looking, he salvages the job himself. When it comes to cooking the slices gently just until they have turned clear she seems to stab at them with the spoon, bullying them over the heat in the skillet until they begin to crisp and brown. Next time, he thinks, he will ask her merely to light the oven for him: the one thing that he cannot do so easily. After a while she allows him to take over. He gives her only the simplest instructions: stripping the leaves from the woody stalks of thyme, washing the figs (which the recipe does not even ask for).

Both of them are silent now. As he works the bad thoughts, the pain, recede into the background. He concentrates absolutely on the task at hand. The new but not unfamiliar rhythm of it. He knows it, like a secret language. It exists already in his hands. The satisfaction of watching them become something, all these separate things. All because he wills them to be more than they are. The meat turning from pink to golden, the sauce coating it with a glossy, perfumed sheen. The sweet, the savoury, intermingling.

It is the beginning of an obsession – or, rather, the evolution of one. With Nur *hanım*'s help he works his way through the book, through the recipes, that is, with ingredients that are not impossible to source in the city now. He learns that the cooking itself is one thing, there is the pleasure in his growing skill, in the confidence of his hands. But there is also the reaction, the pleasure of seeing his creations enjoyed. Sometimes, Nur *hanım* invites the neighbours from the rest of the building to enjoy the food. Only a short while ago he would have felt a kind of despair at the idea of being forced to share. Now there is only a pride. It is a different sort of fullness. His hunger, the hunger that could not be sated, begins to diminish.

Nur

The boy is a quicker, more innately adept student than she. Her hands, so clever in other ways – writing a letter, embroidering linen – are clumsy and inarticulate in the kitchen. He has a natural understanding of flavour, too. She has to work harder at it. She is impatient, too: she has no time for the dishes that require long cooking – he approaches them with a kind of reverence. While the absence of a particular ingredient has her throwing up her hands in defeat, he is able to improvise. He begins to suggest adaptations, improvements. Wouldn't this taste better stippled with the warmth of some dried chilli? Perhaps mint, with its sharper note, would be a more faithful accompaniment than parsley, which is lost in the dish? She watched and marvels at him, this boy who so recently seemed to have forgotten how to spell his own name, as he annotates the pages with his childish, newly confident hand. It is a humbling thing to observe his discovery of this new part of himself.

Taste, she discovers, has the same memory-invoking powers as scent. Without quite realising it, she is recreating the flavours of her youth.

A morsel of *borek* – a modest enough confection of pastry and cheese – can taste simultaneously of love, death, loss. A spoonful of *imam bayildi*, aubergines simmered to velvet tenderness in tomato, oil and spices, brings tears to her eyes. She can taste in it a particular winter night: the first snow in the city. Cold air seeping through gaps in old wood, pressing its frozen breath against the thin panes of glass. They huddled close around the table. Beyond the window the snow fell thick, silent as a secret. Then Fatima had produced this dish, each spoonful kindling warmth in the belly. The cold had seemed to retreat by a degree. The candlelight now seemed to contain a specific, golden heat. The scene beyond the windows became more remote, more magical.

She had been thirteen. There had still been the childish excitement, the thought of the fresh-fallen whiteness that would await her the next morning – but tempered, too, by the awareness of approaching adulthood. A time when one would need to be seemly, decorous. How many more snows would she see before this? It might be only one. It did not come every year: this strange miracle.

But tomorrow she and her little brother could have a snowball fight. She knew, though, that he would aim to miss. Sometimes he was too gentle for his own good.

That all of this, this concentration of memory, could be unleashed by such humble ingredients, such innocuous preparations . . . it is a kind of sorcery.

So much of the old life is gone – never to be recaptured. The house, the fine things, all are beyond her reach now. But food, even at its most extravagant, is an economical refinement.

For the boy, it is different. It does not have the same taint. For him she suspects it may be a way of forgetting. So he plunges forward, an adventurer, all excitement. She trails after him cautiously, wincing at shadows, knowing they may expand into further deep chasms of memory.

George

There are thirty beds in the ward, fifteen currently occupied. Several of them, poor beggars, are practically insensible with malaria – one very bad. A syphilis case – too much time spent in Pera brothels. Two dysentery. And one man, seconded to the Allied fire brigade, so badly burned on one side that he has the look of being partially skinned, with the muscle exposed raw and livid pink. He was trapped beneath the fallen spar of a flaming building – a wonder, really, that he survived at all.

There are cases that no amount of fortitude can improve; their fate is already sealed. But for those borderline states, when the patient hovers on that thin precipice between life and death, sheer will can make the difference. George knows this, because he has seen it time and again. The struggle, or the acceptance. There is no shame in either, contrary to what many believe.

The burned man, Lockett, spends most days sitting up in bed smoking a cigar and reading the foreign newspapers that George procures for him. He looks as relaxed as a man can look, and if one approaches him from the right side, one might wonder what such a robust-looking character was doing in a hospital bed. The other side is a different tale, a battlefield of dressings that give him the appearance of being held together with sticking plaster. This is practically the case. It is still not certain that he will live. An infection would finish him. There is the unseen, too. A rattle in the lungs: time will tell whether they are damaged beyond all repair.

'How are you this morning, Lockett?'

'All right, doctor. Was wondering if I could get a bit more of that good old Scottish stuff.'

On the first evenings, to help with the pain – and because he liked the man – George had given him generous draughts of his precious single malt. Now he wonders if it had been a mistake.

'Lockett, it's eleven o'clock in the morning.'

'Well, you can't blame a fellow for trying.'

He had refused to take any morphine for the discomfort, once he came to, saying he had seen 'too many go down a bad road with that stuff'. To George's dwindling supplies of Highland gold, however, he has no such objection.

'A coffee, perhaps?'

'Is it that filthy local stuff?'

'Yes. Though I've actually started to think it superior.'

'You've been here too long, doc. You're going native. But . . . oh, go on, why not? It isn't as though a chap has any other options, is it?' He peers ruefully up at George, one eye lidded with intact, pale skin, the other ringed with raw red. If there is a message of entreaty in this look, George chooses not to receive it.

He climbs down to the kitchen on the floor below. Here is a huge Ottoman stove, enamelled in sky blue, for even the most mundane items in this house have a claim to beauty.

It is a formidable, unfamiliar thing with several ovens and six hot plates. Here, presumably, magnificent spreads were once prepared. It seems the sort of house in which such feasts would have been eaten. George has only dared to make coffee upon the smallest plate . . . though, if truth be told, his culinary skill does not extend much further. He bought a small copper pot from the great bazaar in Stamboul – and the coffee, too, following his nose to a stall where men ground the new-roasted beans before one's eyes, packaging it into plump, fragrant parcels.

He measures out the fine grounds, a few spoonfuls of sugar, pours in the water. He isn't absolutely certain he has the method right yet. Every time he stops for a cup on the street he scrutinises the particular blend of flavours and decides how he will better his own recipe. This is how his mind works. He is not creative in any sense, but he can analyse and improve. It has served him well as a medical man; has helped him refine the optimum dosage of quinine without eating into precious, limited supply, to discover the most effective tourniquet for a newly severed limb. He pours two cups of the stuff, watches the brown foam rise to the surface.

Lockett gives his a dubious sniff, places it beside him to cool. George takes the first hot sip. This first mouthful is still something of a shock, the taste like a distillation of earth with only the sweetness of the sugar to make it bearable. Then he begins to savour it.

'How did you get this then? Stuck here with us strays?'

'What do you mean? I'm an MO – that's what I do.'

'No, I mean Constant' of course' – the soldiers' abbreviation. 'Couldn't believe it when I got shipped off here. Thought I was on my way home.'

George sips – too much – scalds his tongue. 'I volunteered, actually.'

'You volunteered?' Lockett frowns up at him. 'Are you mad, doc? What was it . . . the money?'

'I suppose it was. Or something like that.'

Not a complete lie. The money was an attraction, but it was not much more than he could have made with a new placement in England, from the comfort of his own home. But then there had been the challenge of setting up and running his own hospital – that had beckoned to him. So, too, the revelation of proper beds and almost-adequate resources after so many years beneath canvas, eking out supplies.

And yet, if he were to be honest with himself, none of these was quite the reason.

That afternoon, Sister comes to tell him that the man with yellow fever – the doomed case – has died. Will he come and take a look, to verify? And then, really, in this heat, the body . . .

He goes into the ward to see. The fellow lies there, his eyes rolled back into his head. This might mean – thankfully, perhaps – that he was in the grip of delirium while he died. While George was exploring the city, this man was slipping from life. There was nothing more they could have done for him. The rest was the body's work, whether it had enough fight in it.

The man volunteered to come out here, like George. He remembers their conversation now: the man half in the grip of fever, with a too-bright light behind the eyes. He had wanted to see a little more of the world, before settling down for good. It is no greater or lesser tragedy than any of the deaths George has witnessed. But perhaps there is an added poignancy, in the fellow eluding death in the conflagration, only to die here in otherwise benign circumstances.

His family will not have been prepared for it. Undoubtedly, since the war spared him, they may have decided that he had luck on his side: a common enough fallacy.

George looks again at the figure on the bed. The strangeness of this experience has not left him, not since that day at medical college in Edinburgh, when they were first let into the room with no less than thirty cadavers – old and young, fat and thin, male and female – but all alike in one terrible respect. Far more akin in death than they would ever have been in life. The idea that these forms had once been living, breathing, thinking, loving. It seemed so . . . unlikely. The experience became even more uncanny, he would discover, when you had actually known the person. In the dissection room, that day, he had become an atheist.

He walks out into the garden of the hospital. The heat has slipped from its daily peak, the air is heavy with the scent of warm fig leaves. The afternoon has taken on the bluish tint beneath which it will slip, imperceptibly at first – and then suddenly, all at once – into evening. The Bosphorus, drowsy, purplish, only faintly stirring, ranges before him across to the Asian shore. Not such a bad place to die, he thinks: at the meeting of continents, in the cradle of civilisations, beneath this infinite sky. So different to the sky at home, hemmed and softened by cloud. The cemetery is in a good spot, too. They had to bury some of the first prisoners of war handed back to them: the most malnourished, the most diseased. The family will have somewhere to visit.

He makes himself a cigarette. For a man with no religion, this is something of a ritual. He lights it, draws on it, and with the first exhalation expels the thing into the air. It has worked in far more trying times than this.

The Boy

The older lady frightens him. She reminds him of what he
has learned of the sultans of history. Some of them were not
averse to drowning little boys in order to make sure, for
example, that their sons became rulers. But perhaps sometimes they did it just for a whim, when things got boring in
the imperial harem. Nur *hanım* did not teach them this at
school, but small boys have ways of learning things. They
put them in sacks, he knows, like unwanted kittens. The old
woman has no son, and no throne to protect – but he is not
absolutely sure that he wouldn't put it past her. She seems
to live in history, too: she talks more often of the past than
she does of the now. In her presence he slows his steps, lowers
his voice. She is to him unfathomably old. To him Nur *hanım*
is old – and yet this lady is *infinitely* more so.

He does not think she likes him very much. He has heard
himself referred to by her as 'the boy'. Only ten days ago
she discovered him playing with some small animals of green
stone that were, apparently, extremely rare and precious. The
trunk of the elephant had, unfortunately, parted ways with

the body. There would probably not be significant qualms about the drowning. He is most nervous when they are alone in the apartment together, like today.

He has decided to make stuffed cabbage leaves: a new recipe from the book. He and Nur are meant to be making these together. She does not like him using the stove. But she is delivering her embroideries to the seller at the bazaar, and it is raining heavily outside, so there will be no one playing in the street. The morning stretches interminably before him in the way that hours do when one is young and has so many of them left to use up.

A careful perusal of the recipe has told him that he will not need to use the stove too much. Most of this is in the preparation. Besides, it always seems to be Nur who burns herself against the handle of a pot, or scalds herself with steam – not him. He begins to set out his ingredients: the rice, the onions, the cabbages, the nuts and raisins, the olive oil. He has climbed onto the stool, and is just preparing the pot for the cabbage when he hears something that makes his skin prickle with fear.

'What are you doing, boy?'

He turns and sees her in the archway. One hand leans her weight heavily upon her cane, the other holds aloft one of her cigarettes. The mingled scent of these and the *oud* that she wears at throat and wrists is uniquely hers.

'I – I'm cooking, *hanım*.'

'At the stove?'

'Yes.'

She raises an eyebrow. He braces himself for the reprimand. To his surprise, it does not come. She blows out a thin stream of smoke.

'What are you making?'

'*Lahana dolması, hanım*.'

'Ah. They are my favourite. I suppose you were making them for me?'

Nur *hanım* has always been rigorous on the importance of telling the truth. 'No.'

Her eyebrows come together. He feels that despite his best efforts he may not have said the right thing.

'And how are you making them?'

He shows her the book.

'Oh.' She shakes her head. 'No, one does not require a book for such a recipe. Such things are simply *known*.'

He watches as she unties the scarf from about her neck, and begins to remove the dazzling rings from her fingers. He has an uneasy premonition. If he were not standing on the stool, he would take a step back.

'Are you frightened of me, boy?'

He wavers. This time he is determined to get it right. 'No.'

'Good.' She moves forward. The cane is forgotten, resting against the wall. When she wills it, it seems, she is rather steady upon her feet. 'I am going to help you make them.' She shakes her sleeves back from her wrists. 'Needless to say we will not be using a recipe book.'

'But—'

'For someone like me, such a thing is in the blood. You, perhaps, would not understand. You are not a woman, nor are you properly a Turk. But we have been making these things since the beginning of time. To use someone else's instructions would be an embarrassment.'

He lets her join him. What else can he do?

He quickly sees, to his horror, that she is not doing anything as the recipe says it should be done.

'Of course,' she tells him as she begins to boil a huge quantity of rice, which the book says should be mixed first with the nuts and oil, 'I have never actually *made* this dish myself. In the past' – *her beloved past* – 'we had a woman who did this sort of thing for us.'

'The book—'

'But that does not matter,' she insists, 'such things are beyond practice. They belong to a different, deeper kind of understanding.'

The room has filled with the refuse-stink of the cabbage. He is certain that it is cooked far beyond the tenderness demanded by the recipe. The leaves have lost any hint of green, and seem to be fast approaching brown. But he is too afraid to tell her. The rice, too, appears overcooked. And there is so much of it: far more than will be needed to fill the leaves. Nur *hanım* will not be happy, she despises waste.

It is only when she takes the onion that he has so carefully filleted and chopped, and begins to mix it – raw – into the rice that he feels compelled to break his silence.

'But,' he says, 'the onion is not cooked.'

'Well,' she says, and takes a breath, as though she is about to issue one of her proclamations. Then she seems to waver. For the first time, she looks a little unsure. 'What does it say, there, in that book?'

He draws it toward him. 'That the onion should be cooked.'

'I see—'

But now he has the momentum, ' . . . and the rice should be mixed with the nuts and oil first . . . and the cabbage should only be simmered until tender.'

Both look toward the pot containing the cabbage, where the water has acquired an unhealthy yellow foam.

'Ah.' In a different voice, a general acknowledging the wisdom of an inferior, she says, 'Shall we begin again?'

The Prisoner

They were suffering, the Armenians. At the beginning they had railed against the soldiers, pleaded with them. Now they didn't have the energy to resist. They were, on the whole, silent, save for the occasional low, almost animal moan of discomfort – shocked and then exhausted into accepting their fate.

But some of them could not keep up. They kept stumbling over their own feet. The shoes many of them wore had only been good for a day of walking. Now half of the group walked on the burning ground on their bare soles. They were poor country people, of course, that was part of it. Perhaps they did not have good shoes. But it might also have been the thing he had suspected: that none of them had really believed in what was happening to them. They had not properly prepared themselves.

In those first days they seemed to treat it as a misunderstanding that might at any second be realised, that the whole thing would be called off. They would be allowed to return home. Home was all they knew. He had very little knowledge of this south-eastern part of the Empire, other than the names of towns – Mosul, Kirkuk – and rivers – the Tigris, the Euphrates – learned from a map. But he had more than these people, for whom the next village, a day on the back of a mule, might have been the farthest they had ever travelled. They had been walking for three weeks now. Or was it four? He had long ago lost track of the days.

One might almost feel sorry for them. But you could not think like that about an order. And these were traitors . . . murderers. By association, of course. And the fact was: they, the officers, were suffering too. Their feet were blistered and swollen, too, their bellies were empty, their eyes also blinded by the bright, scorched, unending wastes over which they travelled. So when the stragglers at the back began to lag behind, to fall down, they became less and less patient. *They* weren't allowed to lie down in the dirt and cry out with their pain, they had no one from whom they could beg mercy. So it became easy not to care for these stragglers, indeed, to begin to blame them. Their moans were merely another physical affliction: worse than the rest of it, somehow. And then it became clear how easily the problem could be dealt with; unlike the other afflictions over which they had no control.

A bullet, carefully aimed, where the spine met the skull. Then more silence: not just from the one who had been silenced forever but from all of them, silence of shock and fear.

At first it was only the most brutal among them who did the silencing. The ones whose hatred was a deep, established thing. At first you merely observed. And then you realised that to observe and say nothing was as bad as being complicit, even worse. So you became complicit.

There was a woman whose bare feet were so badly blistered that she could hardly walk. She kept falling down. She had two children, a very small boy and a slightly older girl: she had carried them most of the way. She tried to crawl instead of walk. One of the soldiers prodded her with his bayonet, ordered her to stand.

At one point they came across the Tigris, moving sluggishly through the boiling land. Suddenly, the woman with the blistered feet veered off toward it. There was a moment of stunned silence.

'Hey!' the superior shouted to him. 'Stop her!'

'I think she wants to cool her feet.'

'Don't we all? And she's not: she's going to jump in. Look! What are you waiting for – go!'

He went after her. Suddenly, perhaps in anticipation of the water, she was moving quickly. A grotesque drunk man's stagger on her broken feet.

'Come back!' he shouted. She paid him no heed.

'She cannot get away,' the officer shouted after him. 'All must be accounted for.'

'Stop!' he called to her. 'I order you to stop!'

Still, no response. It was as though she could not hear him, perhaps she was beyond hearing. If anything she picked up speed – still running with that odd, lopsided, staggering gait, dragging her children who were stumbling, struggling to keep up.

'Stop!'

She continued to run.

It was the action of a moment, without thought. He raised his gun and aimed for that spot at the back of the neck and fired and the front of her head exploded outwards.

He felt something inside him fracture.

Later he would know it. That was the moment. Despite everything he might still have returned to him, the man he used to be, before that. After it, there could be no way back. And that was before the bullets began to run out, and became a precious commodity. Other means had to be found. The butts of rifles. A large enough rock. His bare hands.

Some of them went mad with what they had done. Often they were the ones who committed the worst acts. A kind of frenzy overtook them. It was a dislocation of the self. You could almost hear it. But though the thing inside him had fractured, he did not go mad. He envied them, because there was a kind of refuge in their madness, a lack of culpability. And sometimes he envied the dead more than the mad because they were blameless; now, if they had committed crimes then at least they had paid for them with their own blood. He envied Babek, who he had pitied, because he had never been asked to sacrifice this much. He had died without this burden upon him, without ever discovering the extent of his own potential depravity, without ever knowing what evil might exist within himself.

One night he staggered out of camp. He was thinking of that river, the Tigris, only a few miles away.

He had the half-formed idea of washing himself until all of it came off. And then diving in, though he had never been a strong swimmer, and letting it carry him away somewhere . . . to a place of peace.

He walked on his broken schoolteacher's shoes for hours, but he did not find the water. So he walked further, into the night. He realised dimly that he must have missed the river, might indeed have been walking in the wrong direction entirely. But he could not stop. He walked until the first pink-tinged fingertips of dawn began to creep beneath the curtain of the night.

He only stopped walking when he heard the shout: 'Halt! Who goes there?'

He had not discovered the river but he had found the enemy. The British, at the grisly end of their Mesapotamian campaign. Tired and sick and ready for retreat – and certainly not expecting anything like this, this unexpected boon. An enemy soldier practically offering himself up to be taken as a prisoner of war.

Anyone would think the fellow had gone completely mad.

The Traveller

I remember an almost impossible place, where you could walk over a bridge and hear fifteen different languages spoken at once; where you could cross between two continents in the time it took to eat a warm *simit*, to smoke a single cigarette.

I read of it obsessively in books. I discovered swathes of history. Byzantium: a great, sophisticated, democratic metropolis when most of England, which thought of itself as so ancient and civilised, had been little more than a collection of mud huts. The Romans had come and made it the new, eastern jewel of their empire. The emperor had loved it more than Rome, and had given it his name: Constantine. He had made it a place of pomp and splendour, colonnades and bathhouses and statues. Which would be crushed to rubble by the victorious Mehmet the Conqueror and his army. The Ottomans. Who would in their turn build structures of incomparable beauty: mosques with airy, burnished domes, minarets so delicate they looked as though they would not be able to stand the weight of the clouds they seemed to hold aloft.

And yet I did not find within these pages the truth of the place I was looking for. That city was a living place, full of creatures: stray cats sleeping in the midday sun; dogs roaming the streets, as gnarled and characterful in appearance as the old men who sat watching them. A sudden confetti of doves alighting in a garden beside the Bosphorus.

A city full of scents, too. Some of them bad: mackerel left out too long upon the quay; the unwashed bodies of people who had arrived upon huge ships and had no proper place to lay their heads. The smell of burned things, the peculiar odour of an entire life gone up in an evil greasy smoke: books and bedding and furniture and house and worse. But good scents, too: warm savoury fig leaves and jasmine flowers – tiny white stars against old stone – and the brine of the sea and the toasting of bread and the burned caramel of coffee and the pure sugar cloud that floated through the open door of a confectioner's shop.

I wake and for several moments do not know where I am. A ship, I think – the listing motion, the feeling of confinement. Then I discover my surroundings: the dense foam cushion of the couchette beneath me, the small shard of dusty light beneath the window blind. I pull the cord, roll it up.

I am unprepared for the splendour of the view that greets me. When I last looked out all was in darkness, lit by the occasional bright flare of a signal box, the night trundling by. The rain continuing, but as a desultory drizzle, as though it had run out of enthusiasm for the task. Anything could have been beyond the track, but one assumed it was much of the same unremarkable, interminable pastoral.

Now, the mountains.

An early morning sky of a billowing softness, nursery blue, with a powder smudge of pink at the horizon. Cloud obscures the lower slopes but the ridge rises out of it, the sun just beginning to find the peaks. They seem less to reflect it than to glow from within like melted metal. They are lethal, beautiful. The quality of the light. The air smells, tastes different too. I open the little flap of a window as far as it will go and drink it in.

Something has opened in my chest at the sight of the mountains. Difficult to tell in this moment whether it is grief, or joy, or some strange amalgam of the two. My face tightens with cold, and I realise, lifting a hand to it, that my cheeks are wet with tears.

A journey, almost a lifetime ago. Days of travel . . . different countries, a whole continent's worth of them. Speeding me away from that place. Fields and villages and great old gilded cities. Then these mountains. Set apart from the rest, looking down at me impassively. Then I understood quite how far I had come. That I was never going back.

I decide to go in search of some breakfast. I dress clumsily – the fastening of each button seems to be accompanied by a purposeful lurch of the train that sends me crashing into the couchette or the washstand – and make my way unsteadily through the sleeping carriage. At intervals half-open doors disclose scenes of unwitting intimacy: stirring forms beneath sheets, sleep-rumpled pyjama-clad bodies. The eye is drawn to these revelations even as one tries not to look. I feel a peculiar tenderness for these strangers, there is familiarity in their unguardedness. All of us, I think, share a certain vulnerability on waking: it is always something of a shock.

I walk the length of the train, through the couchette cars and the second-class carriages in which the passengers doze in strange contortions: I do not envy them their fractured night's sleep. I discover that there does not appear to be a dining car at all. What a fall from former glory has occurred here, to this train that was once a moving Grand Hotel. With the shutters up throughout the train now the landscape seems to enter the carriage, almost to overwhelm it. It feels more as though we are floating through it than travelling on solid ground. I see businessmen who seem to be making a studied effort not to look out of the windows, as though to be awed by the scenery is really somewhat déclassé. But I see, too, small faces pressed against the glass.

Back in the couchette, galvanised by coffee and a stale bread roll, I open my suitcase. I lift it out, and lay it upon the bed. It is perhaps two metres in length, but the fabric is so fine that it takes up less room than a paperback when folded. As it unfurls the sunlight catches on gold thread. The hues are ecstatically vivid, despite the age of the piece. It is hand-sewn. The stitching, though neat and tiny, bears the unmistakable evidence of human imperfection. I trace it with a finger. I feel the peculiar intimacy of it, my hand so near to the place where, decades ago, another hand worked its talent into the cloth. Fingers tight about the needle, gripping, piercing.

Over the years it has travelled with me everywhere, improving every space in which it has been placed. Illicitly loud against regulation linen. Glowing with an almost preternatural brightness from a wall in London, the colours filling the room like light passed through stained glass, bleeding into the grey day outside. And now, the uninspiring Formica and chipboard interior of a train berth: ridiculous splendour, the whole space seeming to shrink and gather about it.

Threads have come loose and small stains have appeared over time but it has never been washed or mended. I could not bear it. I could not stand the idea that some essence might be removed in the cleaning of it: the spirit of a place, of the person who made it. I could not bear the thought that the sanctity of its creation would be compromised by the work of a stranger.

It is something tangible. Made by her. Almost a part of her. It is like the relic of magic left in the hands of the narrator at the end of a fairy tale. It means that I did not imagine any of it. It makes her real.

The Boy

For some time he has carried around in him a kernel of pain, like a hot stone. Normally it sits in his chest, somewhere between his lungs. In the day he can manage it. When his mind is busy, at school. When he is cooking, particularly. But at times, when he is trying to sleep, and finds himself alone in the dark with his thoughts and no distractions, it seems to grow. At these times it feels that it is taking control of him, that it is almost bigger than him. He wonders how it is that his body remembers to breathe or swallow, or any of the other things that keep him alive. Because his head is full with it, his thoughts are blotted out by it. It is no real cause for alarm, then, when the pain grows. It is in his head now, and his stomach, and his limbs ache with it. All of this is new. But still he does not call out to Nur *hanım*, or to either of the older ladies. Instead he shuts his eyes.

Incredible heat. From everywhere the sound of screaming and the howls of dogs, ringing feet on the cobblestones. In the street: old men in nightshirts, women staggering about with armfuls of screaming children, their faces horrible with fear. Every so often there is a roar and a *whoooooomp* and a vast, fiery object falls as though thrown from the sky itself: a fiery timber, a shower of red-hot roof tiles. The sky is as light as day. About him everything is movement – the flames, the running. But he is to stay here hidden from the fire's sight – understand? – until they return. And he will stay here, for two more days, as the *tulumba* eventually bring the blaze under control. As the neighbourhood is revealed in its new incarnation: a no-place, a black, matchstick city, disgorging the occasional plume of dark smoke. His only disobedience will be to move back inside when it becomes too cold to remain outdoors.

No one is coming. They have forgotten him. There are things he knows, terrible things, but that he cannot look at, not now, not ever.

But now he hears it. Someone calling his name. He opens his eyes. It takes a moment to understand where he is.

Even when she found him, she had been calm. Her voice had soothed him. For the first time he sees her frightened.

'Where is the pain?' she says, loudly, almost harshly. 'Show me. Here? And here?' She presses a hand against his forehead, snatches it away just as quickly. Then, with a hitch in her voice, 'I am going to get help. Do you understand?'

Nur

'It must be something he ate,' her grandmother decides. And then, with unusual tenderness, 'It is my fault, I cooked with him.'

Yet he ate very little at supper: Nur was surprised by his lack of appetite. She had almost mentioned it, but decided to let it pass.

Now she remembers the time she discovered him digging for roots in the school's small garden, eating his discoveries indiscriminately. She had dragged him up by his armpits: didn't he understand that he could poison himself?

Could he have done such a thing again? Not now, surely . . . but then with his fondness for food, his eagerness to experiment? If he has poisoned himself it will only get worse, she should take him to see someone, immediately. Now that she has decided she feels a new calm, almost a coldness. They need a doctor.

'I'm going out,' she tells her grandmother who – inexplicably – is now offering the boy a puff on one of her 'restorative' cigarettes, and looking faintly cross when he shakes his head.

She'll go to Mustafa Bey, her father's old friend: one of the kindest men, and most knowledgable. He only lives a few streets away – he too has fallen upon shortened times.

'No,' her grandmother says, scandalised. 'You cannot go out at this time. Send for . . .' she seems to grasp for a few moments for a name, a fragment from the past. Defeated, remembering where she is, she lapses into a silent consent.

'I'll be careful.'

'You will wear a veil.' Her grandmother stands.

'*Büyükanne*, I don't—'

'It is one thing for you to be walking the streets bare-faced in the day, even if it is one thing I heartily disapprove of. It is another for you to go out at night. It makes a certain impression, Nur, on a particular sort of person. I will not have you in danger.'

There are times when it is better not to argue.

Behind the veil the dim-lit streets become the shifting landscape of a dream. It is quiet with the particular intensity of the deepest hours of the night, and despite her purpose and urgency, Nur is unnerved. She cannot think of a time in her whole life in this teeming city when she has been so alone. The cobbles sheen with rain, slick and perilous underfoot. A sound comes, a note of utter desolation. It is only the yowling of a cat – but, disembodied, it has a strange power. It is like a distillation of the hour itself.

When she reaches Mustafa Bey's house, she is struck by the certainty that no one is inside. All of the houses are shut up for the night, of course, but this one, she feels, has the particular blankness of an empty building. All the same, she knocks on the door – what else can she do? When no answer comes, she knocks harder – using both fists.

From the house next door, from behind the obscuring

screen of a *keyf*, comes a woman's voice. 'What are you doing out there? Don't you know people are trying to sleep?'

Nur recognises the voice. It is the widow who visits her mother and grandmother to share neighbourhood gossip.

'It's me,' she calls, 'Nur.'

'Little Nur. But what are you doing, out at this hour?'

'I'm looking for Mustafa Bey.'

'Well, you won't find him here.'

'Why not?'

'Oh, you haven't heard?' The delight in being the first to impart the news. 'He and his wife have gone to Damascus, to live with their relatives there. Last week. After their Irfan died, you understand . . . the city holds too many memories.'

So she hurries on to the Red Crescent hospital near the quays, but even before she arrives she can hear the chaos, can see a crowd of the sick and injured waiting in the street outside. The new arrivals in the city: there are too many of them for the city to cope. Some are so ill that they are lying in the street, barely sensible.

She tries to think, but her mind is clouded by panic. She looks behind her, to the night-time glimmer of the Bosphorus. The ferries are still running. She knows, suddenly, where she must go.

George

He opens his eyes, and finds himself in a darkness as absolute as when they were closed. The sound – he thinks it might have been gunfire in the dream – resolves itself into an urgent knocking. He fumbles with the lamp, fingers clumsy, goes pyjama-clad to the door. Sister Agnes is on the other side; she half-falls into the room. Her look, as she surveys him, suggests that she had hitherto expected a doctor to be immaculately presented at all times, fully dressed and ready for duty.

'One of the patients?'

'Someone here to see you.' A faint note of scandal. 'An Ottoman. A woman.'

He dresses quickly, wondering what on earth this can all be about. A Turkish woman, here? And at this time of night?

In the hallway is a slim, veiled figure. In the uncertain light from the lantern she appears rather ghoulish; he feels a small thrill of disquiet. She lifts her veil.

'You.' He recognises her instantly – but he cannot make any sense of her presence here.

She comes towards him like a wraith, white-faced. 'I need your help.'

He is surprised by the meagreness of her lodgings. Neither neighbourhood or house seems to match her: the fine bearing, the fluency and intelligence of her speech. Nor the regal poise of the old woman, who looks at him as she might a grocery boy and who wears several rings inlaid with what appear to be vast emeralds and yellow diamonds.

When he sees these baubles, utterly incongruous with the dingy room, he thinks he understands.

He bends over the boy, and there is an intake of breath from the old woman, as though he were a vampire about to drink the child's blood. When he'd arrived, the boy was retching a thin stream of bile. But in the last few minutes his eyes have rolled back into his head. George thinks he has an idea of the complaint. He just needs to make certain. He touches a hand to the forehead. It is boiling hot, his hand comes away slick with sweat.

There is a scream – and then a hard blow catches him on the back of his head: such a surprise that he stumbles, almost pitching forward across the prone child. He turns, and finds the old woman looking back at him with menace in her eyes.

'*Büyükanne! Bunu yapma!* Stop that!' The woman, Nur, turns to him. 'I'm so sorry. She does not understand. She sees only an enemy.'

He rubs the back of his head. He feels a little stunned. Quite incredible, that there should be such power in one of those frail old hands. She keeps the hand aloft, threateningly. Her expression tells him that she will not hesitate to strike again.

Keeping a wary eye upon her, he speaks to the younger woman.

'I'm fairly certain that it is malaria. The fever, the vomiting, it all makes sense.'

'What can be done?'

'Quinine, rest, fluids.' He looks her in the eye. 'I have to warn you. Your son is in a precarious state. You must prepare yourself for the fact that he may not recover.'

Her mouth is a thin line, and her hand is at her throat. He can see the struggle, her fear and grief. But she merely nods.

'And he will have to come with me. To the hospital.'

Now she is unable to hold her silence. 'He cannot remain here? I can watch over him.'

'No. I cannot ensure that he will receive adequate treatment if he is here. He needs to be observed constantly. Even the slightest change, invisible to one who is not a doctor, could be fatal.'

He is purposefully brutal, he needs her to understand that there is no argument against his taking the boy with him, now. He has been here before with worried mothers.

She nods, and he is impressed again by her self-possession. 'Then you must do it.'

The Boy

The man who takes him from Nur is very tall, and his face is in shadow, and he speaks in a foreign language. He does recognise some of these words. But the pain and confusion is too great for him to decipher them.

The next thing he remembers: being lifted, carried. The great expanse of water, black as a concentration of the night itself. He has seen fishermen throwing catch thought too small, or diseased, back into the waves. Perhaps this will happen to him.

The crossing: a swarm of stars above, clusters of brilliance that seem to shift and sway. Every movement of the boat is pain, but he clenches himself against it and thinks only of the stars. Somewhere behind them – beyond them – he knows that his mother and father are watching. If they are waiting for him on the other side it will not be so bad.

Then he is being carried again, and leaves are brushing his face and the sky is obscured. Nur *hanım* is gone, she has given him to the foreign stranger.

He understands. He has made too much trouble for her.

She is giving him up. He cannot help crying out in fear and loss. He knows he will be ashamed of this later: crying out like a baby!

Nur

Back at the apartment, in the secret dark of the kitchen, Nur sits down upon a chair and stares at a spot before her; seeing nothing. She feels the pressure of tears, but the ability to find this release – the talent – long ago deserted her. When she is finally returned to herself she discovers that her hands are clasped about her lower abdomen, as though there were still something there to protect.

The infinite variety of loss. When one has lost little, one cannot understand this. One thinks the thing must be of a type, only varying in scale and quality. She has become an expert. A connoisseur.

Her father, emphatically lost. A grave to visit, at Eyüp. Her mother, lost in all but her physical self. A brother, lying broken in some forgotten waste of the Empire: the loneliness of the body; too horrible to think of.

Her secret loss. A gain discovered only after the knowledge of its losing, when the blood came. A terrifying quantity; the death of an unknown part of herself. How to begin to grieve it?

Now a new loss has presented itself, if only as a possibility. She does not know, seeing this new one appear, if she can contain another within her. Because each grief is not something to be experienced and overcome, like a severe but finite bout of illness. She has learned this. It is absorbed into the self, it becomes a part of the self. A change occurs; mysterious, intangible, but definite. The person is altered forever by it.

PART TWO

The Prisoner

'I noticed that you do not sleep. Sometimes at night you cry out.'

He glanced over to where the speaker was sitting. The man did not look quite like the other prisoners. After so long in this British prison camp in the Egyptian desert, with poor food, disease rife, blistering heat and perhaps worst of all a monotony of existence that ate at the soul, many of the men had acquired the look of the walking dead.

And yet this man, though thin, his cheeks drawn, had something almost elegant about him. Unlike most of them he had not long ago decided to neglect his appearance. His hair was carefully combed, his cheeks freshly shaven, his moustache newly waxed. He had a gleam in his eye that could be described either as enlightened . . . or, less kindly, fanatical. This in itself was a novelty. So many of the men's eyes were cloudy with boredom or hunger or the beginnings of the blindness that had blighted so many of them: a condition that even their captors did not seem to have intended, or to understand.

He thought: what could be the harm in talking of it, in such a place? For so long it had been stoppered up inside him, poisoning him from within.

'I have done terrible things. Evil things.'

'And what are they?' The man, though only ten or so years his senior, had an almost fatherly air.

He hesitated.

'However bad they may be, I am certain I may have heard worse.'

As he admitted them, those deeds that he could actually bring himself to talk of, he found that he could hardly believe in them . . . that if he had not actually been there himself to witness them, to commit them, he would think that they had to be unspeakable lies. But he could feel them in him; a deep sickness, deeper than flesh and bone, a poison that would destroy him from within.

Finally the man put up a hand. 'It is enough. I know what it is you speak of.'

'You too were involved?'

The man did not appear to have heard him. 'But at a time like this what is important is how one may justify the act.'

'I'm not sure that there can be any—'

The man stopped him with a brief motion of his hand. There was an innate authority in the gesture, an assumption that he would be obeyed, and the idea came to him that this prisoner had been no ordinary soldier before his capture.

'For too long this Empire has been a sick, tired, lumbering thing. Those differences that once made us strong are now destroying us: when something is so fractured it cannot be efficient, or strong. To move forward, we need to be whole, uniform. Our differences are weaknesses because they represent a conflict of interest. Do you see?'

'I'm not certain.'

'War means doing terrible things for a just, even noble, cause. The smallest boy knows this. Every army has killed traitors of its cause. What happened to the Armenians was yet another tragic, but necessary, by-product of the war. There is no virtue in tormenting yourself.'

That night he lay in his cot, thinking of what the officer had told him. For months he had thought of himself as something less than human, denatured by the hideousness of his acts. But now he had been presented with a new possibility: that these acts were not merely justifiable, but perhaps even worthy of praise.

It would explain everything; it would make it all condonable. But that was too easy. He could not believe in it: could he? He wished that he could. If he could he might be able to find some relief. The thing that had seemed so senseless, a random flowering of evil – inside himself as much as without – might acquire meaning and definition. He might even be able to sleep again; to stop fantasising about ways to end the play of horror within his mind.

It was a seductive possibility. It was as though a mirror had been held up to him in which everything was reversed. In which he was not a monster but a hero; in which his acts were not cowardly but courageous. Acts that an ordinary man might not have had the strength of character to commit.

But it could not be true. Could it?

And yet each day, over the weeks that followed, he sought out the officer. He found that merely to hear the man speak was soothing. He was *so certain*. Another version of events. It might be a fiction but it was a comforting fiction at least. It glittered to him in his dark place.

With enough retellings, it ceased to be merely a story.

Here is something true: it is not difficult to believe in a better version of oneself. A man must be very strong-willed indeed if he is to refuse to accept another's idea of him as heroic, not monstrous.

Gradually his own memories began to acquire the shimmer of unreality. The things that had happened – that he had done – became like a bad dream. They were a nightmare that pervaded every moment of his waking life, yes, but perhaps not quite so vividly as they once had. Where they had him so firmly in their grip he now found himself able to halt them for a time, to ask questions of them.

What this man offered was an antidote to that poison that had gone deep inside him. He was like a dying man – thinking himself too far gone for help but willing to try anything. So he grasped for it. Of course he did.

A new system of belief. This was what it was. In order to follow it, he had to give himself over to it completely. Like any new convert he had to forget everything he had believed before, to leave behind that weaker, questioning part that would in the end have destroyed him.

He had horrified himself with thoughts of how his family would react, if they knew what he had done. Now he saw that such fears were irrelevant. Ordinary people like his mother, his sister, could never be expected to understand. He had been involved in something that defied comprehension; something much larger than all of them.

Some in the camp had peculiar obsessions. There was an officer who had never played a musical instrument before but became fixated by the idea of making himself a lute. Somehow he even infected a couple of their British captors with his dream. They brought materials for him: a file, plywood, glue. He worked tirelessly in a corner of the sleeping block, which became known as the 'Egyptian Lunatic Asylum'. His hands became a map of welts and cuts; he had only a penknife to work with. No one really thought the thing would be completed, but perhaps that was no bad thing if it kept him occupied.

Even when – despite all the odds – it was finished, he spent several weeks refining the thing. Smoothing edges, tightening strings, fashioning a plectrum, adding a *gergi*. Now all were interested, invested in the fate of the lute.

Finally, he had to accept that there was no way in which it could be bettered. His work was done. All celebrated the triumph with him. They gathered about, and asked him to play for them. But he could not play – he was just the maker. A captain who could took over and regaled them with songs from their homeland. The lute maker retreated into a corner with the rest of them and sang along too, with a smile of deepest contentment upon his face.

Within a week, he was dead from dysentery. It was bad luck, some said. At least he had managed to finish his little project. But they all knew the truth of it, really. He had lost his purpose.

What was *his* purpose?

His was this new system of belief. It had its own language; comprised of words such as *necessary*, and *righteous*. Phrases such as: *the future of the nation state, the Turkish people*. He was not alone. Such phrases were murmured in the camp refectory as the unchanging daily slop was spooned onto their plates, or in the communal washrooms as men rinsed their wasted bodies. These were slogans of pride at a time when dignity had otherwise been lost. For some, as for him, it was a new creed. For others it might have been little more than a mechanism of survival. You lived here either in a state of fervent belief and hope, or you despaired and died. It was as simple as that.

Sometimes, still, in moments of weakness, doubts would creep in. There was perhaps some small part of him that obstinately refused to be convinced. That reminded him, for example, of the Armenian children in his class: of his favourite pupil; that clever, naughty boy who had always had an answer for everything. He would wonder what had become of them, of their families. But he learned to stifle this part. It would endanger the whole construction: if he let it it would destroy it and, in the process, it would destroy him.

This thing had forged him into someone new. It had been terrible, but in the same way that fire is terrible and yet is used to temper metal, to separate the ore from the baser bedrock, to strengthen and refine.

He understood that now.

Nur

At times this city seems more beautiful than she has ever seen it. Perhaps it is the season; still hot, but the sun of autumn has a maturity and resonance that it lacks at other times of the year. All colour is more vivid beneath it. The sky of late afternoon is so intensely blue it seems almost violet, and the light kindles intimations of gold in old stone. The Bosphorus basks in it, too, performing sedate transformations: from the pale, whitish mauve of early morning, through the deep navy of noon, the evening silver.

The city has revealed itself as a turncoat; it does not care for them, for all they have lost. It will endure after those who live within it now perish. It has continued its existence in tranquility, feeding contentedly from the wellspring of time – even as marauding armies have arrived at its gates ready to waste and conquer, even as fire has rained from the sky. Perhaps this has always been the unspoken agreement between the city and its inhabitants. They are birds resting upon an ancient bough. If the wind blows too hard for them to keep their footing it . . . well, it cannot be blamed on the tree, can it?

When she arrives at the old house she sees several white-robed figures, two playing a game of chess, the others making suggestions; a couple stand a little way off, smoking pipes.

They are enjoying the shade thrown by the elegant umbrella pine that she used to climb as a child. She can still recall the rough texture of the bark against her bare shins and feet, the perfume of the sap discovered later in sticky clumps in the hair, between fingers and toes. At the sight of them, within her, that familiar kindling of useless fury.

When they catch sight of her, all talk stops. She would like to believe it is because they have felt the hot touch of her anger. She knows the truth is that she is a spectacle, a curiosity. As she makes her way to the door she feels their eyes upon her: an intruder in their sanctuary. Then one says something, a little too loudly for her not to hear, but too quiet for her to make out. Laughter follows. By the time she has made it to the door her self-possession has almost deserted her.

The same nurse, wearing the same air of vague disapproval, comes to meet her.

'I'll tell the doctor. He may not allow a visit so early. The' – a fractional pause – 'patient may not be ready.'

Nur waits, feeling chastised, beneath the silent scrutiny of the white-robed figures.

It is the first time she has entered the house in five years. When her chest begins to burn she realises that she has been holding her breath. The smell of the place is the thing that catches her first. There are new notes: something antiseptic, the nostril-sting of detergent, the unmistakable, indefinable smell of sickness – something stale. But beneath all of this there is the scent of her home. Familiar as a loved one.

The nurse has returned.

'Follow me.'

She hesitates.

The nurse beckons her forward with an impatient motion.

Nur suspects the woman thinks her a little mad. She imagines that she must look a little mad – particularly when she steps over the threshold, and the act alone summons the sting of tears.

But there is also curiosity. It is immediately clear that the *selamlik*, visible through the open door off the hallway, is almost untouched. Here the men used to gather: her father and uncles and other guests, later her brothers. She risks a step nearer. She is almost certain that she can still detect the scent of her father's particular brand of tobacco. The room is full of ghosts.

The *haremlik* is a different matter. It has been colonised by the living – and the dying. The room that was once the exclusive sanctuary of women is now a sleeping place for foreign men: sick ones, but the enemy nevertheless. It has been renamed, too. This, the nurse explains, leading her briskly through, is 'the ward'. Temporary beds line both walls. All about her are prone forms, more or less dressed than the robed man she met in the gardens. An expanse of livid flesh draws the eye, though. She cannot help but look, sees a figure who has been very badly burned, resists the involuntary impulse of pity. This man has fresh linen, a Bosphorus breeze through an open window. All the comforts her former home can provide. And he is alive; albeit barely. Her brother, for all she knows, did not even have a funeral shroud.

Beyond the *haremlik* is the *sofa*, the masterpiece of the house, with its tiled garden and mosaic floor. She sees that at some point the fountain, visible through the open doors, has ceased to flow. Powered by some miracle of hydraulics fed from the Bosphorus outside, it was her father's pride.

He used to say that the sound of the flowing water was the most peaceful he knew, a mimicry of the great channel just beyond.

All of it is so familiar and so strange. How is it that inanimate wood and stone feel so like some extension of bone and flesh? She moves into the *sofa*, looks instinctively toward the great windows. There is the view she remembers.

Upon one of the divans in the *sofa* she sees a pile of books. Herodotus, a couple of English novels. Her father's books. Enemy hands, enemy eyes have perused them.

'Hello.'

Nur turns. The English doctor stands in the doorway, a slight frown. She stifles her anger. For the first time she is properly aware of the extraordinary position necessity has left her in. At best, one avoids even being seen by the occupiers. At the very least, one avoids being noticed by them. And she has wandered voluntarily into their midst.

'He's a tough little chap,' he says, leading her through. 'I've heard grown men cry from the pain of it. Not a whimper from your son. He's had a deal of morphine, so he won't be himself. But he has been awake today.'

She follows him, silent. The less she says, she thinks, the better. This way he may not see her hatred. And this way she may still be able to look at herself in a mirror and not see a traitor.

The boy is on his own, in what used to be her father's study: he is a slender white hillock beneath the sheet, only the fine fronds of his dark hair visible above it. Here is another assault of memory: it comes in the scent of old paper and tobacco, which somehow remain years after the source of them has gone. He sits up in bed, looking at her with eyes that have a curious, unnatural brightness.

'I thought he'd prefer to be in here, you see. Not out in

the ward with the men. Though I may have to move him, if there is a need for a quarantine case.' He looks about at the walls, which bear the pale rectangular reminders of the paintings that once hung there.

'I think this used to be a study, or perhaps a library. It has that scent to it.' Curious that he should have noticed it too. 'This was a house, you see.'

'Yes,' Nur says. Here is where my father used to sit and read for hours. Just beyond is the room in which my mother and grandmother and I and my aunts and my cousins drank rose-scented sherbet, and had the luxury of being bored. Afternoons – filled with the murmur of women and the smoke of perfumed cigarettes – that felt as though they would keep happening forever.

'Nur *hanım*?' The form beneath the sheet stirs, a face emerges. His skin is still bleached of colour, but it has lost the yellowish cast.

The doctor helps him to sit, with a care that she decides is nothing more than professional creed, arranging cushions behind him.

'How are you feeling?' she asks.

'Hungry,' he says, in English.

She laughs – she cannot help it – and at exactly the same time she hears the English doctor's bark of a laugh, too.

Her face is hot. Some nameless unpatriotic slippage has just occurred.

The doctor clears his throat. 'He is doing very well, everything considered. I shall leave you two, now.'

'Thank you.'

'I'll be outside. On the terrace, if you need me.' For a large man she is impressed by how silently he moves, a doctor's trick, perhaps.

'I brought you something.'

She hands it to the boy, gratified to see the new animation in his face, the small flicker of childish greed at the prospect of a present. He unwraps it.

'Do you recognise it? I brought it so it would remind you of home.'

It unfurls from the paper; an exclamation of colour against the sterile white of the bedspread. He traces the gilt thread with a slow finger. He nods, solemn. 'Thank you.'

She allows herself to believe that he is, truly, pleased with her gift. 'It doesn't hurt too much?'

'No. He,' he points at the door through which the man has gone, 'gave me the medicine. I can see colours behind my eyes.' He shuts them, to illustrate this.

'Well, that's for the pain.'

'I know. I'd like to be a doctor, one day. Why are you frowning?'

'Not a *chef de cuisine*?'

'Oh.' He thinks. 'Perhaps both.' And then, seriously, 'Am I coming home?'

'As soon as you are well enough, I promise.' The same question has been on her mind. She will remove him from the Englishman's care as soon as she can be certain he is free from danger.

'To your home?'

She frowns. 'It is your home now, too. Not just my home.'

'Oh.' This seems to satisfy him somewhat.

She wonders what has brought this on. She supposes it is the first time he has spent any significant time away from her, or the apartment, since that dreadful night. He is still not quite himself, she notices. Some of his sentences disintegrate into incoherence. When she begins to fear she is tiring him, she decides to leave.

She goes to find the doctor. She knows she must thank

him, however much she would like to leave without it. It is not just her innate politeness; it is a safeguard of sorts. She needs to make sure that he will treat the boy as well as he would treat one of his own men.

He is smoking a cigarette. Behind him is a waterfall of green: the wisteria. The last of the summer flowers are still scattered about his feet, purple leached to pale brown. And beyond the wisteria the merciless beauty of the Bosphorus. It seems incredible to her that this was once a view she took for granted.

'I wanted to thank you,' she says.

He withdraws the cigarette and blows smoke over his shoulder, so that it cannot land on her. The fingers which grip the cigarette are articulate, rather elegant. And yet, she reminds herself, they are the hands of little better than a butcher. She has eyes, she can see the uniform; he may be a doctor now, but he is a soldier too. His title is still an elegant euphemism for murderer.

'It will need to be several weeks, at least.' His voice is slightly roughened by the tobacco.

'Weeks?'

He nods, grave. 'More, if possible: I would like to keep an eye on him. This case – I fear it has all of the hallmarks of the worst kind, cerebral. And he is very young.'

'But he seems so much improved, already.'

'I know that this is a difficult thing for a mother to hear, but I must tell you that he may never be completely cured of it. The virus often lives on, in the body. The best we can do is monitor him now, whilst he is still in such danger.'

She cannot absorb it. She will need to repeat it all to herself, later, to make sense of it.

'Surely he cannot stay here for that long. I cannot imagine that it would be allowed—'

He interrupts swiftly. 'I am in charge of this hospital. And I say that we have room for him here.'

'Oh . . .' She is at a loss. With no small effort she forces herself to say it: 'Thank you.'

He gives a slight smile, just enough to show the teeth. His incisors are slightly too long. The teeth of a predator, she thinks. She does not smile back.

'I had meant to ask you,' he says. 'Where did you learn such excellent English?'

This pretence of interest – as though they are equals. Or, more likely, it is meant to patronise: as one might congratulate a pet upon the learning of a trick. 'My father sent me to the British school.'

My father, the Anglophile. The reason for so much of our trouble.

A bank account seized; a house sequestered; a whole family suspected of enemy espionage. Even with her father dying, hardly capable of any treachery even if he had wanted to be. Even after his death, in the first year of the conflict, they had remained beneath suspicion. Even with her brother fighting for their country in the war. The state's suspicion had cast a long shadow.

'Would you like a cigarette? I can make you one.'

'Oh,' she says, so taken aback that she forgets to immediately refuse. She doesn't smoke them now; they are too expensive. Her grandmother, in the time before, had worn a small pair of golden tongs on a chain about her waist. When she rolled herself a cigarette there was a ritual to it. First came the tobacco, stored in an embroidered silk bag, then a leaf of fine pink tissue paper from the tiny book she kept about her person. She would roll the tobacco into a tiny, neat tube – no small feat with hands as gnarled as hers. Then those tongs would be used to lift it, lit, to her lips so she need no more stain her fingers. There was a grace to her movements that Nur knew she would never possess; she did not have the patience.

He is still waiting. She senses that he would like to continue the conversation, that within that little metal box is also the proffered possibility of an impossible accord. She wonders if he realises this too.

'No,' she says, 'thank you.'

He can afford to appear generous if he wishes: he is the occupier. He makes the rules. These possibilities are closed to her. His freedom to act in this way, in any way he wants, is only another means by which to wield his power. And for this pretence of friendship she decides to hate him a little more.

George

'I'm going to help you to sit up.'

He arranges the pillows, careful with his movements lest they cause any pain. The boy watches, silent. The fever-glaze has gone, there is a new curiosity. This, the advent of consciousness, is the first time he has really seen the boy. Before that he was a case, an urgent one.

His eyes sting. He rubs them, and they only feel worse. He waited with the child through the night, watching for any sign of the fever mutating, worsening. He has done the same a hundred – a thousand – times before, beneath canvas in the Mesapotamian desert, in a temporary barracks beside the Caspian Sea: a marshland place so famously rife with the disease that Alexander the Great sent his unwanted generals there to die. He has watched men return entirely to themselves only to fall suddenly, fatally, back into the clutches of the thing.

He is still not certain that the boy will survive; he chose not to tell the mother this. He senses that she has suffered enough; she wears it upon her like a cloak.

'Is there pain?'

A hesitation. He thinks perhaps the boy does not understand. He gestures at his head, his stomach, pantomimes a wince.

'Some pain,' the child says, articulating as precisely as a judge. It is said bravely: I am suffering, but I am not going to complain about it. Beneath his eyes are bruise-like impressions. Not, George thinks, so much the mark of his recent condition as a more general, long-term malaise: poor nutrition, general fatigue. He saw it in the faces of the Russian children on the refugee ships. He does not know the mother at all, but he has some idea of the sort of person she might be. He can imagine that not being able to feed her son properly would pain her.

Now the boy is looking about himself, with wonder and poorly concealed fear. He understands. He has experienced the same phenomenon almost daily across the span of the last five years. At least now he is static, for however long it may prove to be. When they were on the move it could take a good ten minutes of careful thought. He would stitch together the memories of the previous day – adding these to the ache in his legs, the temperature of the air trapped beneath the canvas. Even then, one could not always be certain. The desert could be a different place from one day to another.

'You are in the hospital,' he says. 'You have a rather bad case of malaria.' He stops, not sure how much the boy understands.

The child blinks, tries to shift himself to sit up.

'No, let me help you. There.'

'Thank you.' Then, rather formally, 'I'm sorry. My English is not good.'

He has to work not to laugh. 'It's a sight better than my Turkish, I can assure you. I'm impressed that a boy of – how old are you? How . . . many years do you have? Eight?'

'Seven.'

He is taken aback. Eight had been a wild overestimation, to flatter the child. He had thought five at the very most. Malnutrition, most likely, has stunted the boy's growth.

'You are a soldier?'

'I'm a doctor.'

'You are in the army?'

'Yes, but my job is slightly different to the others'. I'm there to save lives.'

'For the soldiers in your army.'

'Not necessarily.'

'You saved other soldiers?'

'Several.'

Mere skeletons, George remembers, in a worse state, if that was possible, than their own men. Ruined by frostbite and dysentery. The Ottomans had won Gallipoli. They had won it with sheer numbers. Men used like bullets; launched toward the enemy, never expected to return.

The boy is looking up at him with a mixture of fascination and fear. George wonders what tales he has heard of the British army. Nothing good, that is for certain. A sudden inspiration. 'Do you like animals? Animals, you know?' He makes a puppet from his hand, his fingers four running legs.

The boy nods, suspicious.

'And birds?'

Another nod.

'There was a desert we passed through. The Mesapotamian desert. And then, suddenly, the rains came, and it wasn't a desert any more. Suddenly there were flowers – orchids, such a bright purple that they looked like tiny coloured lights in the grass – and thousands of birds came to feed from the insects that came for them. Can you imagine it? Thousands.'

The boy does not say anything. George isn't even sure he

understands. But perhaps it doesn't matter. The memory is, really, a selfish indulgence. He remembers the particular green of the grasses: it was like seeing the colour, really *seeing* it, for the first time. 'And there were great plump birds called partridges, and smaller ones, grouse. And in the swamplands there were boars. Boars. Do you know what that means?'

The boy shakes his head.

'Like a pig, but with lots of hair, and tusks.' George finds himself pushing back the front of his nose to make a snout, grunting. He feels ridiculous. He has no idea what Bill would make of this, if he were to come in now. But he is rewarded when the boy smiles for the first time since his arrival at the hospital.

'You saw it? That animal?'

'Oh yes, of course.' He didn't, actually. They remained mythical: which made a kind of sense; it was the land of myth. There, oil seeped up through the ground unchecked, a concentration of ancient power. The locals paid it no heed; it was of little use to them. Later, when they travelled through the Paitak Pass with the Persian mountains sheering up before them, palely-red, impenetrable, they climbed a narrow road built originally by Alexander the Great on his way to India. Some of the very stones on which they trod had been laid by men more than two thousand years ago. It was impossible, knowing this, not to feel your own utter insubstantiality. One small footnote in a much larger narrative that contained nobler campaigns, greater bravery, more impossible feats. There was some comfort in it, too. When you were so aware of your own smallness, it seemed to matter less if you were soon to drop dead a few miles up the road of the malaria you were suddenly certain you had contracted.

'The swifts were my favourite, though,' he tells the boy now. 'They're a kind of bird . . . with a forked tail, like this.'

In a snatched half hour of idleness he had liked to lie on his back and watch the swifts' movements. They could move together at will, as one, in perfect synchronicity, through some silent, mysterious knowledge. It moved him, though he could not quite say why. They came here because their ancestors had come, for thousands of years.

The boy's eyes are almost closed, he sees. But he thinks that he might still be listening, so he continues, all the same.

'In the evening they came to eat the insects. They were so fast, so precise. Like a needle moving, like this.' He makes the darting movements with his hands. Then, hardly conscious of what they are doing, his fingers move to the embroidery that has slipped to the end of the bed. The gilt thread is rough against his fingertips. He can see that needle moving too, so fast, so precise.

The boy is fully asleep now. That is good; he needs to rest. And yet he feels a strange kind of loneliness, left as he is now with his recollections.

He had envied those swifts. To live in such a state of grace, unhampered by heat or cold, or all the problems that humans created for themselves in the needless complexity of their lives. Animals did not recognise the boundaries between lands – or rather, only the borders created by the seasons, the abundance or scarcity of food. Man had been like that once. Where had it gone so wrong? Long, long before this: before Alexander the Great, perhaps.

And where did it go wrong for him? His own slide from grace, hidden beneath a cloak of duty? Rather easier to pinpoint. It is going to be even easier to convince himself that he is doing the right thing, the moral thing, now there is a child to look after.

But the truth remains: Medical Officer George Monroe is, in fact, a coward.

The Traveller

From Lausanne to Venice there is a restaurant car. I sit and have a glass of white wine and a meal of tough chicken, slightly raw potatoes and green beans that have been over-cooked into limp greyness. I eat as much of it as I can stomach, and promise myself that I will make up for the deprivation when I reach my destination. I can still taste the memory of the food there: that alchemy of sweet and sour, fruit and meat together, the sumptuousness of the oil.

I take a sip of the wine. It, too, is indifferent – but there is a certain decadence to it, this lunchtime drink, with the splendour of the countryside rushing by. An afternoon sleep-iness comes over me: what is it about travelling that makes one so tired? All I have done since this morning is sit. But I did not sleep well last night on my hard foam bed. It was partly the discomfort and the racket of rain on the glass, partly the volume of my own thoughts. There is an emotional density to this journey, a burden I will carry all the way there.

Around me are pairings or quartets of diners. For the first

time I wonder what they make of me. A lonely soul, perhaps, on a solitary journey.

I know exactly what is necessary to remove the sour after-taste of the wine. Back in the couchette, I take from my suitcase a wooden box. Upon it is the image of a magnificent building, but faded over the years so that only the faint impressions of the gilded domes remain. The clever sliding mechanism of the lid still works smoothly, however. I draw it back to reveal the plump, sugar-dusted cubes within and allow myself one. I am getting stout: a combination of too much food and increasing age. No sign of the slim young man who had no fear of running to fat.

I let the sweetness and the delicate perfume fill my mouth before I chew. It is the perfect consistency, yielding, but not too soft, this piece studded with pistachio nuts. For a long time I could only find in England that insulting translation of *loukoum*, the stuff they call 'Turkish delight': food dye, cheap sugar syrup, that overpowering hit of synthetic rose.

It took me a long time to source *loukoum* like this, the proper sort, which we could serve to customers with their coffee after a meal. That would be worthy of keeping inside this box.

The Boy

Behind his eyelids the swarm of stars remains, like a secret. The doctor gave him liquid from a spoon. It killed the pain, and summoned the stars. No: now the stars are changing shape, breaking apart, elongating. They are becoming small, fast birds with forked tails – thousands of them. They move beneath his eyelids and he watches them, half in awe, half afraid . . . though he cannot say why.

The doctor has grey eyes. He is about the same age as the boy's father was, but he is much taller. He does not wear this height like a threat. And yet the man – the doctor – is English. The boy knows some English, he learned it at school. The enemy are English. He knows this, and Nur knows this. He wonders how she could have forgotten. Perhaps because she was so frightened. But he cannot help wondering again if this is her way of getting rid of him. Perhaps the old woman complained, because he criticised her cooking. He doesn't want to believe it, but enough terrible things have happened to him in his short life already that he knows anything is possible.

The enemy kill Ottoman men. He isn't sure how they feel about Ottoman boys – but then he isn't really an Ottoman boy, as the old lady is fond of telling him.

The doctor seems kind. He likes birds. But already he has learned that things – and people – are often not what they seem. He will be ready, ready to run if he has to. At least, he *will* be ready, only after he has had a little more of this strange, bird-strewn sleep . . .

Nur

It is difficult to ignore the fact that the boy seems like a shadow of his usual self. Today she sits with him for only half an hour before he drifts into sleep. She cannot decide whether she should stay a little longer, in case he wakes again, or leave.

There are noises from the ward on one side, but on the other silence. This door, she knows, leads through to the *sofa* – once her favourite room in the house. Holding her breath, she gives the door a little push. It is empty.

The walls are covered in hundreds of painted tiles; an indoor painted garden of cypresses, vines, hyacinths, violets, dog roses, cherry blossom, pomegranate flowers. All of which, at various times of the year, could once be found in the real garden without. As the waters of the Bosphorus shift beyond the windows, an interplay of light and shadow occurs within: something more than a mere reflection. More a sympathetic reply – as one dancer might echo, but not match, the movements of a partner.

In the centre of the room is a *şadırvan*, a marble fountain, with the edges of the bowl scalloped like the inside of a shell.

Once the water fell from it in a silver stream. If one sat on the divans that line the room it was almost impossible not to be lulled into a state of tranquillity. The water is stopped now.

There is an austerity in the room today. With the fountain silenced, the walls gleaming frigidly, the atmosphere is that of a beautiful mausoleum. The shadows moving upon the walls seem now like trapped memories.

There is a sound behind her; she turns. It is the English doctor, stepping through the door.

'This is my favourite room,' he says.

His possession of it, his choosing of it. She could not speak even if she wanted to, all that could come out, she feels, would be the hard gust of her anger.

He pushes a hand through his hair. 'I like watching the ships,' he says, 'passing up and down the Bosphorus. Imagining where they are travelling to and from. Though most of them, I fear, are full of refugees these days.'

It does not soften her anger, this knowledge that he shares her old pastime. It only makes her own experience seem inauthentic, somehow, less uniquely hers. She is so intent on not hearing him, not letting his words settle upon her, that it is some time before she realises he has stopped talking. He is looking at her, instead, curiously.

'This is my house.' She isn't even certain that she says it aloud or inside her mind – only realises he has heard when he makes a polite cough of surprise, an Englishman's cough. These English, with their civility – politely colonising half the world.

'I beg your pardon,' he says. 'But I thought—'

'This is my house. It was my house, my family's. It was taken from us by our government, and then by you from them. Your army took it.' She is almost pointing at him. Her use of the second person is no mistake: she wants him to feel the wrong of it. 'You were not content with merely taking the city; you had to take people's homes.'

A long silence as he digests this.

'Well—' he says, and falters. He seems stunned.

Now she is frightened: she has gone too far. He would have had to have been deaf not to have heard the threat in her tone. She waits, as is her lot as the conquered, to see what he will do with her.

George

Her house. Now he understands. Her face on that first morning, coming to visit the boy. Ah, but before that, too – when he had found her barefoot on the jetty, and Rawlings had thought her mad. She had been paying a visit to her past. Now he has the cipher with which to translate the expression she had worn, stepping inside. Sorrow, curiosity, a kind of hunger.

Now he is confronted with her anger. He had thought Bill ridiculous, talking of that first visit by her as though it were a threat. Now he sees that he has underestimated her. There is something dangerous about her fury. He should reprimand her. But he cannot quite bring himself to do so.

Instead he looks about and through this new lens sees it as a reflection of her. The elegance, the refinement.

How strange it must be to see it so transformed, into a place of white linen and prone male forms, scented with the alkaline tang of the iodine, and the smoke of Lockett's cigars.

'I had not considered,' he says, 'I was told that it had belonged to a . . .' he stops, and thinks better of speaking the word, the one the general had used: traitor. 'That it belonged to someone the Ottoman government – your government – did not get along with. But I had assumed, I suppose, that they were dead.'

'My father is dead,' she says, and at his expression, 'illness, not by their hand, although . . .' She stops herself, and lapses into silence, lost to some private inner reckoning.

'When did you leave?'

'During the war. We were given a day to leave. We took the things that were the lightest, and the most valuable. The rest we left.'

'You must take them now. I will help you.'

'No.'

'You do not want them?'

'No.'

He struggles to understand. 'Because . . .?'

'We have no room for them. You have seen where I live.'

Yet he does not think she has quite told him the truth. 'You could sell them.'

'Some foreign books, some English paintings? No one wants such things. Not for anything more than a few *piastres*, at least, and I am not willing to sell them for that.'

He thinks perhaps he has pressed her harder than he should, but he cannot help himself. 'It seems a brave thing to do, then, to leave them in a deserted house, where any thief might have helped themselves.'

She takes a breath. 'I left them here,' she says, 'because with them, we remain. And one day we will return.'

He nods. Now he understands.

'It is our home. It does not change because we no longer live here.'

'Of course not.' He agrees because it seems necessary, but he is not sure he can quite see the truth of it. There is something pitiful in the attempt to leave a mark of ownership upon the house in this way. These things have seemed to him like the possessions of someone dead. Even now, knowing that they belong to her, that feeling remains. They have the cold, finite quality of artefacts on display in a museum.

As he sees it, all they seem to do is emphasise the loss of it – the disappearance of the life that was once here. He had felt that sense of trespass before, when the house was anonymous, when for all he knew its inhabitants were dead or gone far away. He cannot imagine what it must be to see your family home colonised by the enemy and with it every memory created within its walls. He has always been able to think of his work almost entirely as a force for good, set apart from the politics of war. Now, for the first time ever, perhaps, he is oddly unsure.

The Prisoner

He expected a throng. A cheering crowd. He is not alone; they have all believed it. They have waited for it through the strange, interminable journey. Every one of the men on board is up on deck for this moment. They are the long-lost war heroes.

Three years have passed since the end of the war. Four since the British captured him, by that river, in hell. The monotony of incarceration, of desert heat, of other bodies in close proximity. No word from the outside world: as though the world had forgotten them. And yet he has been grateful, in an odd way, for these years. They have given him the time to relearn everything that happened. To reforge himself.

Finally they are home.

The city, beautiful as ever, is slumbering beneath a warm autumn morning. But it seems too quiet. Like a place slumbering beneath a spell. No crowds. Only a smattering of khaki-clad British on the quay to receive them. From this distance the British soldiers are tiny figures, dwarfed by the hull. And yet their upturned gazes seem to absorb the ship, to take possession of it. It is theirs.

A little further off stand a smattering of locals, but they do not cheer or wave. They look up at the ship and its cargo in silence, as though staring at a phantasm, some strange mirage from the past.

It is late afternoon before anything happens. Finally, four officers board the ship: two British, two Ottomans. One man calls out to the Ottoman officers: 'You may not recognise us, but we are your brothers.' They avoid catching his eye.

In contrast with these two men, red-fezzed, immaculately uniformed, they can see how much they have all changed. They have not had the yardstick for comparison, until now they have only had one another. And they are all pitiful: sunburned, emaciated, though perhaps most of all those who have been blinded, and stare about with milky unseeing eyes, who cannot even see their beloved city; struck down as they have been with the mysterious disease for which no cause or cure could be found.

They are allowed from the ship, finally, if they can provide an address in the city. For a few moments he is struck dumb. The words will not come to him, only the idea of a place. Water, calm, trees. It seems impossible, now, an idyll – like somewhere glimpsed in a picture book. The version of himself that lived in that place is very far away now, too. The officer waits, eyebrows raised. When finally he produces it, from some hidden well of memory, the man hardly seems convinced. But he is allowed from the ship.

In the streets people glance at him and look quickly away, some flinch involuntarily with shock. He catches a glimpse of himself in a gilt mirror outside a stall and sees a haunt-eyed spectre. He looks like a wretch, a beggar. He reminds himself of all that he has done, all that he has sacrificed. *I am not to be pitied*, he tells them silently. *I am to be thanked, praised . . . but not pitied.*

He knows what he is. He is an embarrassment to them. They would rather not see him in their streets. He is like one of the stray dogs. Not so long ago, the Mayor of Constantinople ordered the removal of every one of the animals, which had been inhabitants of the city for as long as anyone could remember. Some eighty thousand of them were rounded up and taken on boats to the most inhospitable of the Princes' Islands, Hayırsızada, a sharp spine of rock rising from the Marmara Sea. Most of the dogs had died of thirst and starvation – some had even drowned trying to swim the distance to the boats that had abandoned them. Those few that did not die had lived off the seagulls they managed to catch – and each other. In the end these survivors were brought back, returned to the streets where they now lived as a reproach to the city's mistake. This is he: a bitter reminder, a source of shame.

He makes his way to the white house like one in a dream.

There it is, unchanged. Home.

He can hear the sound of their voices.

The reckoning will come now. Will they see the change in him? Will they know what he has done? This is the first proper test of his new conviction. He summons the words of the new language to himself. Necessity. Righteous. The Future of the Nation. He begins to stride toward the house.

But there is something wrong. It is an animal knowledge at first that tells him this, deeper than thought – like a bad note scented on the air. Then he realises that the voices are wrong. He sees white-clad figures, men, a number of them. He sees khaki green. He hunkers down, out of sight. He catches the words now: a foreign language. He sits and watches and is filled with a terrible new understanding. This latest, worst trespass: the colonisation of his past. The one thing that had been left good and whole. He will find some way to revenge this.

Nur

On her way to deliver her embroideries she stops at Haci Bekir – the best confectionary shop in the city. The scent of powdered sugar makes her mouth water.

This errand is performed, oddly enough, on her grand-mother's instructions. 'The Englishman has done us a favour, now we must show our gratitude. That is the way of things. Really you should have done this on the first visit, *canım*. I am surprised at you.'

'But *Büyükanne*,' she had said, 'he is our enemy. Surely it would look—'

'I am thinking precisely of how it would look, girl. It is only right. We cannot allow our standards to slip merely because the enemy is boorish and uncivilised and has no sense of decorum. We can show them up by our example: it is the last weapon available to us. And,' – this part reluctantly – 'though it no doubt cost him very little, because the enemy may do as he likes, he has shown us a kindness.'

Nur is not convinced that she can quite share her

grandmother's view, but she sees that there might be wisdom in the act.

She was rude to the English doctor; she let her anger get the better of her. She cannot afford to fall from his favour, not with the boy so ill. If she cannot quite bring herself to be civil to him in her speech then a gift is a less complicated way of currying favour.

She steps inside, and asks the man behind the counter for some *loukoum*, studded with slivers of pistachio. The smallest box, because it is all that she can afford. At least it is beautiful with a painted design of the Aya Sofia. But then as an afterthought, with a slight thrill at her recklessness, she buys another box: rose-scented, her favourite.

She has never actually set foot in the shop before. In the time before, Fatima would procure them. The quantity that she now holds in two twists of gilt-printed paper would seem laughable in comparison to the pounds of the stuff Fatima would return with, to fill the silver bowls throughout the house. They would eat several pieces with every cup of coffee, and spare no thought for the cost. A time of plenty in everything.

Except . . . in that time she could not have gone to the shop, even had she wanted or needed to, without receiving the inevitable dark looks. And with her face uncovered? Unthinkable. A woman of good family would not behave in such a manner.

She takes one of the sweets from the bag on her way back and holds it in her mouth, savouring the sugared fragrance, before she allows herself to chew it. Here is another observation: when one is not used to having them every day, one tastes the sweetness all the more vividly.

This flavour is of a time, too. Drowsy, lazy hours. Days spooling ahead. Sometimes pleasurably, sometimes filled with ennui, and a strange melancholy. Then time had been meted out in great handfuls. There had been a surfeit; one struggled to use it all up. From the early morning call of the milk seller to the evening one of the yoghurt seller, the hours had seemed to billow out before her, empty.

In that time before, Nur might have done one modestly significant thing with her day. She might have finished a new book or she and her mother might have gone for a drive out to the old walls of the city, or one of the picnic spots beside the Bosphorus. Or attempted to paint the scene from the terrace, which she had never managed to represent to her satisfaction. One could not paint the wind, that was the thing.

There were days when she lay in bed and glanced back over the span of hours and could remember nothing at all taking place . . . as though she had passed all the time in a dream state, punctuated only by meals, by aimless wanderings in the garden. Or she had spent the day imagining what she would be doing if she had a life in the world beyond – if she were a man, perhaps. A cold understanding would come over her: this was how her whole life would be, meted out in pockets of ennui. When leisure was the thing that took up all of one's time, it ceased to be easy. It became an art. In the imperial harems the women had become grand masters at it.

It was important to cultivate a rich inner life; to sustain one through hours of boredom and solitude. Some women conjured fantasy lovers, spending so long deciding upon the peculiarities of their beauty, the sound of their voice, the shape of their hands and form that they knew them far more intimately than they did any living person. Some imagined journeying to exotic lands, unencumbered by any of the practical inconveniences of travel. Nur once heard it said that a woman's sphere is actually less constrained than a man's. Because whilst he may travel outside in the physical world, her internal world is limitless, set only by the boundaries of her imagination. This life within the mind is a skill that men do not always take the time to learn . . . unless, perhaps, they are of a particularly spiritual bent.

Nur was not convinced. She could not quite bear the idea that everything she had learned in the long years at the British school would be for nothing. All the languages she might never speak, the history, the arithmetic for which she would have no use . . . the study of atlases which would now only serve to remind her of all that space she would not have the opportunity to explore, all those places she would never visit. Knowledge stoppered up inside her, with no outlet, rotting like something left in a jar. Or worse, poisoning her from within, infecting that inner life with the taint of disappointed hope.

Difficult to imagine now, that luxury of being bored.

As she makes her way down toward Galata bridge she hears her name called.

She turns. A little way below her on the cobbled slope stands a man: she does not recognise him at first, though there is something familiar.

She looks again. It is her cousin Hüseyin, her mother's nephew. The most obvious of the changes is the absence of his once luxurious moustaches. Without them he appears younger, more handsome, but his face has lost a certain gravitas. There is more to it than this. His clothes are different, too: the foreign tailoring gives him a different shape. Most of all, he has exchanged a fez for a dark felt affair with a slender brim.

'You look so different,' she says. 'I hardly knew you.'

'And so do you.'

In her surprise at seeing him, in noting the changes in him, she has forgotten how she herself might appear to him. She is aware now of the cheap cotton gloves with the stain on the thumb, the outdated dress, the worn leather of her shoes, the twice-mended dress. The greater losses, too: which she feels must be written upon her face.

He is a man; there is a brief hope that he will not note these things as a woman might.

'How have you been keeping?' he asks. She hears the pity in it, and understands that her hope has been in vain.

'We have survived.'

'Your husband?' A moment while he searches for the name. 'Enver?'

She shakes her head. 'Killed. At Gallipoli.'

'Oh, my dear Nur. A widow, so young. They say they fought very bravely there.'

She has to quash the sudden flood of her anger: what would he know of bravery? 'So they tell us,' she says.

'And Kerem?'

'We had a note from the War Ministry. Missing, presumed lost: near the Russian border.'

'So perhaps—'

She cuts him off. 'That was four years ago. We had little hope at the beginning, now we have none at all.'

His face seems to lose all colour. 'I am so sorry.'

'It is not your fault.' And what she does not say aloud: 'It is nothing to do with you, in fact. You made certain of that by staying away.'

'I should have come back.'

She does not know how to reply. Her innate politeness would never allow her to admit that she agrees, that she has judged him for having stayed away.

'You see,' he says, 'it was a little more difficult. My

circumstances have changed. I have got married myself. My wife is an American. I must return to her soon.'

A gust of rage has passed through Nur, and for a moment she cannot bring herself to smile, as she knows she should, let alone speak. He has been halfway across the world falling in love, while her brother was dying for his country. There are times at which her emotions come so close to the surface, when she has very little control over them. Finally, she manages to say: 'I must congratulate you. I suppose you will bring her here to meet us?'

'Oh . . . one day. It will be quite a change for her. America is such a new place. It's so different to here, where everyone lives surrounded by the past. You know, it doesn't feel as though it has changed at all.' Perhaps realising what he has said, he gives an awkward little cough.

With an effort she manages to take pity on him. 'Are you staying long?'

'I return to New York at the end of the autumn,' he says. 'I have come here to sell the house, more than anything else. It seems useless to have such a large property here, merely gathering dust.'

Nur nods. Within her the rage threatens itself again.

'How is my aunt?' he asks now. 'And your father's mother? We must come and pay a visit.'

'No,' Nur says, before she has even thought about a reply.

He looks surprised, a little hurt.

'My mother is not well, at present,' she says. And before he can ask, 'Not in her body – in her mind. From the day Kerem left for war she was not herself. But on the day we had that notice from the Ministry it was as though we lost her for good, too.' He nods. She sees, almost to her gratification, that his eyes are wet with tears. 'So I do not think it would be the best time for it.'

He inclines his head. 'Of course.'

Now would be the time to tell him of their changed circumstances. But she discovers that she cannot do it. Especially in the face of this evident prosperity. She could ask him for money. It would be his duty to give it, to help this branch of his family. It would be madness not to ask. She would not have to spend a *piastre* of it on herself – she could save it all for her grandmother, her mother, the boy. And yet she cannot do it. Her pride will simply not allow it.

'We went for supper with a British friend of mine last night,' Hüseyin says. 'I met him in New York. We went to one of the *meyhanes* in Galata. This city seems to have turned into a madhouse.'

'A British friend?' Nur cannot conceal her surprise.

'Yes. He has always been my friend, he remains so. Your father – as I recall – had many British acquaintances.'

'None of whom we would speak to or even think of any more. I am sure the feeling is mutual.'

'You surprise me, Nur. I did not know you thought in such black and white terms.'

'You were not here,' she is surprised by the tremble of anger in her voice, 'when everything *became* black and white.'

If he feels the slight, he does not show it. 'And you think it is now?'

'More so, yes.'

'I would not be so sure. None of us are innocent in this.' He covers his mouth with his hand, smoothes the place where his moustaches would have been.

'Tell me, the thing that you are deciding whether or not to say.'

'There are stories, of terrible things.'

'What do you mean?'

'By our army, Nur. You wouldn't hear them, here, of course. But in other newspapers – American, French – there are detailed accounts.'

She is not sure that she wants to hear any more, and yet cannot stop herself from asking. 'Accounts of what?'

'It is not the sort of knowledge you need to bear.'

'I cannot judge that for myself?'

'Goodness,' he says, almost smiling. 'You have certainly changed. What happened to my shy little cousin?'

'A war.'

He stops smiling. 'All right – I confess, I do not want to speak of it, not in detail.'

'You cannot allege a thing, like that, without telling me something.'

'In the East, mainly. Massacres, Nur – not of soldiers, but of civilians. Our own people. Ottoman citizens. The Armenians. They say they marched them into the desert. People saw . . .' he leaves a pause, as though for things unsaid, too terrible to be said, 'evidence.' The word, in its sterility, is chilling. 'And those that survived, that managed to escape, are talking of it. Some believe that they are still going on, even now. The atrocities.'

'That is absurd. I would know of it.'

'Not necessarily, Nur. Sometimes it is possible to be too close to something: so much so that one is prevented from seeing the whole.'

She thinks of the boy. A shiver of fear. 'No. I cannot believe it. It is easy for them, the "Allies", to make up whatever they choose now they have won.' But she realises dimly that her skin has gone cold, and there is a bubble of nausea in her throat. Because if it is a lie, who would be able to make up such a thing, even in the interests of making the other side look worse? In most rumours, she knows, there are seeds of truth. But what she says is, 'Why would I have heard nothing of it?'

'The question is would you have heard *anything* of it? People hear – and tell – what they want to.'

'Why are you telling me?' She forgets briefly that it was she who demanded it. She feels that the thing has entered her like a poison.

'All I am trying to say is that when one sees them from a distance, these last few years, it seems that none of us are innocent.'

There is a long silence. Nur thinks of many sharp retorts with which to fill it, mainly upon the theme of everything being easy from a distance.

'Well,' Hüseyin says, briskly, 'I hope to see you again soon, little Nur.'

'And you, cousin.'

But as she walks away she is thinking something quite different. That she would be quite content never to see him again, in all his wholeness and prosperity. And his accusations of atrocities – accusations which somehow seem to include herself, her brother, everyone else who was not lucky enough to escape the war, like him. They cannot be true. Can they?

George

'I'm not sure I can come today.' At the weekends George, Bill and a couple of others, Briggs and Howarth, have taken to exploring the city and beyond.

'Why?' Bill asks.

'The child – he's still running a temperature.'

'Oh for goodness' sake, Monroe. The Sisters are more than capable.' Bill narrows his eyes. 'You know, I'm not even sure you'd exhibit the same concern for one of our own. What is so special about this boy?'

'Fine.' He holds up his hands, in surrender. Bill is an understanding man. But George understands that it is in the best interests of all not to create too much of a commotion around his newest patient.

They take an early ferry from the quay at Galata. At the kiosk, trying to pay for tickets, the man tells them: 'No, Englishmen. You do not need to pay.' He is unsmiling as he says it. It is not meant as a gesture of goodwill, George is certain. It is more like an accusation.

On the water the light is blue, the air cool with the new

breath of autumn. They are observed with furtive curiosity by the other passengers. A small boy strains away from his mother's embrace to get a clearer look. She gathers him tight against her, administers a sharp reprimand.

George looks with equal interest at his fellow passengers. His eye is drawn to an elderly couple in one of the corner seats at the back: he in the signature red fez, she in a dark headscarf. There is a quiet tenderness about them, though they barely touch. It is something in the way their bodies incline toward one another, in the way the man seems anxious that she not miss any sight on the banks as they pass. He watches them until Bill gives him a nudge and he comes, with a jolt, back into an awareness of himself.

The great wide sweep of the Bosphorus is all serenity. Hard to imagine that a fearsome crosswise current stirs beneath the surface. The men have been warned about it: to take care when swimming. They say a man drowned here, just beyond the stately beauty of Arnavutköy village, trying to save a child. Did the child survive? George feels an important need to know.

On the horizon appears an apparition: a flock of white geese. No – sharpening into focus: a flotilla of sails. They draw nearer silently, inexorably. From a distance the *kayıks* appear unmanned, so many *Mary Celeste*s. Then George can make out the men sitting within them, can hear the commotion of them, the chatter and shouts. Fishermen, returning with the dawn catch from the Black Sea.

He is reminded now of something the burn victim, Nicholls, told him. He insisted that it had happened to a friend of his, but it is so fantastic a story that he cannot believe it to be anything other than apocryphal.

Not so long ago, the patient said, two rather surprised fishermen netted a live bear in the waters of the Golden

Horn. There was a – relatively – logical explanation for it. A group of British soldiers, Rawling's friend included, had bought a bear from an entertainer in Stamboul, and taken it to their barracks in Pera. The story was that it had discovered the regiment's beer supplies, which one suspected was less accidental than professed. It had escaped its new owners and gone carousing alone in the streets. Like many humans, it had been filled with a mistaken idea of its own skill and agility, and had climbed onto a railing beside the channel, to walk along it in the manner of a tightrope artist. A six-hundred-pound, inebriated bear does not make the best gymnast. It had been very lucky that the fishermen had decided to set out earlier than their fellows, in the hopes of scoring the catch of the day. That had certainly been achieved.

It is a funny story, but it is also further evidence of the state of the men. He has seen it in the Pera nightclubs: the behaviour growing ever more outrageous. They are growing bored now, restive, glutted with the idea of themselves as conquering heroes and homesick for England. It makes for a rather volatile combination.

On either side of the water the land sheers up, densely forested: it has a muscular beauty. Near to the waterfront the elegant wooden houses cluster, some three storeys high, exquisite with fretwork and the white and green tracery of jasmine. The breeze comes to them over the water laden with its perfume. In the street one finds this scent often, usually before seeing the white flowers clustering around a door, massing across ancient stone. It provides a welcome balm to the odour of refuse ripening in the heat: a caress to follow an insult.

Some of the waterside houses have small balconies. On one stands a figure – far off, but the long skirts reveal that she is female. As they draw closer George sees that she is veiled. When the ferry passes she retreats indoors. He is certain that all the Ottoman warmongers must have lived in the clamour of the great city, not here, with nothing but the sounds of the birds and the water. Only thoughts of peace could exist here. Some are less well-cared-for. The greyish-brown of the old wood is exposed beneath the paint, splintering away from the frame. Balconies loll drunkenly. The houses here are made all the more melancholy by the vestiges of their former beauty. A hush seems to hang over them, a pall of history.

'Çay! Çay! Kahve! Kahve!' One of the ferry-hands makes a slow circuit of the passengers, offering tea and coffee, the round sesame-studded *simit* breads that they sell in hot piles on the street. Suddenly every one of them is famished: they order confusedly. Just as the drinks are handed to them the ferry makes an unfortunate lurch: Howarth deposits the hot contents of his cup into his crotch with an oath that George is glad probably won't be translated by any of their fellow passengers. For a minute or so they are all laughing too hard to be of much help to him; finally Bill leans across to proffer his napkin.

They disembark at the last stop before the channel widens into the haze of the Black Sea. The stop is a small fishing village; a straggle of houses and a couple of simple wooden jetties for moorings. Above here, Bill tells them learnedly, is the Byzantine fortress.

They climb out of the place, upwards, with the heat building until it begins to feel suffocating. The cool of that first hour on the ferry is hard to imagine now. The scent of the hot vegetation rises about them. A small gecko runs out across George's foot – anticipating a snake, he jumps back. The other men laugh at him. They climb until his clothes stick to him with sweat. They have all become soft, he realises; they have not had this much exertion since the war itself.

Suddenly Bill gives a shout. They follow his arm and see ahead of them, up the path, great gun emplacements pointed toward the sea. As they look closer, they see that the surrounding hillside all about has been pockmarked by shells, huge chunks of ground torn up, the grasses only just beginning to cover them. Closer still, and they see the Turkish script at the base of the emplacements: the stars and crescents stamped into the stone.

'I didn't know we bombed the Bosphorus.'

'Not just the Bosphorus, doc,' Howarth tells him, cheerily. 'The city, too.'

George thinks of the crowds milling daily over bridges and in marketplaces, funnelled through the thin cobbled streets at the heart of the city, and feels a little sick.

They descend by a different path to a rocky beach. As they near the water, all of them, by some unspoken agreement, begin to unfasten shoes and roll off socks. All, that is, except for Bill, who decides to remove everything he is wearing. He stands there, scrawny and pale, with a bib of red where the sun has caught him above his shirt collar, and everything above his collarbone an entirely different colour to all below, proud as an emperor. This is enough to make them laugh. But even more so when a small *kayık* with three figures in it – three women – appears round the nub of the headland.

Instantly Bill is transformed into a cringing, shrinking figure, hopping across the sharp stones to cower behind a screen of rocks which are not quite up to the task. No one thinks to tell him that while most of him is hidden the entirety of his white backside emerges above the rocks like a strange beached sea-creature. Perhaps even if they wanted to they could not form the words: they are beside themselves. George cannot remember the last time he laughed quite like this – stomach clenched in an almost-agony, gasping for breath. Every time he thinks he has recovered himself the images will return: the scurry across the hot beach, the coquettish emergence of Bill's white bottom.

The *kayık* has disappeared from view – it never did come near enough for there to be any real danger of embarrassment. Now they wade into the water and remove their clothes surreptitiously, piling them on a large flat rock that emerges in a dry shelf. It is mercifully cold, despite the heat of the day; a preparation is still required before the plunge. They become schoolboys for a time, splashing and jostling – teasing Bill until the joke has been fully used up, as though it is some precious rationed commodity from which they must take every morsel. Then, little by little, each enters his own private realm.

George turns onto his back and sculls a little way away from the group. The sky above him is vast. It is a strange tension of opposites: his body held in the water's cold grip, his face warmed by the sun. From the shore, faint but distinct, comes the scent of pine and herb. Heaven, he thinks, would be something rather like this – at least in his book. After this thought, inevitably, comes a small splash of guilt. But he has to strain, almost, to feel it. Home seems so far away – and somehow hardly real, as dreamlike a place as Constantinople would have seemed had he tried to fathom its existence back in London.

'Gawd,' Briggs says, scattering these thoughts like a pebble pitched into a shoal of fish. 'I'm starved.'

'You always are.'

'A tapeworm, probably . . .'

'Take that back, you scoundrel. I have a healthy appetite, that's all. A man's appetite. And the food here: all that spice.

Like trying to eat something splashed with a woman's *parfum*. Give me . . . roast beef and potatoes, no flavouring but gravy.'

'Fish pie.'

'Kidneys in brown butter.'

Groans of agony and pleasure.

They want to go home, George thinks. They've stayed on, what . . . for an adventure? A chance to see more of the world? A little extra in the pay packet? They don't have any vestige of this thing that exists within him. The desire to stay. Or, to call it by its proper name, the fear of return.

On the journey back, Bill makes his thoughts on the new patient's arrival clear. This is a hospital for officers of the British army, not for small Turkish boys.

George is circumspect enough to know that he might have felt the same if the situation had been reversed.

'I could not refuse.'

'No,' Bill said. 'But you should explain now that you will need to move him. The Red Cross are taking in refugees, locals – they would take him.'

George respects Bill too much to think of reminding him that he is of an inferior rank. More than this, he knows that Bill is right. 'I need to keep him at least until we can be certain he is clear from danger.'

'Because every time you let her into the hospital you expose us to more risk. What if, one day, she decides to bring a gun with her? She – yes – a woman, could kill most of the men in the ward before we had time to stop her. How do you know that it hasn't been her plan all along? That the child isn't merely a ruse?'

George is irritated. 'You are starting to sound rather paranoid, Bill. Perhaps you've had too much sun.'

'I think perhaps you are the one who has been dazzled, Monroe.'

'What do you mean by that, exactly?'

Perhaps Bill decides that he has made his point, or perhaps he remembers that George outranks him. Because now he says, placatory, 'I understand that you feel a duty of care. But afterward?'

'I will consider the Red Cross.'

This is the first time he can remember lying to Bill. They have shared more than most brothers. He has told the man his fears. They have wept together. George has even shared with him his personal burden of guilt. And about that Bill – though he perhaps did not understand, or approve – kept his counsel.

Why the lie? Why the certainty?

It is due partly to the child, he knows, the responsibility he feels for this young patient. It has awoken something latent in him. And it is due partly to her, the mother. Perhaps if she had fallen to her knees and begged and wept, it would in fact have been different. It is her fortitude that compels him to do this thing for her.

Nur

In the small hours of the night she wakes to hear a tapping downstairs – so quiet that at first she dismisses it as a percussion of the wind. But it persists, soft, but too regular to be any fluke. Someone is outside. Her first thought is of the boy, the doctor; something is wrong. She dresses, and hurries down, opens the heavy door as quietly as she is able. She is so surprised by the sight of the figure on the other side that at first she cannot make sense of it. She steps back, goes automatically to close the door again, believing it must be an apparition, some figment of her dream carried over into life. This is not the first time she has thought she has seen him . . . in the streets of the city, boarding a ferry, through a window. But he has always eluded her before; whenever he has come close enough for her to see his features they have resolved themselves into those of a stranger and her mistake has been evident. She has accepted that all she has seen is an imprint of memory, a ghost. But now he is near enough that there can be no mistake; she can see the mole on his cheek, the double fold of the eyelid of his right eye that does not quite match the left.

He puts out a hand, holds the door.

'It's me, Nur.' The voice is his and yet not his – there is a new, raw quality to it. 'Let me in, quickly. I don't want to draw any more attention to myself than I have to.'

She steps back without saying a word, still half certain that if she speaks it will all become real, he will disappear back into memory. But he follows her in, a presence coherent enough to move the air.

Now, in the lantern light, she is surprised that she recognised him at all. He looks like a beggar, worse than the ragged Russian White Army officers seen on street corners. His hair is matted, it does not look like human hair at all, but the rough bristles of an ill-kept mule. There is more grey in it than black. In each cheek there is a crease, a worn fold. There are black patches upon his cheekbones, as though the skin there has died, or is in the process of rotting away. His lips are scabbed, ulcerated, as though they have decided to part ways with his face. Oddly enough, these changes in him persuade her that he is no apparition. Because, if he were, he would surely appear as his old self, whole, the one known to her.

Her little brother.

She risks speech. 'But where—'

He makes a motion for her to be silent, pulls the door closed behind him. He moves like an animal. Just above the stink of sweat and unwashed flesh she detects the metallic odour of alcohol, the anise tang of *raki*.

'I went to the old house first.' His voice has been changed too, is low, harsh, and it too speaks of pain. There is nothing of the old affection in it. It will come, she decides, one cannot expect it yet. Now she realises that they have not even embraced yet, have not exchanged the expected words of love. They will come.

'Where have you been?'

'In hell. There were men there, Nur, at the house. Englishmen—'

'We thought you had been killed.'

'I think perhaps I was. Or something like it.' There is a rattle in his voice that seems to come from somewhere deep in his lungs.

Now the stifled joy rises in her. 'They said missing in action. But we couldn't let ourselves believe it. So many were really dead. Missing came to mean—'

He has raised a hand to silence her again, as though he has been continuing a separate conversation in his own mind.

'I have been in the desert. A prisoner of the British army: the same one that has taken over our city.'

'Of course.'

'For four years. They did not think to let us come home when the war ended. They let us rot in there for another three years after the Armistice was signed.'

'Oh, Kerem . . .'

'The people here looked at me in the streets like I was an animal. They backed away from me; small children pointed at me. Is that how we welcome our war heroes? I have done things . . . things that should be asked of no human being: but necessary things, for the good of all. And this is how I am received.'

'What things, Kerem?'

Even as she asks it she isn't entirely sure that she wants to know. He does not hear her, or he chooses not to – either way she cannot help feeling relieved that he doesn't answer.

She would like to embrace him but she senses that he would not allow it.

'I have maggots in my feet, Nur, fleas in my hair. I am disgusting, yes: I can see that you think it, just as the people in the street thought it. But this is what they made of me.'

199

'We will get you clean. You are home now, Kerem.'

Perhaps he does not hear or feel the tenderness in her voice; he shows no sign of it. Instead, he says: 'This is not my home. This is a hovel.'

She frowns to bring him into focus, trying to overlay this new character, this stranger, upon the image of the former. He is different in almost every respect. She cannot believe the changes in him. He was so mild before; allowing others to make decisions on his behalf. But this must always have been in him, mustn't it, written in secret somewhere? This latent fire.

'I cannot believe it, Kerem. I'm – so happy.' She isn't, though she knows that she should feel unmitigated joy. Instead it is something more akin to fear; she is too unnerved by the change in him. But perhaps if she keeps saying it, with enough conviction, it will become true. Besides, he doesn't seem to have heard her. He stares, blankly, at the portrait of himself hung upon one wall. She wonders what he is thinking, if he is considering this change too.

Finally, he speaks. 'It is late now. I've travelled a long way. Every part of me is in pain. We can talk properly in the morning.'

'Of course.'

She cannot sleep. The night sounds visit her: the screech of a cat fight, the haunting call of an owl. She lies, wide-eyed, exhausted but relentlessly awake, and waits for dawn. She cannot shake the feeling that there is a strange presence in the house, that something has come back with him. It does not feel like a homecoming.

In the morning her mother sits silent in her corner. She does not take her eyes from Kerem, except, occasionally, to glance up at the treasured portrait of him, smiling down at them. Nur cannot begin to guess at what is occurring inside her mind. In some lucid part of it is she recognising him, celebrating his return? Or is she seeing all that is different in him? Is is she trying to reconcile this wasted spectre with the ruddy painted youth upon the wall, who now seems almost to be flaunting his health, his wholeness. When Nur had dared to imagine her brother's homecoming, in the early time before she resigned herself to his loss, she thought of it as the key that would unlock her mother's silence, return her to herself. Somehow, she had thought, everything else would be easier to bear with him restored to them. She sees now what a foolish dream that had been. Because in that version he had been a little thinner, a little older, but unmistakably himself.

Even her grandmother is uncharacteristically quiet. Before she understood that this is what a homecoming might look like, Nur would have expected her to shout the triumph of her grandson's survival from the rooftop, to summon their neighbours to come and bear witness to the war hero returned. Instead she sits in her chair, twisting the brilliant rings upon her fingers. And unlike Nur's mother, she hardly looks at Kerem: when she does it is with an expression of bemusement, even pain. Nur has never seen her so discomfited.

In the light the state of his physical degradation is all the more evident. Nur finds herself emptying most of their weekly supply of yoghurt into a plate in front of him, drizzling it with ladlefuls of honey, several handfuls of nuts – cutting him a third of their weekly loaf and insisting they have plenty. He eats like a starving man – which of course he no doubt is – unaware of his surroundings, of anything at all, until the food is gone. Then he seems to surface. He is more beautiful with the thinness. It almost hurts to look at him.

There is so much she would like to ask him; about the places and things he has seen. It would be a way of understanding him, the changes that have occurred in him. But she senses there is also much that she is afraid to learn. The greatest change, the one that unnerves her most, is not something external. These physical blights will heal with time. The thing that Nur feels, as only a sister can, is something beneath the skin. She can find no trace here of the gentle brother she knew, the man who only ever wanted to share his learning with others. Someone – something – new and fierce has taken his place. She thinks of the old stories, of *djinns* who could take any form, including those of humans – those of loved ones. There was often something striking about them that would give them away, though. Some quirk that had not been present in the original . . . the eyes, often it was that. She understands this now as she never has before. Because there is something different about his eyes: or perhaps behind them.

She would not admit it to anyone, even if she had anyone to whom she could speak of it. But the truth is this: this man sitting at the table is a stranger. And he frightens her.

The Prisoner

To come home and discover this: his family living like paupers. His mother an invalid. She has become a mad old woman. She stares blankly ahead, as though the mind has long ago taken flight of the corporeal self. He sits beside her, tries to coax some sign of animation from her.

He reaches out a hand, to touch her arm. She flinches away with such force that the pitcher of water beside her is knocked to the ground with the terrible crash of breaking pottery. The blank-eyed look has briefly given way to one of terror.

'*Djinn*,' she hisses, accusingly. '*Djinn!*' And he knows that she truly believes that she is looking at a demon. He feels a shadow of the old horror creep into the room. He sees a woman beside a river, and other faces, old, and young . . .

'No,' he shouts, as she begins to wail. 'No – *Anne*, please!'

Nur rushes into the room. She hunkers down, strokes her mother's hair, soothes her, murmurs words that are almost like song – a lullaby. She turns and looks at him with unbearable pity. 'It will take time, Kerem. For her to understand . . . to come back to herself.'

He sees that his sister has covered her hair with her veil, as though ready to go out. There is a paper bag in her hands.

'Where are you going?'

She gives a small, involuntary flinch – so small that perhaps only a brother would notice it. He is sure before she even speaks that it will be a lie. 'To the school. I am teaching there now, Kerem. I am not sure I am as good at it as you, though. The children—'

'And what are you holding?' He snatches for one of the boxes before she can stop him, prises it open. Inside he sees a box of *loukoum*.

'For the class,' she says.

He lets her go. But he thinks to himself: a tiny box of *loukoum*. For a whole class of schoolchildren?

Nur

The lie felt necessary. How could she tell Kerem the truth, so soon, after learning where he has been? This does not help her to feel better about telling it.

She presents the painted box of *loukoum* to the doctor.

'It's a gift. A small one. To say thank you.' It seems so meagre, suddenly. She is embarrassed: both by its modesty and by the act itself. This is a mistake, she realises; her grandmother has got it wrong. The small twist of paper now seems to have a power, a meaning, that she had not antici-pated. She thinks of how she herself would look upon it: an Ottoman woman giving a gift to the occupier. There are still dark looks revered for women who comport themselves in this way, and her grandmother is an expert in the art.

She thinks, too, of how Kerem would see it. The old version of him might have understood: but not the new. Only a few hours in his company has been enough to teach her that this new brother is a man of hard lines; without compromise.

Even the doctor seems embarrassed. 'Ah, thank you,' he

says. His hand feints toward the box, wavers, and then he takes it. There is a contact of skin that both flinch away from; she feels the shock of it, this infringement, pass through her. 'But you should not have . . .' he stops himself. 'Thank you. It is some time since I received a present.' He holds it loosely in his hands, as though he might be expected to give it back, she thinks. The pretty painted box looks ridiculous against the khaki of his uniform.

With his loss of composure, she regains her own. 'It's *loukoum*,' she says. 'You have it with coffee – though of course you can eat it however you prefer.'

'Thank you,' he says, again, now turning it carefully over in his hands as though it is something precious.

She becomes aware that the filigreed windows of the old *haremlik*, now the ward, look out onto where they stand. She is aware that any one of the men in the ward might look out and see them.

'Shall I take you to the patient?' he asks, as though he has sensed this new unease in her.

'Yes, please.'

The boy is awake, and in more discomfort today – she can see it in his face as soon as she enters the room. She opens the box of rose-scented *loukoum* she has bought for him, but he only eats one piece. The taste hardly seems to make any impression upon him.

It frightens her, because it reminds her of the time when he was like this before. Insensible, unresponding. Weeks of it. Eventually, with what feels almost like a physical effort, she manages to wrest a smile from him with a story about her grandmother trying to make coffee, and blaming the stove, the pot, the coffee and even the weather for the unsatisfactory result.

The smile has cost him, it seems; within a few minutes he

is asleep. She looks at him and cannot imagine how she might care any more for him.

'He's doing well, despite appearances. I had to lower the dose of the morphine, so that it cannot become a habit. He is feeling the pain of it properly for the first time since he fell ill.'

'He seems very tired.' She catches herself. It sounds like a complaint.

But he merely inclines his head. 'He will be. His body has a great deal of work to do.' A slight smile. 'But he is recovering from it as well as any patient I have seen.'

She remembers, suddenly, exactly what he is: an army doctor. Her mind gropes toward what he might have seen – illness, yes, but also blood, death . . . and then stops fast. It has come too close to what she saw, one terrible day in Mahmut Paşa market. She has not forgotten it.

'I wanted to ask,' he shifts his weight from one foot to the other. 'Will you come and have some of this . . .'

'*Loukoum.*'

'*Loukoum* with me?'

'Oh,' she readies herself to decline.

'If I were to insist?'

'Then it is your right,' she says, under her breath, in Turkish, 'as the occupier.' Victory, indeed an entire war, has bought him the ability to insist upon something, and see it done.

He frowns. 'Pardon?' He hasn't understood, of course. But as though he sees it too he says, quickly, 'What I mean is that you would do me a very great honour, in sharing it. I have bought a coffee pot, taught myself to make it in the Turkish way.'

There is something almost pitiable in it. She thinks suddenly of her father. It is almost as though he is here with them, in the same room. 'Surely, *canım*,' he says, 'you aren't going to deny a person the companionship of a cup of coffee? Even a sworn enemy deserves as much.' And so – not without a note of misgiving – she assents.

He shows her out onto the terrace, and she tries to make herself appear at ease, as though she does not already regret agreeing to it. The invocation of her father is no excuse: he never knew what it was to live like this, beneath the yoke of another people. The fictions we tell ourselves, she thinks, to give credence to our own actions. But there is nothing she can do now that the decision has been made.

He has placed some rather ugly chairs out here, a small wrought-iron table. But as she sits she reluctantly sees the genius in it: the elevation here provides the perfect view out onto the Bosphorus, framed by the hanging fronds of wisteria. It both amazes and annoys her that none of them, in the whole long years of living here, thought to do the same.

She steels herself to look about at the garden she knows so well. The last vestiges of petals cling to the roses in the flowerbeds. Curious, she sees, that someone has been weeding: the soil appears freshly turned. Someone must be looking after it, though not as attentively as they might; otherwise the dead roses would have been picked before they could scatter themselves. In the days of living here, they had been arranged throughout the house in huge bouquets, so that for two months the air was scented with them.

The pomegranate tree is painful to look at: the waste of it, the ripe fruits left unpicked. Holes in the skins gape through the bright centres where the birds have clearly taken their fill of the seeds within. If she were braver, she would ask him for a couple to take home, or she would simply smuggle them out. She knows that she will not: she is too hamstrung by her own sense of propriety.

A creak, and she turns to see the doors opening; the nurse

emerges, carrying a tray. The doctor follows behind. Nur does not think she mistakes the reprimand in the woman's look; it is not wholly unlike her grandmother's. If she were in any doubt as to whether she has done the right thing in accepting his invitation, now she has her answer.

'She doesn't let me carry the tray,' the doctor tells her, sitting, once the nurse has gone. He is a tall man, and upon the small seat his knee comes too close to her own. She swings hers away. 'She tells me I'll drop it. Thank goodness she at least lets me perform the operations.'

The *loukoum* have been placed upon a small plate: the one she ate from as a child, she sees with a small shock, with its border of red running chickens. In the middle the sweets look almost obscenely pink and succulent. He pours out the coffee in a steady stream. She can smell the quality of it; the best kind. She has not had coffee like this in years.

Suddenly there is a loud commotion beside them, and his hand wavers, spilling coffee into the saucer.

'Damn.' And then, quickly, repentant, 'Sorry. I have grown so used to the company of soldiers.'

She is hardly listening; she is distracted by the same disturbance that caused his slip. Several sheets of furled white paper have just appeared to blow into the garden. She blinks, and sees them for what they really are.

'They must have been pets,' the doctor says, cleaning a cup with a napkin, passing it to her. She waits until he has placed it on the table before her, his hands back at work pouring the next cup, before she reaches for it. 'But they're half-wild now—'And then he stops and seems to remember.

'They were,' she says. 'They were my mother's doves.'

He seems to be deciding whether to speak, to allude again to her loss. She is relieved when he seems to think better of it. Instead they watch the birds together in silence.

They are certainly not the same fat, snowy creatures they once were. Their plumage is marred by stains, their forms leaner. They watch the table, with its bounty of *loukoum*, with a sharp interest that reminds her of the seagulls that fly in from the Sea of Marmara, pestering the mackerel sellers on the quays. Once, they would have flown to her mother's hands. Now they keep a wary distance, probing the wet ground for grubs a few metres away. And then she watches as they discover the pomegranate tree; begin tearing at the red globes with their beaks. She tries not to resent them their feast.

She sips her coffee – because the quicker she drinks it the faster this awkward encounter will be done with – and burns her tongue. At the same time she is surprised: he has managed to make it almost perfectly, though it is a little too sugared for her taste.

'Please,' he says, 'do not be too kind with me. What do you make of it?'

'It is well made. Perhaps a little too weak, a little too sweet.'

He nods, absorbing this.

'I am sorry, that was impolite.'

'No, no . . . otherwise how do I improve?' He smiles.

It is the smile that returns her to herself. For a few minutes she had forgotten precisely whom she is sitting with.

It is such a delicate balance. She must be cordial enough with this man that he continues to treat the boy. She does not think he is the sort of man to behave heartlessly. And she finds it difficult to associate the figure before her with the blood-soaked enemy of her imagination. But she must never forget her hatred; it is the last powerful thing left to the conquered.

She stands, makes her excuses. When he has gone inside

she turns and leaves through the garden. Here, in full view of the windows should anyone choose to look out, she pulls six pomegranates from the tree, almost more than she can hold. The feral doves squawk in indignation. The fruits are so ripe that the juice seeps from them, staining the palms of her hands like blood. They are hers. She smiles. They will taste even better for the circumstances of their procurement.

No, she has not forgotten.

The day the English planes came to Mahmut Paşa, she had been on her way to try and find bread. The place she normally went to had not had any for days. The city's biggest market-place seemed as good a hope as any. Inconveniently in these last weeks she had seemed hungrier than ever, her body turned traitor on her.

Three shapes, travelling at incredible speed, like shards of thrown metal. The noise had come a breath later, and it was this noise that made sense of the shapes, gave them scope and dimension. She was riveted where she stood. They grew from the sky, they seemed to be trying to land. She was not yet afraid; she gaped at the spectacle like a child at *Ramazan* fireworks.

When someone shouted, 'English planes!' all she could think was . . . *but how absurd*. Unthinkable: England was thousands of miles from here, a continent's breadth away. But when people had begun running toward her, away from the marketplace, she too had turned and attempted to run. No singular decision of her own, rather some herd instinct. She had only taken three quick steps when she was thrown forward by the air itself, landing without even the time for her body to react, even to put out her hands. The side of her jaw and her hip had hit the pavement together, and the shock of it exploded through her skeleton. A brief carnival of colour behind the eyes; then nothing at all.

Perhaps she only lost consciousness for several seconds, but by the time she opened her eyes the world had changed. There seemed to be a curious stillness. Quiet, too, but that was perhaps the note in her ears, a shrill mind-bound scream of shock, that drowned out all else. As she sat up the pain in her jaw had finally arrived – pain that made her feel furious, though she could not say at who. She could not remember who to blame for it.

Curious: there was a horse, a mere few feet away, sleeping in the street. Had anyone else seen it? She looked about, to find the owner. There he was. Sitting awkwardly, legs out in front of him. He seemed curiously sanguine. Did he not mind? Then she discerned the fact that half his head was missing, realised that he would not be minding anything at all. Beyond him other forms, remnants of forms. The eye snagged upon them even as it tried not to see. The line drawn by death had ended just before the place where she had fallen. If she had walked here a little faster, or left a little earlier, or turned to run with a little more hesitation, she would not be here to dimly notice the blood soaking into the muslin of her headscarf, the pain between her hips that would have made her cry out if she had been able to make a sound.

When the scream in her mind had finally lessened – it did not stop properly for days – she heard the sirens of the ambulances. When they ran out of space, trucks, mules, lemonade sellers' carts. The dead, who would not know the indignity of it, piled high, to be collected when lives had been saved.

She had got up on her feet, and had walked home, though there had been a pain at the very centre of her which made it difficult.

At the door her mother had screamed, and screamed. Nur

had been amazed that she had somehow been able to hear and echo the noise in her head. It was only when she undressed that she understood that she was covered in blood; most of it not her own. But when she stripped to her undergarments she found more blood, dark and clotted, much thicker than the rest. This, unmistakably, was her own. Finally, but too late, certain things made sense to her: changes she had noticed in her person. She had wondered. But it was only now that she discovered for certain, in this moment of loss, that she had been going to have a child.

She heard later that the planes had been trying to bomb the War Office. This was what people said because it was not quite believable that they could have been aiming for a marketplace of unguarded civilians. Nur knows nothing of the machines, does not know how exactly they find a target.

But she was there. Saw how close they came; saw the intent in them.

Nur

Her grandmother is in one of her sulks this evening. Nur feels it as soon as she enters the room.

'What is it, *Büyükanne*?'

Her grandmother gestures, with one hand, her rings flashing magnificently. (Nur has long ago given up on persuading her to sell these baubles.) 'This horrid apartment. This dust and gloom.'

Nur feels an apology form on her lips, and swallows it just in time. There are other things to feel guilty about, perhaps, but not this.

'I was beautiful, once. Did you know that?'

'Yes, *Büyükanne*. Of course you were. You are beautiful now.'

'Oh, stop it, you naughty girl! I don't stand in for flattery.' She bats her hand. But her mood has lightened by a degree. 'Have I ever told you of the moonlight picnic we had once, at the Sweet Waters of Europe?'

Nur pretends to think. 'No, *Büyükanne*. I don't believe you have.' She knows the story so well she might have been there herself. It has the vibrancy of one of her own memories.

Wrapped in silks, veiled in *yashmaks*, the women sit in long *kayıks*, attended by many pairs of oarsmen. Other crafts follow in a winding procession, some packed with musicians to serenade them. Young men follow in their own *kayıks*, try to glimpse the famous beauties. They will be disappointed; the women are scrupulously covered. The boats themselves are decorated with fabulously ornate cloths: silk, embroidered with fishes picked out in real silver and gold thread. When the moonlight catches them, fracturing off the water, they really seem to swim.

And there is her grandmother, in the first of the *kayıks*. Upon her feet she wears slippers of the softest white chamois leather. They are the sort of shoes that tell any onlooker an immediate story: here is a young woman who never has to step in dirt.

An exquisite ruby ring upon the slender little finger of her left hand, but no more adornment in the way of jewellery. She does not need anything further yet – that is something to be saved for old age, when lost brilliance in the self can be compensated for in a dazzle of gems.

'And a single-flounced dress of Chinese mulberry silk,' her grandmother is saying. Her eyes are closed. She, like Nur, is watching the party make its stately process toward the bank. 'And over that a jacket. A *salta*, that was what it was called. But what colour?' she seems to falter. 'I can't remember. It will come to me. Blue? No, I never wore it – it washed out my complexion. Red? No . . . that doesn't seem right either – I used to have such beautiful red hair.'

With a little shiver of irritation she opens her eyes.

'Green?' Nur supplies.

'Oh clever girl. But how *did* you guess?'

There is a thud from above them. Someone is up there on the roof.

Her grandmother grimaces. 'It's your brother, Nur.' She does not say his name so often, these days, Nur has noticed. And it is only when she speaks of her grandson that her poise seems to desert her. 'He smelled of alcohol. The shame of it, Nur!'

'He has suffered a great deal, *Büyükanne*.'

'That's certainly true. I think he may have the camp madness. Fatima *hanım*' – the butcher's wife – 'told me of it. Her friend's nephew came back with it. And he was blinded, too: he is quite a pitiful sight to behold.' The pity is undermined by an unfortunate hint of *Schadenfreude*, compounded when she says, 'Thank goodness, at least, he is still a handsome man.'

Nur cannot quite agree. Because if anything, as he grows healthier in body, that thing that is changed in him seems to strengthen, too.

She goes to find him, up on the roof.

He is sitting hunched in one corner. 'Kerem?' she whispers.

The sun is setting somewhere in the west. It is sunk too low to be seen but it has stained the sky with streaks of vermillion fire.

'Kerem?'

Perhaps he did not see her the first time, because she sees him start. He turns toward her. His expression terrifies her. It is a look of profoundest agony.

She goes to sit beside him.

'Kerem,' she says, after a while. 'While you were in . . .' she shies away from saying it: the war. 'While you were away. Perhaps, if you speak of it . . .'

'I cannot.'

'Not now, maybe. But in the future . . .'

'I cannot speak of it, Nur.'

He turns to look at her. There is a plea in his expression,

an entreaty, but she cannot interpret it. It is too soon for him, she thinks. There will be other opportunities: he is returned, now. She thinks of the boy, how long it has taken him to recover from his illness. Well, this thing in Kerem is like an illness – though somewhere deep within, not visible to the human eye. They have time, now. That is the thing to remember.

So instead they sit together in silence, as the world around them grows dark.

Later, she finds herself wondering what life would have been like if Enver had not been killed in those first weeks at Gallipoli, if he had returned to her, like Kerem. How would the war have changed him? Her husband did not have Kerem's gentleness in the first place, after all. Would he, therefore, have fared better . . . or worse?

She finds the miniature, in her small wooden box of keep-sakes. She tries to remember this face attached to a body – but comes up against difficulties. A . . . scent. How had he smelled? Of tobacco and cologne? She tries to recall flesh and weight and presence.

But whenever she attempts this a strange thing happens in her mind. She does not see the man she married, the man in this miniature. Instead, she sees at first a thin figure, feet and nose too large for the rest of him. An oddly pointed head, fine black hair cut straight across the brow. This is Enver the child, as he once was, the only time at which she might have been able to say she properly knew him.

Her brother had told her of an incident in which Enver tripped and smacked the side of his head hard against a chair. His father had stood over him as his face worked, saying: 'A real man does not cry, Enver. He thinks what lessons his pain can teach him.'

By the year before the war, he was, according to her grand-mother, 'extremely charming and clever'. This claim had been filtered through Enver's mother herself, so had to be put under some scrutiny. Nur had also been presented with this minia-ture. One thing she had to admit was that he had grown into the large nose; it now gave the face a distinguished aspect. But the resemblance to his father was now all too clear. His father, too, had been a handsome man. It lent a new arrogance to the face. She thought she might have been better disposed to him had he lost rather than gained in this respect.

She had had a brief, guilty hope that the declaration of war might put the wedding off. He was in the first of the age groups to be summoned for enlistment. But no, in fact, the ceremony was brought forward. He wanted to go to war a married man. She had wondered whether this was some superstition on his part. It could not be anything to do with her – he had not seen her since girlhood. Later, more pity-ingly, she wondered if perhaps he had not wanted to die without becoming fully a man.

A wedding bed scattered with sesame seeds to ward off the evil eye. An Armenian tradition, originally, but absorbed into the ways of the city for all to use. The ritual of the bath; the bathhouse itself like a temple to cleanliness. The soaking in fast-flowing water, the rub-down, the pillows of blossoming scented lather. Her hair washed in rosewater, dried, dressed. A white dress, embroidered with green and silver threads. Sitting for two long days in this confection spread about her like sea foam, her vision obscured by the two silver tinsels hanging down from her headdress so that whenever she moved she saw a shower of stars. At one point the boredom, and the odd experience of being stared at by so many strangers, had seemed suddenly hilarious. She had begun to grin, and found it difficult to stop her shoulders shaking, no matter how hard she fixed her attention upon a crack in the tiles at her feet. Her grandmother had given her a look that could have turned flesh to stone. A bride should be retiring, silent, modest.

Him stooping to lift the veil to look at her for a couple of minutes. His face oddly expressionless: what did he see in her? She was so distracted by the experience that she forgot to look at him, to take in his features – the changes in the boy she had once known. It only occurred to her later that it might have been the same for him.

She had not had time to discover how the life between boyhood and manhood had shaped him. He had been kind enough; but many husbands are in the first weeks of marriage.

Did he love her? Did she love him? The thought was laughable: they had known each other for such a short time. The only sort of love she knew was that of her family, and that was a thing of history and blood, forged and complicated across a lifetime, knotted and detailed and multicoloured as a *kilim* rug.

He had desired her: she had seen it on the nights when they had been together. She had felt the power that she wielded over him. But it was not a real power, not like that commanded by men: it was a fleeting conjuring.

What of her desire? His was worn upon his body, there was no mistaking it. Perhaps a woman's was a more change-able, elusive thing. She has read of it in books, has learned of its power. Anna Karenina, Emma Bovary, the wife of Shah Zaman in *One Thousand and One Nights* – all of them driven rather wild by it. And yet books are not always the most trustworthy teacher. Do they speak of the universal experience, or its extremes? This was not the sort of thing she could ever have spoken to her father about, no matter their rigorous discussions of other literary themes.

Her mother, her grandmother: unthinkable. If one had a sister, perhaps then. She did not think she had felt it. On those nights there had been something. A brief, purely sensory pleasure, like the stroking of the tender underside of the arm, or the hair. But the discomfort had always outweighed it. Perhaps, with time, she could have felt it. With knowing him better. But they had not had that time.

He died almost instantly. There had been a letter from one of the men in his company at Gallipoli, too, 'to the widow of Enver'. She wondered if he had shared her name with them at all, or kept it to himself like a secret. Her sadness surprised her. She mourned – not him, exactly – but the man she had never had a chance to know. Even the description of his death carried a distance. It was a panacea, a sop for grieving wives and daughters and sisters to cherish like a keepsake.

He died bravely for the Empire, with a smile upon his face.

The Prisoner

In the dark apartment he turns onto his side and coughs like
an old man, spits bile onto the floorboards.

His sister is changed beyond all recognition too. A widow
now. No, but that is not the most significant difference. She
is altered in almost every respect. All her old softness is gone.
In the absence of the men, she has taken all responsibility
upon herself. Even now, upon his return, she does not seem
ready to yield it up to him. She goes out into the streets with
her face uncovered, she teaches at his school.

He feels betrayed when he thinks of her there. He suspects
that if he were his former self, perhaps, he would thank her
for it – for continuing his work after he was thought gone.
But he cannot do it, cannot feel it. All he can do is resent
her her vocation, her busy, exhausting life.

He catches himself. He: a schoolteacher, now? The thought
is absurd.

He has tried to find employment. But has no one told
him about the influx of Russians with their impeccable
manners, their attractive air of tragedy? Or the Turkish

refugees ousted from lands that are now being called Greek? The restauranteur, the coffee shop owner – even the oil-smeared chief stevedore on the quays – look upon his wasted form, and pallor warily, as though it might be something catching. Little do they know that before them stands a war hero: a man with ten times the strength of will they possess, who has seen and done things they cannot imagine. He is filled with an urge to scream it at them, these small men who pity him. His hatred for them almost surpasses his hatred of the enemy. To these people he is part of the past; as much of an embarrassment as the eunuchs who walk the city's streets. Once these figures had held the invisible reins of power in the sultan's court – they had been purveyors of messages and gossip, the grand masters of intrigue. Now they are viewed as part of the old Empire: outmoded, vaguely shameful, a reminder of archaic ideals. And just as they are immediately recognised in the street by their soft bulk, their hairlessness, his wasted form marks him out as one of those few who returned from hell. It is more convenient to forget men like him ever existed.

For all his deprivations in the prison camp he had something there that he seems to lack now. Purpose. There, with the officer's help, he had been able to see it all so clearly. Now the old doubts are returning, beginning to plague him. At night he tries to stave off sleep, because when he does faces visit him: terrible images that he had thought he had managed to escape. Sometimes, when he does sleep, he finds himself waking drenched in sweat; sometimes he wakes crying out. On the first night this happened, Nur came to him, and asked him what she could do for him. He hates the pity in her expression; in some moments he can believe that he hates her. She thinks that she has had a hard life since the war began: she has no conception of the things that have been asked of him, the invisible parts of himself that he has been forced to sacrifice.

Now he sleeps on the roof. He claims that it is because he likes the hard surface, for sleeping. The truth is that the proximity of those who knew and loved the old version of himself is almost unbearable.

Upon one tawdry wall hangs a portrait of himself that his mother had commissioned a few months before he left for the front. In this portrait of himself: hatted, straight-backed, faintly moustached (the days before he could grow facial hair in earnest) is represented an image that he could no more return to than if he had lost both of his legs. They have kept it there to taunt him, to torture him. He reminds himself how much better he is now; how much stronger, how necessary were the things he has done: all things that he thought he knew for certain when he was inside the camp. But it is more difficult than it was before. Most of all when he sees the way his sister looks at him, as though she suspects the thing that is fundamentally changed about him. As though she fears him.

Well, she has a secret too. He has noticed that she is gone from the house for hours at a time, often returning only when it is growing dark. She cannot have been at the school for all this time, he has realised, or delivering linens at the bazaar. There is something else that is occupying her time, though no mention of it is made.

So he follows her. Across the channel of the Bosphorus on the ferry – concealed in the crowd, head lowered, so that she will not spot him: though those around him do, moving a little further away from him as if he carries a disease. Even if he had not taken such precautions he does not think she would notice him: she appears lost to her own thoughts, her eyes trained upon the approaching bank.

There is only one place where she could be going – and yet this makes no sense. He has seen the enemy there, with his own eyes. But he watches, and follows, and hides and waits. And there he witnesses her betrayal.

The Traveller

In Italy the colours of buildings have changed subtly: now there is burnt sienna, orange-red, shutters painted deep green. Even the gloomiest suburbs have a certain romance to them for the foreigner; because they are different and strange in subtle ways.

At the next table sit the couple I glimpsed on the platform in Paris; she of the pale pink coat. Undiscouraged by the terrible main course they have ordered the equally awful pudding: a cream and sponge confection in glass saucers. They feed this to each other from the spoon, seemingly with no awareness of its lack of culinary merit. Their gaze slides, rarely, to the scene beyond the windows – but nowhere else. Nothing seems to dim their excitement for this journey, for each other; it is like watching children – a voluptuous delight. I do not resent them, though the sight gives me an ache. It does not come to all, what they have. For some of us it beckons, but remains forever out of reach: an impossible promise.

As we approach Milan the sky is palest gold, the trees intricate black cut-outs against it. I have always thought that

Milan has much more in common with the cities of Austria and Switzerland than it does with those of the south of the country. It is a sober, cooler place; it rains often. Bisected by fast roads and the rattle of trams; seamed with money. The passengers who embark are almost exclusively well-dressed. The women are fur-clad, exquisitely shod. But perhaps the men are chicer still: they wear their suits with a panache that is out of the reach of any Englishman and pastel-coloured scarves of softest wool. But I remember a time when it seemed that an Italian man wore one thing only: a uniform of khaki green serge, just like any Englishman.

Venice, at dusk. For such a jewel of history and art the station is a surprisingly tawdry place. It has begun to rain, and I can see small clusters of umbrella-hawkers touting their wares. This is where the honeymoon couple disembark. He carries the three cases, elegant monogrammed affairs. There is something almost old-fashioned about them, especially beside the lank-haired, paisley-clad twenty-year-olds who can be only a decade younger.

They are just before me. I watch as they are swallowed by the crowd and feel a strange sorrow at the loss of them, never to be seen again.

I have booked a hotel here for the night to break the journey, and Venice is roughly the midpoint, if one takes into account the ferry from London. I am ready for a respite. My body aches as though I have travelled the entire distance on foot.

It is raining when I exit the station, raining as I leave my hotel – where my room is not quite ready for me – and make my way along the edges of the smaller canals toward St Mark's Square. People hurry by beneath umbrellas; their faces wear this weather as a personal affront. The canals are swollen, precarious. Everything seems made of water; the city looks like a painting in which the colours are beginning to run.

As I look up at the famous basilica a shift occurs. The many fluted domes and elegant, filigree spires suddenly make it appear not like a Christian place of worship but rather the temple to another great faith. For a moment it feels as though I might not be in this Italian city at all, but already arrived at my destination. I know that the Silk Road came to an end here: bringing with it from the East silk, yes, but also foodstuffs, language and, it now appears, buildings. In a way, I think, this church is what I have been trying to do with the restaurant on a humbler scale. It is a reconstruction, a translation, of a remembered, faraway place.

Looking for shelter from the rain I discover a small but rather grand cafe, the interior gleaming with gilt and velvet. It seems an overpriced bauble, but perhaps at least authentically so: the date on the menu passed to me by a surly waiter reads 1720.

The doors release a fug of steam. I am shown to a red plush banquette in one of the gilt-and-mirror salons. Behind me is a *trompe l'œil* scene of a ravishing damozel: pale rounded shoulders and dark regard, black hair falling the length of her nude back to her waist. She reminds me a little of paintings I have seen of women of the 'Orient': lurid French and English fantasies of reclining women, surrounded by fruits and attendants, a sense of inaction and surfeit. I wonder what one Ottoman woman in particular would have made of such a representation. She would not have liked it, I know this much. I think perhaps it is the impression of languor, of idleness, that might have angered her most. She was never idle. She did not understand what it was to give up on anything.

I see the waiter's eyes snag on the suitcase, as though he is deciding whether or not he can bring himself to serve the owner of such a decrepit object. I was afraid of leaving it at the hotel. This may seem absurd: who would attempt to steal such a woeful piece of luggage? Still, to me the value of the contents means that it was not a risk worth taking.

When he has departed as quickly as his patent Oxfords will carry him, I open the bag and remove the next item. It is a first edition. A profound Sèvres blue with a gold embossed filigree pattern: a rather nice match to the gilt-and-pastel splendour of the cafe itself. I read it a long, long time ago: so much so that the story, in my mind, has become a little hazy. It had begun to bleed into other memories assimilated from that time. I am no longer quite sure whether, for example, it was the book's protagonist who travelled the Mesapotamian desert and climbed the Persian mountains, and once stayed in a town beside the Caspian Sea and saw a White Russian Army officer shoot his own reflection in a mirror, because all was lost. And whether he once lay upon his back outside his tent and watched the birds and longed for their grace and freedom. It is sometimes difficult to be certain what from that time is a fiction and what is real. My memory is not as it was. So much has happened in between.

My coffee comes, short and strong, with a delicate rime of brownish foam. I take a sip and it is perfect; only the Italians understand coffee like the Turkish, in my opinion. But Turkish is my favourite.

I open the front cover. A distinctive scent, still trapped in these pages: smoke.

Just inside the cover is a colourful chart of the world, according to which this train journey is only a thumbnail in length. And there, written in elegant blue ink, unmistakable, is her name.

Nur

'How is he today?'

'Much improved – you will see that for yourself. He's more talkative, interested in everything.'

Nur is somewhat thrown by this. It doesn't sound quite like the description of the little boy she knows. It sounds more like the child she knew before the war.

For a long time, after the terrible day, there had been no glimmer of the boy he had been. She wondered if that child had sunk completely from view – never to return. There were things that could change a person absolutely. And in childhood one was more malleable, more impressionable in character and mind; the change might be all the more devastating.

She read to him, in Turkish and English. He listened, she thought, but without expression. She kept finding some previously unnoticed horror in the pages. Death and violence had hidden in these books without her seeing them properly before. There were whole passages that had to be discounted and stories ended up making little sense, though it did not seem to register upon him.

She was fairly certain that she was the only person alive who cared about his fate. It was her duty to safeguard that fate, however inexpertly she did it.

'We've been playing dominoes,' the doctor says, surprising her out of her thoughts. 'I taught him. It's not a difficult game, but I'm still impressed by how he has taken to it. He's very quick.'

'I know.'

'Should I not have done so?'

'No. Of course you must do as you like. He is in your care.'

Her own emotions, clearly, have been more visible than she thought. When the doctor speaks like this she feels an indistinct apprehension. It is like the coffee, of the last visit. It is the idea of boundaries being crossed, the complication of relations, that makes her uncomfortable. She understands that she should be grateful to him for keeping the boy entertained. And yet he is still her enemy.

The enemy wears a uniform, he is fair-haired, he speaks with the same accent. And yet she cannot make that figure coalesce with the man before her, rocking slightly on his heels, a little sunburned across cheek and brow, running a hand through his hair to make it stand on end.

Away from this place, she can. She can imagine any number of things, in fact: that his agreement to treat the boy is merely another assertion of superiority. She can convince herself he will use this favour for leverage in some manner. She thinks of her brother – incarcerated for *four years* in a British jail. Something inside Kerem is broken. And whatever it was that caused it happened in the war, or perhaps in that very jail, at the hands of Englishmen like this.

Away from this place she can convince herself that she must remove the boy from his care immediately, no matter the consequences. Because for her to even look at an Englishman – let alone speak to him, drink coffee with him – makes her a traitor to her own family.

And yet confronted by the reality of the doctor, this infuriating affability, she finds that she cannot hold onto her convictions with the same vigour. It would make it so much easier, she thinks, if he could be a little less pleasant. If he could provide her with something to dislike that she could feed and water until it grew into hatred.

He has said something, she realises. 'Pardon?'

'He tells me that you play backgammon.'

'Not now. I used to play with my father.'

'How does he know about it?'

Because he knows about everything, Nur thinks – he misses nothing. Sometimes she wishes he were just a little less observant. 'I have a set in the house. It was one of the things I took from here when we left. I should have sold it, but I couldn't.'

'No one wanted it? I'm surprised.'

'No, I suppose I mean that I wouldn't. I wouldn't sell it.'

'Ah.'

He leads her through to the boy. She sees that he is sitting up in bed, and that he is eating: a plate of eggs, with the softest white bread, the sort that is impossible to find in the city now. There is a new fullness in his face. He looks almost better than he did before the illness. He looks like a different child. He has not noticed her yet: he is too intent upon his breakfast.

She glances at the doctor and finds that he is watching her. It seems that he sees everything. That whilst this transformation should make her happy, she feels instead an urgent sadness.

'I need to step outside,' she whispers to the doctor, stiffly. 'I apologise.'

She looks toward the sweep of the Bosphorus, changeable by the hour and yet in the essentials unchanged. Her breath returns gradually to its rhythm, the central calm restoring. It has passed. She would like a mirror, to see how visibly this thing has marked itself upon her face, but perhaps it is a good thing that she cannot see herself.

A selfish sadness, she thinks. It should not matter to her that she herself has been unable to enact this change in the boy – only that someone has, and that he is so much improved for it.

The door opens.

'I don't mean to intrude . . .' he steps carefully. 'I wanted to check if there was a problem.'

'Yes, of course. It was a surprise, to see him looking so well. I am – very happy.' It sounds like a lie, which is absurd.

'I have to congratulate you,' he says. 'He is a clever child, but he has been taught excellently, too.'

She does not want this kindness. She feels its power to destabilise.

'Thank you,' she says, as coldly as she is able. Then, unable to help herself. 'I have not seen such bread in this city since before the war.'

'Pardon?'

She almost says the thing she has been thinking: I supposed that if one has occupied a place, one has access to the very best of everything. Her sense of preservation prevents her.

He is watching her, frowning, as though trying to decipher her expression. She will not allow it. She makes her face a mask.

'I will take you back to him,' he says.

'If you do not mind, I would like to speak to him alone.'

'Of course.' He inclines his head. If he is insulted he makes pains not to show it.

This is how it should be; the coffee was a mistake – or, rather, the recognition of a debt owed. A singular instance, not to be repeated.

She sits down beside the boy and takes his hand – warm, faintly clammy.

'I hear you've been learning to play a game?'

'It's called dominoes,' he says, patiently. 'I'm good at them. I've beaten George four times out of six.'

'George?' She is confused by the name. Then she understands – the doctor. So, he and the boy are using first names. Again the sense of trespass.

'Your friend.'

'My *friend*?' She reminds herself that he is only a child, he cannot understand fully. Still, his interpretation profoundly worries her.

'The doctor is not a bad man . . . so far as his kind go,' she says. 'But he is certainly not my friend; he is not your friend. He is our enemy.'

'The war is over now.'

'But our city is occupied by their army. Do you understand? He is an Englishman, and you are an Ottoman boy.'

'No I'm not.'

This gives her brief pause. She has never heard him refer to himself in this way, had not thought the distinction mattered to him – because it has not signified anything to her. It once mattered to her grandmother, of course, as it does to so many. The war made people see one another differently, that was the thing. She thinks, and then tries not to think, of the terrible acts Hüseyin spoke of. It cannot be true. A war changes people, yes, but it does not turn them into animals.

'Next time,' she says, 'when he asks you to play dominoes,

tell him that you would prefer to read.' And before he can protest, 'Look, I've brought you a new book.' It is a collection of fairy tales, some of her favourites. 'I loved these when I was young.'

He does not look absolutely convinced.

'What is the matter?'

With heedless childish honesty, he says, 'I have other books already. I have the recipe book, and George' – that name again – 'has been reading to me from this.'

She looks at it. *Around the World in Eighty Days.* It was her favourite, as a child. She would imagine herself as a female version of the hero, circumnavigating the globe. How simple and attainable that dream had seemed in childhood, before the restrictions and complications that came with adulthood, with war.

'It's wonderful – oh, it's about . . .'

'I know,' she says, 'I know what it's about.' He looks faintly hurt. But then, she thinks, he has hurt her, and in this moment it doesn't seem to matter that he is a child and she a grown woman. And it is her own copy of the book. She recognises the jacket: powder blue with the title picked out in gold embossed letters. Inside the jacket her name is written, in the childish hand of a decade ago. Not a gift from the doctor at all, then, but an appropriation. An occupation. A city, a house and now, it seems, a childhood.

'Well,' she says. 'Of course you must finish that, first. It will help with your English.'

The words are cold and hard as pebbles in her mouth. She is not unaware of the contradiction: she has told him to steer clear of the Englishman, but continue the endeavour to learn his language. The alternative would be to admit that those years of lessons, all her work, has been in vain.

'Thank you,' he says. He takes the book of fairy tales from

her and, with an unlearned, childish grace, says, 'I'm sure I will enjoy these, too.'

She feels her anger ebb.

'Perhaps you could teach me to play dominoes.'

George

She comes to tell him that she is leaving. He realises that he is disappointed – he has hardly had a chance to speak to her this time, other than the odd conversation about the bread. For a second then there had been that expression again, the one she had worn on the jetty, or when he had stooped to retrieve her book. As though – he is fairly certain of this – she rather wanted to spit at his feet like the little boy before the Aya Sofia.

The visit to her son has been good for her. Sensing something like a new lightness in her, he wants to keep her talking, to make her linger. Grasping for a subject, he says, 'I wanted to ask you to explain what these rooms were used for, when you lived here. I suspected, for instance, that the ward was a women's room.'

The stare that he is met with makes him feel all the impertinence of the question. For a moment he thinks that she is not going to deign to answer him.

'Yes,' she says, finally. 'It was.'

'I can see that it must seem very strange—'

'And that room,' she indicates the place where the boy lies, her tone unmistakably dangerous now, 'was my father's study. And through there is the room in which my grandmother smoked her cigarettes . . . that, with the fountain, is where I once deposited some goldfish that I had bought in secret at the bazaar; my father was angry with me. And behind us is the room in which my father died, and on the opposite side of the house is the room in which my brother and I were born. And this, here: this is where we first heard the drums of war, over supper, the last time were were all together as a family. Is that enough for you? Or must you have more still?'

He knows that he should not allow her to get away with this last challenge. Locals have been arrested for less. She seems to be waiting for him to act, almost curious to see what the repercussion will be.

'You should not speak to me like that,' he says. 'I cannot allow it.'

'I apologise.' And yet there is no hint of remorse in her tone.

But he cannot make himself feel the outrage that he knows he should. Mainly because her own outrage, at seeing her house colonised like this, can only seem reasonable to him. And though it was all said in accusation, he now has a picture before him that he feels privileged to glimpse. Of this building as a living place: domestic joy and tragedy, all the mess and splendour of life.

'Thank you,' he says. 'I accept your apology.' At this the mutinous look returns to her expression again. She is usually so careful, but at this moment he could imagine her as the saboteur Bill suspects her of being. He does not want her to say something regrettable, now, that will force him to act. So he says, 'And I apologise too. I should not have asked you to speak of that time. I understand that it must have caused you pain.'

She closes her eyes. When she opens them again she looks directly at him and nods. 'Thank you.'

A strange pause occurs, now. There is an unexpected frankness in it; he realises that this may be the first time they have looked at each other properly. Usually she keeps her eyes averted from his face, as though there is something objectionable in it: which he supposes, as the face of the enemy, there must be. This look seems to redress the balance. In it, they become equals.

He watches her go, from behind the shutters, where she will not be able to turn and see him; he feels a voyeur. She moves quickly, as though the lawn is a no-man's land in which it is unsafe to linger.

She has come nearly every day. And he is glad of it. He enjoys her company in spite of the hostility. For so long he has had the company of men: men who talk and think in the same way as one another; who all come from something like the same background. Her company is more than a refreshment; it is a challenge. It shakes the complacency from him. The thought in itself is a surprise. As a doctor, and as someone who has become fond of the boy, he wishes him a quick recovery. But he does not regret that, while the child remains, he will have other opportunities to talk to her.

Nur

'I know where you have been, sister.'

'What do you mean?' She sounds like someone with a secret; she can hear it in her voice.

'I've followed you. You've been back to the house, the one that is now filled with the enemy's men. I saw you go inside. I saw you speaking with one of them.'

She feels a flush creeping up the side of her neck, and puts a hand there to cover it. She laughs, too, to disguise her fear. The sound is unconvincing; it has no humour in it.

'I don't see anything to laugh about. What is it that you find amusing?'

'Nothing. I . . .' She falters. 'What has happened to you, Kerem? Ever since you have been back you have seemed' – she searches for a word. Angry. Cold. Dangerous. 'So different.'

'I might ask you the same question.'

He is looking at her now with something almost like hatred.

She had thought that once Kerem had started to put on

weight he might look better, a little more like himself. His cheeks are fuller, his hair is brushed, his various sores are healing. What she had not understood was that the real difference lay in something less tangible, something behind the eyes. The experience of looking at him now is perhaps even more uncanny than it was before. Because, now, in more forgiving light, he looks like the Kerem of before. One might almost believe him unchanged. Until one sees the eyes.

She tells him of the boy, the illness, the necessity. Surely, now, he will understand. But there is that coldness in her stomach again, almost like fear. Absurd: she must not be afraid of her own brother, however much he has changed.

'Which boy?'

She tells him.

'The Armenian boy?'

She does not like the way he says this. She does not like the fact that he feels the need to ask it. 'He was very ill,' she says, 'and the English doctor agreed to look at him.'

'What about Mustafa Bey? Why did you not ask him?'

'He has gone to Damascus. And the Red Crescent hospital was full. It was the middle of the night – I couldn't think what else to do.'

'You went to an English hospital in the middle of the night. For an Armenian child.'

'It was an emergency – if you had been here, you would know.'

He frowns. 'If I had been here.' The way he says it turns her own words into an accusation.

'That wasn't what I meant. All I meant was that everything is different here now.'

'Why did they take the boy? Why would a British hospital – an army hospital – take a stranger in?'

She had been expecting this, and dreading it.

Before she can answer, as judiciously as she can, her grand-mother speaks. 'Nur knows the doctor there. The Englishman.'

'You know an Englishman?'

'I do not know him. I met him.' Quickly, before he can infer anything from this, 'It was an accident. In the street: I dropped something I was carrying, he picked it up.'

'The same sort of Englishman,' he says, conversationally, 'who killed our men? Who would have tried to kill me, if I had been sent to a different front? Who has butchered our country, who has stolen our capital? You . . . ah . . . *met* him.'

She hates the emphasis, the suggestion of something sordid.

'Did our men die for nothing?'

'No, I would not—'

'Did I nearly die for nothing?'

'No, Kerem, of course—'

'Then listen to me now, Nur. You must have nothing more to do with them. You must stop this; now. Otherwise—'

She hears the threat, but it remains unspoken, and somehow more menacing for it.

'It must stop. Do you understand?'

George

That evening, he has a visit from one Major Harding. 'There's been a report that you have a Turkish child here, is that correct?'

'A report from whom?'

'Please, Captain, just answer the damned question.'

But George knows the source – or is almost certain that he does. The second lieutenant that he discharged yesterday. Who had questioned every decision George had made with regards to his condition, because he 'knows a little about the subject myself' – though on probing this revealed itself to be a year at St Thomas', after which he had dropped out.

The main problem, George knows, is that his condition had humiliated and pained him. In insisting that the boil had to be lanced, George had become his chief torturer. No grown man wanted to yield up his pride like that – George himself would have had difficulties with it.

He had complained the morning after the boy had been admitted. 'This is an army hospital,' George had heard him say to his neighbour in a not-quite undertone. 'A British army hospital. We cannot be letting every sort in here.'

'Yes,' he says, finally, because he sees little purpose in dissembling. 'A child was brought here in the middle of the night – an emergency.'

'There are other places for the native population.'

'What should I have done? Turn away the child? Have an innocent's death on my conscience – on the conscience, I might add, of the British army?'

'Your focus should be upon your patients. What if your attention were taken by this Turk child, and you failed to notice the deterioration of one of the other cases?'

George draws himself up. 'It would not happen. Because, as I am sure you will see upon my record, I am an excellent doctor. I would never endanger the safety of my patients.'

'Good. Because if it were to come out that you had prior-itised the child's care . . . well, I think all I need say is that I do not know if there is a specific court-martial for such an offence – it being such a rare thing – but I am sure that one could be created, quickly enough.'

Nur

Nur goes to the hospital to bring the boy home. It is against her better judgement, but there was something in the way Kerem spoke to her that frightened her. It had been . . . yes, something like a threat.

She is making her way past the cloud pine in the garden when a strange creature emerges through the rose bushes in front of her.

She stares at it for a couple of seconds, trying to make sense of the sight. It is one of the strays, the old ginger tom, but he seems to have something caught about his neck – a great collar of material. He must have become tangled in it. She should try to take it off him. She approaches him. He watches warily but does not back away, as if to show her that he is not afraid.

'I wouldn't do that if I were you.' She turns to see the doctor, approaching from the house. 'He's not in a very good mood at the moment.'

'He has something caught about his neck.'

'I put it there.'

'But why?' She is ready to be offended. She never particularly liked the animal, he seemed a bully; there were terrible night-time fights of which she was certain he was the perpetrator. But this seems a strange and wanton cruelty to inflict upon any animal.

'If you look at his hind leg – there on the left, just above the hip.'

'The fur is gone.'

'Yes, I had to shave it for him. He had a wound – it was a messy cut. So I stitched it, applied iodine.'

'Why?'

'Well,' he shrugs. 'I suppose because I can. I saw it, and knew that I could do something for him.'

There is no boast in the way he says it. It is as though he thinks it is the most simple thing in the world. She has to admit that there is a grace to this attitude. How many men in his position, she thinks, would have done the same thing? One in twenty? A hundred?

She is also thinking that it is exactly the sort of thing her father would have done. There was the donkey he had brought back with him from a trip to the countryside, which he had rescued because it had outlasted its usefulness to the farmer and was going to be killed. It had eaten every single rose from the garden, and knocked her grandmother's favourite statue from its plinth, and once come into the house and left a steaming pile of dung on one of the most precious rugs, but they had kept it until it died a few years later.

'A human,' the doctor says now, 'knows that when they have a wound stitched it is in their best interests. If they are told to leave it alone, to heal, they will. An animal has no such understanding. Hence the collar, otherwise he would have torn all of the stitches back out with his teeth and made the thing far worse. He saw it as a violation, even though I gave him a little Novocaine as an anaesthetic. It was one of the hardest suturing tasks I have ever had to do.'

He pulls back the sleeve of his shirt to reveal a wrist covered by lacerations, just beginning to heal to pale pink.

'You could have caught rabies.'

'I know. Or tetanus. You would think a medical man might know better. What can I say? I am a fool.'

'You are not like most Englishmen.' She did not quite mean to say it out loud.

'In what respect?'

She supposes she meant that he seems to lack the English occupiers' cold formality, their assumed superiority. Of course she cannot say any of this.

'I'm not sure.'

'Well, that may be because I am not English. I'm a Scot. There are many of my countrymen who would demand blood for such a mistake.'

'I see.' As though it would make a difference to her, as though she might see him more kindly in the light of this new knowledge.

He smiles. He is somehow different today, but she cannot decide exactly how. It is a minute or so before she understands that it is because he is wearing neither a uniform or his doctor's coat: rather what appear to be his own clothes; trousers, braces, shirt sleeves. He appears younger: somehow more and less himself. This is the private man. She feels oddly as though she has glimpsed him in a state of undress. The formality of his clothing has thus far provided a certain definition to all of their exchanges. It has made it easier, too, to see him as one of a type: the khaki-clad Englishman, soaked to the top of his fair head in the invisible blood of her countrymen. Well, her imagination will simply have to work harder, that is all.

251

It helps, too, to think of Kerem, watching them from somewhere. It is not unlikely that he has followed her again, to make sure she delivers on her promise. It throws new scrutiny upon her every action. What would he make of this amicable scene: the doctor in this new, casual incarnation?

Now the cat approaches George, and butts his ugly head against his shin. She is amazed at the affection, she would never have thought it possible of the creature.

'I call him the Red Terror. He has become a friend. I like to think that he, too, understands what it is to have been in a war.' And then quickly, 'I should perhaps not make light of it.' When she remains silent. 'You lost someone.'

'My husband,' she hesitates. And my brother, she thinks.

'I'm sorry.'

'It was not by your hand.' She realises that she doesn't absolutely know this to be true.

'No. My role was to tend the wounded,' he says, as if he guesses it and wants to dispel this possibility, 'and the sick. As many sick as wounded – perhaps more.' He seems to be asking something of her, some acknowledgement of his innocence in Enver's fate.

She finds that she cannot give it.

Now the cat, newly tame, it seems, nudges her leg. She looks down, grateful for the interruption.

'I feed him scraps. When I first found him he looked like a collection of twigs with some oilcloth draped over him.'

A sudden memory comes to her. A small boy foraging for scraps in the school's refuse.

He nods, solemnly, and she finds it impossible to suspect him of guile. And then, 'I will take you to the boy.'

'Actually, I have come to take him home.'

He frowns. 'No. As I explained before, that cannot happen for some time. He needs to be here.'

'We can care for him at home.'

'You cannot give him the care he needs. You cannot prevent a relapse – which is likely.'

'You were . . . very kind to treat him. I am grateful. But he should not be here.'

He sighs. 'May I remind you that it was you who brought him here?'

'I was desperate. I did not know what else to do. I thought he was going to die.'

'And now I tell you that he may still die. If he had not been treated here, his life would have been in danger. If he is moved from here, now, his life will be in danger.'

'But it is not right. I cannot imagine your army would allow it.'

Something changes in his expression.

'They have not allowed it?'

'There have been—' he coughs, 'words exchanged. But I explained exactly what I am saying to you now. We would have the death of a child, an innocent, on our conscience. But for you it is so much more than that.' He is scrutinising her face. 'I thought you understood all of this.'

His eyes are pale grey, she sees.

'I do.'

'Then why this insistence, when you know that it is bad for the child?'

'Because it should not be like this. We cannot be . . .' she searches for the word. 'Friends' seems an embarrassing over-statement; again she thinks of Kerem, watching from some hidden place, ' . . . acquaintances. We aren't simply people of different nationalities living side by side: in this city we understand that arrangement, at least.' She feels the anger rise in her. 'But it is different with you. You have occupied us. And before that, you were our enemy.'

She hesitates. Why not? she thinks. It might help him to understand. And so she tells him of the day the English planes came. She does not spare him any detail besides that of her own injury, her own loss, the secret blood that came when she was at home. When she has finished there is a long silence. She thinks – hopes – that she has shocked him.

When he speaks, it is in an undertone. 'I did not know of this. I can only think . . . that it was a mistake.'

'It was no mistake. They came low enough to see our faces, to see who we were. That we were ordinary men and women, not soldiers.'

He does not challenge her again. But then he says, quietly, 'In war, people do terrible things. I will tell you this because I think you can stomach it.'

'I do not think—'

'We were in the desert, it was near fifty degrees centigrade: the most inhospitable place you can imagine. It could be forty miles or more between watering places, more. We were prepared for it, but we were suffering. And then, one day, we saw something that I thought was a hallucination at first, a mirage. A great stream of people. Hundreds of them.'

'What sort of people?'

'Not soldiers. No one, actually, who could have been a soldier. Old men and women. There were children dying, there, then, from heatstroke, malnutrition, exhaustion upon the path.'

'But why?'

'We couldn't understand much of what they told us. But it seemed they had all been forced to leave in a hurry, with no chance to prepare themselves. They were woefully lacking in supplies. Luckier ones rode mules, or cows, the animals salt-crusted in old sweat. But some walked in shoes that were falling apart. Some in bare feet. Do you know what happens to your skin when you walk on sand at that temperature?'

She does not think she wants to hear much more, but he continues, relentlessly. 'We tried to give them aid, food, water, where possible – but many of them were too far gone for help. There was an elderly man. He had fallen, in the dust. I tried to get him to stand up, but he could not. I think, actually, that a kind of peace had come over him. He asked me to go to his bag and retrieve a purse of money. This he was to distribute among those who he felt most needed it. Unfortunately, what they needed wasn't money but shelter, water, food.'

'Who did this to them?' Even as she says it she has a horrible premonition.

'We couldn't be absolutely certain. But we did discover that these, the ones we saw, were the lucky ones. A little further along that road we came across . . . other sights. I will not describe those to you. One thing that we did learn is that they were Armenians. Later, I heard similar tales. Retribution, apparently. But they were ordinary people: just like those you saw in the marketplace. How much do you think they really had to do with it?'

She cannot speak to answer him. She thinks of the boy, an innocent. She thinks of other innocents, like him, but without the chance that has saved him, perhaps, from a terrible fate. She feels sick: not merely in her body, but in some profounder part of herself. Still she does not want to believe in it, but she is already thinking of the thing Hüseyin had alluded to; how somehow he had seemed to hear of this too. She is thinking, and trying not to think, of the boy. What his fate might have been, if things had been only slightly different. She thinks of that one allusion Kerem had made to the things he had had to do. Necessary, he called them. And the change in him. But surely not.

'In the midst of war,' he says, 'I think that people believe they have become part of something greater than themselves. But often they have become something less. Less human. They become part of a machine; and a machine has no morality. I do not speak about any particular army when I say this.' He lowers his voice. 'I could be court-martialled for saying this, but I have little doubt that there have been atrocities committed by all sides. Now we have to relearn how to see one another as people.'

It reminds her of something, she reaches for it. The Persian poet, Rumi. He wrote of seeing each other across states, of seeing them for who they are. Actually: seeing was not the precise word he had used. It was loving.

'I do not mean in any way to paint myself as a hero. Believe me . . . I am not that.' He gives a short, joyless laugh. 'Before, when you told me of your husband, I was perhaps not as honest as I might have been. For these few years at least, half of me has been a soldier; has thought as a soldier. I am certain that I was not involved in any way in his death: I was not part of the main offensives. But I have carried a rifle, a knife. I have not used them as much as some. And I did use them, once, when I had to.' At this she feels the shadow of some unspoken memory pass over their heads. 'But the other half is a doctor. And it is what we are taught. To save life, no matter who our patient is, with no qualifications. And so you see the problem. You brought the boy to me. I have treated him, and he is my patient now. I urge you in the strongest terms not to remove him from my care.'

As she makes the journey back to the apartment she is filled with a new resolve. To make Kerem understand, to appeal to the kind, gentle schoolteacher that must remain in some small hidden part of him. In return, to try to understand him, what has made him the man he is now, even if she is not certain she has the stomach for it. Most importantly, to try to remember how to love him.

The Prisoner

He hears of a place where others like himself congregate. Men who have given everything to their homeland and returned to find themselves shunned by those they fought for, treated not as heroes but pariahs. It is on the outskirts of the city, in Eyüp: conveniently out of the way enough that it has been overlooked by the occupiers who are wary of any gathering of Ottoman men. They have been known to arrest groups in the cafes along the quays, smoking their *narghile* pipes, for the mere crime of 'looking suspicious'.

Here the hopelessness that he feels, hiding in that tawdry place with his grandmother and insensible mother, while his sister goes out into the city . . . here it vanishes. Here his experience, as a soldier, as a survivor, is valued. His physical degradation, his wasted limbs, his scabs, his abscesses, are viewed not as something repellent – he is certain that Nur is disgusted by them, though she tries to hide it from him – but as badges of his endurance. And he is certainly not alone in bearing them. If they were visited in the Russian camps variously by hypothermia, frostbite, malaria, the survivors of the English camps in the desert knew heatstroke and starvation. The starvation was the worst, for if men did not die of it alone it found new ways to blight them. Pellagra: a disease with a rather pretty name, the name of a young woman – yet with consequences as ugly as could be imagined. The skin rotting upon the bone. Its sister, trachoma – which made men go blind. His own various scars will fade, perhaps, but these men will never regain their eyesight.

Mostly the men talk of the past they have shared. They mourn dead friends – so many Babeks – and boast of glorious moments of personal heroism. Or seduction: amorous Russian women in the villages near the prison camps there, whores who refused to take payment from men so virile. Most of these stories are too preposterous to be believed. But no one would think to challenge them. They are the last comfort accorded to their tellers. None of them speaks of the things that happened in East Anatolia, toward the border with Syria; none of them mentions the Armenians. But he thinks that he can see it in some of them; they wear it upon them. When brief mention is made of the names of places – Bitlis, Erzurum, Van – there is an almost palpable tightening of the atmosphere, as though two thirds of the men present are holding their breath.

Perhaps they are all waiting, like him, for one of them to find the courage to speak of it. But none of them does. How would one even begin to articulate it, after all this time? So it lingers about them, shadows in the corners of the room.

'I hoped that I would one day see you here, old friend.'

It is the officer from the prison camp. The elegance that had been palpable even in that desperate place is now evident in the neatly pressed clothes, the small gold ring upon his hand, the expensive shine of his leather shoes. 'The war hero.'

He looks at the man sharply. Is he being mocked? No – he doesn't think so.

'I do not feel that way.'

'No. But you must remember that you are.'

'I keep thinking of them. I know that it was all . . . necessary. But I cannot stop thinking of them – the things that I have done, that I spoke to you of—'

'They must never be spoken of again. These things that were done were to secure the future of our homeland, which we hold more sacred and dear than our very lives. But others will not be able to understand. Our own wives and children will not be able to: because actions that are taken in war are beyond the interpretation of ordinary people. You see that, do you not?'

'I suppose so.'

'Nevertheless, our work is not finished. The enemy lives in our very city, in our houses, drinks in our coffee shops, leers at our women. You know, I suppose, that some of them are even marrying Ottoman women?'

He thinks of his sister, the day he followed her, the English officer.

'It is horrible to contemplate. But we must face up to the realities of our circumstances if we are to bring change.'

'How?'

'They won't be here forever. Soon they will pay for every indignity they have made us suffer. An army is coming for them; even now a rebel government is being formed at Ankara. But there is an army working from within, too. This war has not ended quite yet. There is no glory in it, other than one's own pride in doing a good, and necessary job. Are you interested?'

'What would it involve?'

'Well. Some use words. Several of the men here write for

the rebel press for example. You have seen how much they like to talk, how well they use words. But sometimes I think those words conceal a certain lack; that it is all they know how to do. I do not believe some of them even fought in the war at all, or if they did it was with pens and paper, from behind the safety of their desks. Others are the opposite, merely brutes, with no finesse. You and I are different. What we really need are deeds. Acts.'

'What sort of acts?'

'The sort that show the occupier that we are not afraid, that we have not been cowed yet. The sort that reminds him what it is to live in fear of his enemy.'

George

He has been in a suite at the hotel, treating a Very High Up for a nasty bout of enteritis. On his way downstairs he decides to stop in at the bar for an aperitif. In the early evening the Pera Palace bar crackles with intrigue and – unmistakably – sex. Also the mingled scent of Italian cigars, Turkish cigarettes, English pipes. If Constantinople seems to contain the world in all its heterogeneity, then here is a distillation of the world's seediness and glamour.

As he enters he sees four Italian officers at one table, gossiping like old women. At the next sits a Greek Orthodox priest, black-robed, luxuriously white-bearded, taking tea with two elegant women in beautifully tailored Parisian suits. Just beyond them, on the carpet, is a dark, reddish stain. Fainter now than it was when the blood was first spilled. It has been diluted, by the ministrations of some poor member of staff, from a puce exclamation to a rusty insinuation.

Bill saw it; he had been having a nightcap here when it happened. One minute the man was sipping his drink, he said. The next, calm as you like, another man – suited, bespectacled, ordinary in every degree save for the fact that his outstretched arm had ended in a handgun – had walked up and shot him. Dead. Clean, in the centre of the forehead, so there could be no mistake about it. The lack of fuss. Despite, or perhaps because of, four years of war. Bill said that some in the room hadn't even started at the retort of the gun, and had barely glanced in the direction of the fallen man. He had been a Bolshevik spy, they claimed. The other man was a once lofty White Russian. Or . . . had it been the other way around? George had heard both versions of the story.

'Afterward he disappeared, like smoke.' Perhaps, George thought, being so unremarkable, he had merely taken off his spectacles, flung his gun beneath the nearest armchair (it was found there, later) and sat down to order himself a drink. Perhaps he is here at this very moment. Stranger things, here, might be believed.

In this very salon, no doubt, there are men becoming rich, some from the very pockets of the refugees who arrive at the Tophane quay. The idea that they sell – a new life, a fresh beginning, an existence free from poverty and persecution – as irresistible as it is false.

'Monroe – I thought it was you.'

He glances behind him to see Calvert. He goes over, takes a seat. Calvert, he notices, is most of the way through a bottle of very fine white wine, and beginning to show the effects of the alcohol so markedly that George suspects it may not be his first. He checks his watch – six p.m.

'Goodness, man – what is this in aid of?'

'Nothing.' There are two livid spots of colour on the man's cheeks. 'Damned nothing. But I say, Monroe, it does gall . . . when a man makes a smart gesture and has it refused.'

George looks about the bar. He finds the culprits quickly

enough; there are so few women here, and these are the only two, somehow, that seem eligible. 'Don't look at them.' Calvert sinks a little lower in his seat. 'I do not want them to think I care a fig for their poor manners.'

George covers his mouth and coughs. Behind the shield of his hand, he grins.

Perhaps Calvert sees him. He is sharper than George remembers to give him credit for, even after the good part of a bottle of wine.

'But you don't have these problems,' he says, his tone ominously light. 'Do you, old chap?'

'Calvert, as ever I fear you are too subtle for me. What can you mean?'

'They say one of them comes to visit you at the house. A woman. A Turk.'

'Who told you that?' Not Bill, he thinks, please. He would not have thought that Bill, even with his disapproval of the arrangement, would stoop so low as telling a man like Calvert.

'Rawlings. You remember – you treated him.'

'I remember his pipe. My ward still smells of it.'

'Well, we're in the same digs now. *Sly old fox*, I said. Wouldn't have thought you were the sort, Munroe.'

'It is not at all like that. Rawlings, typically, has got entirely the wrong idea about something that should be extremely clear.'

'He said it was *extremely* clear.'

'Well then I can only say that he has chosen to see precisely what he wanted to see.'

'I should say that whatever you tell me, Munroe, I'm fairly certain I'm not going to be convinced.'

He wishes that he did not feel the need to explain himself to a man like Calvert. He tells himself that it is not merely a matter of pride. A man like Calvert could prove dangerous.

'She came to me because her son needed treatment – very urgently, one of the worst cases of cerebral malaria I have seen since Mesapotamia. I had little choice other than to treat the child. It is what I do.'

'I suppose it doesn't hurt that she is ... how did Rawlings put it? A "looker"?'

'I had not noticed.' Even to his own ears, even though he means it – or at least thinks he means it – it does not ring true.

When he leaves the bar he feels an urgent need for a cigarette. His hands are clumsy with the tobacco, the papers, he makes a mess of the first and has to give up on it. He is quite literally shaking with anger. Partly at Calvert – though mainly at himself. He should not have stooped to trying to explain himself. That is what it is: damaged pride. Not, definitely not, because Calvert's questions came too close to a truth he has worked hard not to acknowledge.

Nur

'An *utter* disgrace,' her grandmother is saying. 'Gül *hanım*, you know, from downstairs, tells me that there are Ottoman women taking their refreshments in the Pera Palace hotel these days, surrounded by the most unsavoury elements. And,' – a scandalised undertone – 'one hears of even worse. One hears the most despicable rumours. They say there are those who have *married* the occupiers. Women from the very oldest families.'

They may not be mere rumours. On perhaps three or four occasions, Nur has seen an Ottoman woman walking with a foreign officer. The first time she saw it she stared for so long and so hard that the woman must have felt her gaze: she looked across at Nur with something like defiance, and Nur was first to drop her eyes. Walking through the old quarter of Fatih, where some of the most illustrious families have lived for centuries, she sees a French officer watering a flowerbed. A woman leans from the shutters above, calling out instructions: a little more for the yellow tulips, which were particularly thirsty. She watches them, realising as she does that what she feels is a sense of trespass, a quiet outrage. Yes: she disapproves.

She had thought little would shock her, in this new reality – in which transgression is now the normal state of affairs. Yet this does. What do these alliances mean? Are they born of convenience, of pragmatism? Matches here have frequently been made on the basis of little more. Yet these, across language, culture, religion, are something new. They are occurring in full defiance of belief, too: a Muslim woman is forbidden from marrying a man of another religion. True, for one from a background such as Nur's this would not necessarily prove an obstacle: her family has never been particularly strict about such dictates of the faith. Her father and mother drank wine, none of them save her long-dead grandfather have ever fully observed *Ramazan*.

How might her life – all of their lives – be different, bettered, if she were to do the same? It would not be so difficult. On every excursion through the busier parts of town she has felt herself observed by the foreign men as an object of curiosity, even of desire. They would have access to better food, better living arrangements; they might even reclaim the old house. She is certain that her mother's condition might be improved by a return to her beloved home. Surely it would be worth being despised for such gains? When she thinks of it like this it seems almost a kind of selfishness that she has not sought out such an arrangement.

And yet she could no more do so than she could walk into one of the new Pera establishments and offer herself up for a more nakedly transactional agreement. She knows that it is not her grandmother's inevitable wrath that would prevent her – or not just, though it is a convenient excuse. It is her own pride.

George

The boy has the book open in front of him.

'Are you enjoying it?'

'I understand the pictures better than the words. There are many I do not know.'

'Of course. But I am impressed that you can read any of it. Where did you learn your English?'

'Nur *hanım*.'

He finds it odd, the way the boy refers to his mother like this. An Ottoman tradition, perhaps, just as the fact that there are no surnames. 'Of course. She is a school-teacher?'

'Yes. Though there are not as many lessons now. Most of the pupils have left.'

'Ah. Well, I am sorry to hear it.' He is; he cannot imagine her, somehow, as a person who would enjoy idleness.

'Now she embroiders linens. For money.'

'I see.' He knows little of this woman, but for some reason the image of her sitting for painstaking hours over an embroi-dery is an incongruous one. He cannot imagine her being still. He sees that the book of fairy tales she brought the boy has remained unopened on the bedside and feels an unexpected pang.

'And what do you normally like reading?' he asks. 'In your own language?'

'Recipes.'

George thinks there must have been a misunderstanding in the boy's translation.

'Recipes,' he says, humouring, 'what sort of recipes?'

The boy looks at him, tolerantly, as though he does not mind dealing with a fool; he has enough time on his hands. 'For food. Instructions for food.'

'Oh,' George says, and, unable to think of anything else to say, 'why?'

Again, the sense that the child is humouring him. 'To cook food from.'

'You cook food?'

'Yes.'

George has never heard of such a thing. Young boys, according to his sphere of knowledge, are interested in the same pastimes he was as a child: mainly sport – in all its wonderful variety – and animals. Specifically dogs. Perhaps horses.

'I did not realise that little boys liked cooking,' he says. 'I think you must be rather unique. But then of course I am no expert.'

The boy listens frowningly; George senses his concentration as he translates the words. Then he says, 'Why? You have no little boy of your own?'

'No,' George says. 'I do not have a son.' The child is still looking at him with that peculiarly bright gaze, which George has only recently come to realise is his own, not the work of the fever. Before it he feels . . . what is the word? Excoriated.

As though a layer of himself had been removed. He thinks of those images produced by the x-radiation machines that reveal the secret inner workings of the self, hidden malignancies. 'I think,' he says conclusively, 'I'll leave you to your books. You will be tired.' He leaves the pile beside the bed, turns to go.

'I could cook for you,' the boy says. 'I have learned the recipes. They're here.' He taps his forehead, for emphasis.

George thinks of the vast stove downstairs, the one Sister Agnes never lets him near, other than to heat coffee, the odd tin of bully beef. She is justified: these, after all, are the extent of his culinary abilities. 'Well,' he says, 'it is very kind of you to offer it. But you are too poorly at the moment to be out of bed.'

It is convenient that it is the case: he doesn't quite know what he would say if the boy were well enough, such is the eagerness in his expression. And he still isn't defeated.

'I can tell you what to buy. You can go to the bazaar.' In his animation his command of the language seems to become even more fluent. 'I can teach you, everything.'

George sees that he has argued himself into a corner. It is absurd: this is a hospital, he a doctor, with responsibilities and very little time to call his own. Moreover it is a military hospital; the child should not even be here. He might say all of this, and be done with it. Yet there is a problem. He wants the boy to like him. Mainly for the simple reason that he likes the child. But there is something else: he cannot shake the idea that if he succeeds, he will prove something about himself to himself. Then, perhaps sensing weakness in his hesitation, the boy grins. George is powerless to do anything but nod.

'All right. Perhaps just once. I have tomorrow morning free. If you tell me the things you need, I can get them.'

He cannot quite believe what he is saying. How the other men would laugh at him if they knew of it.

The bazaar is a labyrinth of roofed alleyways. The clamour inside is subject to odd distortions. Outside it has begun to rain, and the air held within is damp, faintly mist-hung. As one looks about the bright hues seem to bleed, slightly, like watercolour paint. George knows that he is observed as he passes. When he turns, though, the stallholders look away, busying themselves with their piles of goods. He wonders what experience they have had with other British soldiers thus far. He imagines – because it is more likely than the opposite – that there have been abuses of authority. Some of the men seem to be particularly zealous about discovering and stamping out dissent among the local population.

He has decided to walk to the spice bazaar – the Egyptian Spice Bazaar is its proper name – via the Grand Bazaar, which spills into it. There are things he would like to buy here. Tobacco, for example. Perhaps something sweet, too – he has a schoolboy's taste for sugar. But that particularly British fear of being misunderstood, of making a spectacle of himself, prevents him. The sheer scale of the variety on offer, too. The stalls he passes that are selling tobacco seem to have thirty or more varieties; he would not know where to begin. He finds one that smells about right – not too perfumed, not too acrid (he feels suddenly like the Goldilocks of pipe smokers) – and asks the man for a quantity of the stuff.

Now that he has a bag on his arm, that it is clear that he is here as a buyer – not an enforcer of some Allied law – the other stallholders are encouraged. They come forward, making suggestions. In the jewellery bazaar, men approach him with great furtiveness, casting wary looks about them, and then whip away pieces of unremarkable cloth to reveal jewels of staggering size and brilliance: a great square-cut ruby, lucent sapphires, a round, grass-green emerald set with a coruscation of diamonds. Suddenly he understands the secrecy: the value of some of these pieces must be astronomical.

'For your wife?' one man asks, proffering a slim gold bracelet. Then, hedging his bets, '*Pour votre femme?*' and impressively, '*Per tua moglie?*'

'No,' George says, 'no, thank you.' He pushes past the man with more force than is perhaps strictly necessary. He is suddenly tired of this place.

Onwards, driven by the surge of the crowd. Onwards, abandoning any pretence at knowing his route now, accepting that he is truly lost. He strides through these unknown streets and past unfamiliar faces like an automaton with one purpose: to keep moving forward. The crowd demands it, the streets too. He passes two women with their veils thrown back from their faces. One gives him a frank, appraising, amused look. And then suddenly he is out in the open air. By some accident he has found his way into the streets between the two bazaars.

He smells the spices before he sees them. Then they appear before him in bright, impossible cones: mustard yellow, red, umber, greenish brown. Smaller piles of dried rosebuds, so perfectly pink, so tiny and well-shaped that they look hardly real. Herbs: thyme and rosemary . . . and – he hazards a guess, bending near – lavender? No, something else. A foreign musk, lacking that astringent perfume. Tumbles of roots in varying degrees of size and gnarliness. The scent is almost overpowering. The tempered sweetness of aniseed, the warmth of cinnamon, the Christmas pudding spice of nutmeg, the tang of ginger cake. And with these aromas, evanescent, shifting, he catches threads of memory – lost before he can fully examine them.

He looks at his list. Rosewater and saffron, ginger root, cinnamon bark. He has little idea what any of these look like, though he may know some of their flavours. Luckily the stallholders seem to know the names of their spices in English – perhaps in every language, for he hears another conversing in halting French. Some of the items on the list are surprisingly expensive. Of course, having no idea of the market price for such things is hardly a powerful position to negotiate from. Yet he feels oddly satisfied at his success in procuring them. Looking at them – flower stamens, a water made from petals, a twisted tuber, the bark of a tree – he cannot imagine how they will be translated into something edible. He begins to wonder if he has been had for a fool.

He leaves through another entrance and is propelled, blinking, in the newly sunlit air. It might be a different day. Here is an absolute contrast with the chaotic former frenzy of the market. He is suddenly alone, in a street in which the shadows fall blue and dappled, cool as a glass of iced water. Where did the people go? This street has no shops, only a row of shuttered-looking houses. That distinctive Ottoman style, tall and elegant, with an embroidered look to the wood and the upper floor projected precariously above the lower.

There is the sound of water, echoing upon stone – turning the next bend he happens upon a fountain sending out a confident plume of water into a stone trough from a great bronze spout. At the far end is a tiny, black-cloaked figure. An elderly woman, extending one time-clawed foot into the green depths, bending down to wash it. When she has departed he too stoops to the plume of water and cups a hand, sluices the fine layer of perspiration from his face. It is very cold, moss-scented, drawn from some secret underground place. A Roman aqueduct perhaps – they had their way with water. Though they stole it from the Greeks, who were here before. It could be thousands of years old. Or it could be only decades. Impossible to say: everything this city, this place of myth and history, can cloak itself in borrowed age and renown.

Rounding another corner, a shock. A whole street of houses destroyed. He tastes the smoke at the back of his mouth before he understands what it is he is witnessing. He has never seen anything quite like it. Beyond the burned reminders of the walls one can just discern the sorry remains of furniture, old divans, chairs. He stops. One of the shapes – still as all the rest – has a too-organic form; perhaps it is best not to look too closely. It might be, it might not be. People are at least prepared for such eventualities; he has heard that they happen all the time, these fires. The old wooden houses are like tinder boxes. Perhaps this sight becomes less of a shock for those who live in the city because of its ubiquity. But he cannot imagine walking past this with equanimity.

He hurries forward, head bowed, the knowledge of it within him now like a poison, his mood utterly changed.

The Traveller

Mid-afternoon, but already the light beyond the window is beginning to fade. I had a late lunch in the dining car and now find myself alone once more in my cabin with my thoughts. Nothing to do until dinner time except stare down my 'bed' with its thin rectangle of foam, promising even more discomfort come morning. A sleep in a proper bed in Venice did something to alleviate the effects of the couchette. But already, after one night on the thin rectangle of foam, my back has begun its protests. I feel bent out of shape . . . corrugated. It is unfair, really, because it is only through the physical – the disobedience of my body, its various pitiable degradations – that I am reminded I am no longer young.

The landscape beyond the windows has varied little all day: a never-ending pastoral, a patchwork of fields interrupted by the odd town or village or the blank of a brickwork tunnel. I am sure that in summertime it would be lush and green and surpassingly beautiful but at this time of year the farmland is just tilled soil, unvariegated greyish-brown.

Now something has drawn my eye back to the scene. A

change: something more than the mere diminishment of the light. It is imperceptible at first and I am about to look away when I see it – a tiny flake of white, seeming to hover for a second before the glass before it is sucked into the slipstream of the train. Then at once they are everywhere, dancing before the window like spots of pure light.

I have never been able to see it as mere weather – not like sun, or rain. Not since a particular day: which might as well have been the first time I ever properly saw snow. It has always seemed to me more like a quantity of magic seeping into the world.

It is almost completely dark now and the white swarm seems to glow out of it. Time, I think, for an aperitif. I could go to the dining car but somehow there is a greater loneliness in drinking surrounded by strangers than there is in one's own company.

I only have one option with me, and it is probably better suited to after dinner, but it will do. I take it from the case, the old pewter flask – seasoned traveller of continents. I pour myself a sparing quantity of the stuff inside and I can almost taste it before I lift it to my lips, the warm smoke of Scottish peat.

Last night I dreamed about her. For a long time I thought that I hated her for what she had done. For not being strong enough, when I had thought her brave, capable of anything. I thought she had simply given up.

I say it, trying it out, the one rich syllable of it. My voice sounds so strange, so loud in the silence of my cabin, slightly roughened by the whisky. And it is so long since I have spoken this name.

Nur

'How is he today?'

'Markedly improved. In fact, better than that – he's cooking.'

'Cooking?'

'No,' he says quickly. 'He isn't cooking, but he has me doing his bidding, as his proxy if you like.'

She tries not to smile.

'He told me that his favourite book was one of old recipes.'

'Yes, it is. The cook who used to work for my family, Fatima. They were hers.'

'I see.'

'He discovered it. We have been cooking the recipes from it since.'

'He told me.'

It makes her wonder what else the boy has told him. Of her insensible mother, perhaps, or the night-time hours of embroidering . . . or the fact that sometimes she buys three-day-old bread from the baker's and soaks it in water to make it edible. Her pride quails as these possibilities present themselves. She reminds herself that she should just be thankful that Kerem had not arrived before the boy's illness. Children do not always understand the importance of secrecy.

'I have to say,' he says now, 'it has been something of a departure from tinned food and coffee.'

'What has he made for you?'

He tells her.

'I'm afraid you have been poorly used.'

'What do you mean? It was delicious: the men enjoyed it.'

'That was a recipe I told him we could not make, because the ingredients were too expensive. Saffron . . . I cannot imagine what that must have cost you.' She is almost proud of the boy's resourcefulness.

'I got a good price, from the seller.'

'Ah.' She decides not to humiliate him by asking what he paid. 'It is incredible,' she says, 'I cannot get him to remember the succession of the sultans, or his numbers, but he has committed the recipes, every detail, to his mind.'

'It is how interested one is in the subject – it is the same for all of us. At medical school I could never interest myself in the symptoms of certain tropical diseases: they seemed so far beyond anything I would ever experience. Then, when I began to treat men for them – and new ones besides – I suddenly became an expert.'

'Of course.'

'But I cannot think of any other boy his age who can speak another language so fluently. His English is astonishing. It shames me.'

'And French,' she says, and is immediately embarrassed by her boast.

'Which makes him more impressive than any adult Englishman. The strangest thing,' he says, 'I found a whole cache of children's books in English and French here. They were yours?'

'Yes.' She finds that she cannot say any more; there is some obstruction in her throat. Silences have strange power. Some draw people together, like co-conspirators. This one, though, seems to pull something open between them, and each is perhaps a little embarrassed by the familiarity of the last few minutes. They have become strangers again.

'You could come and eat with us here, one evening.'

She suspects that he has only said it to fill the silence, to salvage the accord of a few moments before. 'No,' she says, 'thank you.'

'I apologise,' he says, perhaps only now seeing the impropriety of the invitation. 'I should not have asked it.'

She cannot help wondering whether he would ever have asked one of his countrywomen such a thing. An invitation to a supper of soldiers. She reminds herself that it is meant as a gesture of friendship.

'Unfortunately,' she says, 'I have to cook for my mother, and grandmother. Both of them are even worse cooks than I. But I thank you for the invitation.'

'I should not have made it.'

'Perhaps not. But I know it was well meant. And I admit that I have come to miss his cooking.'

'I do not doubt it. I enjoy his company, too. It is so different to the men – you know they moan a great deal more than he. He is a wonderful child, your son.'

He has used the word before, and she has not corrected him. She has – yes – liked the sound of it. But suddenly it seems a deception.

'I have not been honest with you. Perhaps it does not matter either way. But I feel I should tell you the truth.'

'What do you mean?'
'He is not my son.'

Survival trumps education. Nur had understood this from the first days of the war. She had been left with a class of six or so pupils, because the children came and went depending upon the situation at home or in the city itself.

Some of her pupils, the girls in particular, were kept at home – embroidering linens, selling goods in the streets. Some of them, the families of Greeks, Armenians, Jews, had simply gone. Often without any warning: in times like these people did not politely call upon one, explain that Konstantin or Maria would no longer be attending. They did not write notes. They disappeared as though they had never been.

Only one pupil would be there unfailingly. The day after the bombing in Mahmut Paşa, it had been just the two of them in the classroom. He was quick, and naughty. He had a particular affinity for language, English, French, Latin. She was fond of him, despite herself. He was also listless. She suspected, as the war went on, that this was due to lack of food.

He was the son of two Armenians. The father a barber who her father had sometimes visited, the wife a very talented seamstress, who adjusted clothes for her mother and grand-mother. But it seemed that during the war they had fallen on hard times. There was less call for non-essential luxuries, such as the skill of a tailor. There was less call for the services of an Armenian barber – partly because so many men had gone to war, and because some were boycotting the Armenians, the Greeks, the Jews: saying they were secretly celebrating every victory of the enemy. The apartment they had moved into, according to the butcher's wife downstairs (one of her grandmother's new circle of informants), used to belong to an Armenian family.

'Where did they go?'

'Oh, no one knows. They seemed pleasant enough to me – though I know others disapproved of them. But I suppose it's only right, since the war.'

Her grandmother had nodded, sagely – though Nur suspected she was as ignorant as herself as to exactly what the woman meant. She never showed her ignorance, though: to do so was an admission of weakness. She was like the sultans who had wanted to seem all-knowing, all-powerful.

'Why?' Nur asked the butcher's wife. She did not have the same reservations. 'Why is it only right, since the war?'

'Well.' The woman had seemed momentarily lost for words. 'Well. Because they are the enemy now, of course.' Then, apparently bored, she had segued into some tale about one of their other neighbours berating her husband in the small hours of the morning and how it was 'really too shameful' – both the noise, and the fact that the man just seemed to accept it. But he was clearly a weak sort – he would have been the right age to go to war, had it not been for some dubious story about a problem with his heart.

'But why?' Nur had persisted.

'Why what? I can't presume to know the reason for a man's unmanliness. Perhaps he was at the breast too long as a child.'

'No: why are they now our enemies, the Armenians?'

The woman had given a little shiver of irritation. Nur was reminded of the phase she had gone through as a child: a game of replying to every answer with another question. Her mother had worn the same expression of exasperation as the butcher's wife.

'They're traitors,' the woman said – baldly. 'That's all I know of it, but I do know that it's true. Everyone knows it' – as though Nur had spent the last few years living under a rock – 'everyone knows that it's true.' A cross glance at Nur. 'My Mehmet knows more about it, of course: he goes to the coffeehouse, he hears all about it there. The stories men bring home from the front.'

Nur was almost tempted to ask why her Mehmet, who seemed perfectly strong and capable and the right sort of age, had not gone to the front either. She stopped herself: she knew that she would not like herself if she asked it.

Later she thought of her nurse, Sara, who had been Armenian. She had been a second mother to Nur – quite literally, in the first weeks of her life, when she had been her wet nurse, as was common in families like hers. Even while Nur had been fascinated by her strangeness – the fact that she did not fast at *Ramazan*, or was allowed to drink wine (though she never did), and wore her hair uncovered – she had loved her as though she were family. Impossible to think of someone like Sara as the enemy, just as impossible as to think it of the Armenian children at the school. She had seen allusions to 'Armenian treachery' in the newspapers but had been able to dismiss them. They seemed as likely as the pieces on our 'all-conquering army'. To hear a woman like the butcher's wife talk of it as an established fact: that was a different matter.

She had discovered the boy going through the kitchen refuse at the school, looking for scraps of food. He had a small pile of his treasures beside him: potato peelings, the rough outer layers of onions, the skins of aubergines. When questioned, the story came out. He carried a little bag about with him in his pocket. In it were salt and pepper, a little powdered chilli. With these he could make anything palatable. Roots, or grass, or meat several days past its best: the chilli would disguise the greenish hue, too, if one was squeamish. This vegetable detritus was a comparable luxury. He told her all of this with a note of unmistakable triumph, as though proud of his resourcefulness.

The next day she had brought in some of their bread for him – furtively, because if she was caught she would have had some difficult explanations to make to her mother and grandmother; they had hardly enough to feed themselves. This had continued for some weeks. She had been pleased to see that her gifts seemed to be having some effect: that he seemed to have lost the look of a child marked out for death. She made sure that he ate the food she brought in front of her, because she suspected otherwise that he would take it home to share with his family. This was all very well, perhaps. But it was he who was her responsibility, and he was a six-year-old boy. One had to assume that his parents would be better able to take care of themselves.

One day he had not come in to school. She had not worried immediately. But when three days had passed, with no sign, she began to be uneasy.

She knew where he lived. Samatya, the Armenian quarter of the city since Byzantine times, in Stamboul – on the other side of the Golden Horn. She did not know exactly where, but it was a close community, smaller and even more tight-knit since the earthquake in the last century that had forced so many to leave. His parents had been well-known for a time; hopefully someone would be able to tell her of their fate. She wandered through the neighbourhood and realised that her confidence might have been misplaced: there were so few people in the streets. Hunger did this, and fear.

Turning a corner she had come across a terrible, too-familiar sight: several streets' worth of houses razed by fire. A greasy smoke still rose listlessly from the rubble. Later, she could not be sure exactly why, but she had a sudden certainty that here was the reason for the boy's absence. She had wandered through the ruined place, calling his name. She did not really believe that any use would come of it. But as she had passed one of the buildings on the outskirts of the catastrophe, one which had been only half-consumed by the inferno – so that the theatre-set impression of rooms remained – she had heard a noise. A small, high cry, through one of the blown-out windows. She had assumed that it was a stray cat: Constantinople had always been full of them, and they were at that time more than ever the lords of the street, the only ones who did not seem cowed by the change in the city. Then it came again, and this time there was a different, human quality to it.

Steeling herself against what she might find, she had made her way in through the empty doorframe. She had stopped short, realising her mistake. No one could remain in here. There was only death; she could smell it. A thick fog of grey soot hung suspended in the air, she felt it enveloping her. Remnants of blackened furniture stuck up in places like used matchsticks. The stench was almost overpowering. She was about to leave when the sound came again, and she looked into the dark to see a shape. A child, crouched like an animal, his eyes and teeth seeming to glow from his soot-smeared face. He looked like an entirely different boy at first, it was impossible to recognise him through the dirt. But that was not all there was to it: something had departed him. Or, she thought later, something had entered him. A new darkness, a virus of grief. It would be a long time before she saw anything of the boy he had been before.

There were rumours that the fire had not been an accident. That it had been set to teach a lesson; by those who believed – like the butcher's wife – that the Armenians were an enemy within. She would not allow herself to believe it. Not this. No one could have meant this.

She discovered, later, that he had spent three days in the house, three days with the burned bodies of his parents. She had seen them but only as unthinkable shapes; her mind had not allowed them to be anything else. Even when she knew what they were, for certain, she had been unable to match them to the kind couple she had known. The small man with his quick smile, and his wife, whose laughter came so easily, so generously.

She had picked the boy up in her arms – he did not resist – and carried him from the house like an infant. He was almost as light as one. She had walked with him like this all the way home.

George

He remembers the scene beyond the bazaar, the ruined houses. Despite all that he has seen, he shudders.

He had been so certain that the boy was hers. She had been married before the war, it made sense. But it was more than that: her tenderness with the boy. He thinks of how, when he had told her of the boy's condition, her hand had gone to her abdomen. He wonders at it.

He wonders, too, why she has not corrected him before. Did she think, perhaps, that he would not have offered his help so quickly if he had not believed the child to be hers? Would it have made a difference? He would like to think not. Except that he is not absolutely sure. The truth of his motives, as with so many of one's most significant actions, remains inscrutable even to himself.

Did she think that in some way he would judge her, would think less of her?

The truth is that it is quite the opposite.

* * *

She has come every day. Each time he has noticed, learned, something new in her.

That she is a baffling, complex, mixture of confidence and hesitance, anger and equanimity.

That sometimes, when she has used a particularly difficult word, in English, she allows a momentary pause before continuing, as though waiting for him to correct her. (He never does – he is not certain that it would be well received, despite the apparent invitation, and besides, her command of the language almost outstrips his own.)

That the gloves she wears are of a very fine-looking lace, but that they seemed to have been mended rather clumsily in several places.

That, on the occasions when she has removed them, the beds of her nails have a bluish – almost violet – tint. A sure sign of poor circulation that he should not, as a medical man, find so charming a detail.

That there are three tiny, dark freckles about one of her eyes – though he can never remember which. Like a constellation. No, like a signature, the mark of a master artist proud of his work. He is surprised at himself. He does not normally give way to such ridiculous notions.

That often when he is speaking she frowns at him. He cannot decide if this is her concentrating upon her translation of his words – which he doubts because she is so proficient – or that she is marshalling her dislike of him, of what he stands for. Which seems the more likely.

That her smile is a hard-won thing, but that when it comes it is unmitigated pleasure, all the better for the difficulty in winning it.

There are many other things beside, too many to enumerate. He feels that he could write a paper on them – far more fluently than a treatise on the strains of Mesapotamian malaria, which he is currently attempting.

Difficult to diagnose a complaint in oneself. Even, or perhaps especially, if one is a man of medicine. The best way is to list the symptoms precisely, dispassionately, and then attempt to look upon them as one might the same in a stranger.

He goes to the cupboard, retrieves the precious flask, and pours himself a sparing quantity. He holds the whisky in his mouth, enjoying the burn of it, the clarity it brings to his thoughts.

If he were to list his symptoms now? Anticipation. Heightened awareness of the self and one's own short-comings. Heightened awareness of perfection in another; everything in them appearing fascinating, novel. Increased heart rate. Disturbed dreams. Anxiety. Strange, irrational bouts of euphoria.

He senses that a hundred doctors in the same number would diagnose one complaint. He would do so himself . . . observing these effects in a stranger. But as for himself? Impossible. It cannot be; he cannot allow it to be. Because, if it is, he is in a great deal of trouble.

Snow

The snow takes the city by surprise; a month ago it had been warm. It sweeps from the north of the Black Sea under clouds of palest lavender. It silences the world. It perfects the streets, blanketing unsightly piles of refuse and dirt. The street cats slink through it furtively, as though not wanting to draw its attention upon them. The stray dogs are suspicious of it, fearful: they growl and whimper – one brave pack leader tries to paw the flakes out of the air.

It is beautiful, otherworldly. In some places, perhaps, it becomes mundane, but not here where it visits rarely. Nur steps out into it, a swift breath in at the cold. She wraps her scarf a little higher about her face, and plunges into the swarm of white.

Kerem watches from a window. At one time he might have seen beauty in it – he can hear the delighted cries of children from the street. As he watches, several small figures emerge, clothes dark against it, wrapped in what appears to be every item they own. They kick at the fresh fallen powder, scoop it up into their arms so it fountains down. He sees Nur stop and talk to them and then he sees or perhaps hears her laughter.

He blinks. Because all he can see are the broken bodies of so many men; freezing hard as stone – but not so hard that the dogs will not be able to tear into them. There is a tightness, high in his chest. He closes his eyes and turns from the glass. He will light a cigarette, and then he will go and speak with his friend in the Eyüp coffeehouse.

The boy watches it, from the window of the house on the Bosphorus, transfixed by how it seems to melt into the water, or to be swallowed by it. There have only been three proper snows in his lifetime; it is a miracle. And how quickly the opposite bank is transforming from dark green to white. He would like to go out into it; but he knows that he will not be allowed. His old self would have run and jumped in it, would have built figures from it.

For the doctor, it is still a miracle. He has not seen snow like this for several years. By the time they arrived at those villages beside the Caspian Sea the snow was old and brackish. To those living there it had long ago become a nuisance, not a novelty. This is like the snow of childhood, blanketing the peaks overnight so that he would wake to a world transformed. The red deer moving through it, suddenly exposed. All of the colour gone. A new, more essential beauty. It seemed possessed of its own light, even after darkness fell. He could see it there glowing out at him, like a secret.

He is in the grip of some uncertain emotion.

'Would you like to go outside?'

He has his answer before the boy has even spoken.

'Sister Agnes, I'm taking him out. Could you fetch me some blankets?'

She widens her eyes at him: what madness is this?

He ignores the look.

It is colder than he has expected: the wind funnelled in across the water feels as though it comes straight from Siberia.

'Are you warm enough?'

'Yes.' It comes muffled from beneath a layer of blanket.

'We don't have to stay out here for long.'

It is slow progress; there are already several inches of cover and the wheelchair is unwieldy, even with the small weight within it. In a few minutes, in spite of the cold, George is damp with sweat.

He remembers something, from childhood.

'Look up, into it falling.'

'I cannot.'

The boy, he sees, is so tightly swaddled that he is fixed into position, face forward.

'All right. Look, I'll help you.' With no small effort he tilts the heavy chair back towards him on its wheels, so that the child is facing the sky.

Above them they watch the unwinding vortex of snow like a falling constellation, a fragmenting nebula. The few bare branches are black veins, equally strange. The boy opens his mouth, and catches a flake upon his tongue. George knows the taste of it – the taste of nothing, and yet with a flavour all of its own, metal and something sweet. His eyes burn. Though it may be nothing more than the bitter air.

At some point he catches movement from the corner of his eye, and turns to see a figure approaching through the veil of white. She might be unidentifiable, wrapped so comprehensively in shawls, but he knows from something in the movement that it is her. The rush of joy he feels on seeing her takes him by surprise. It is that which one might feel upon the unexpected arrival of an old friend; even a loved one.

He raises a hand. He doesn't call out – he isn't sure whether she will be able to hear him from this distance and somehow the words won't form themselves anyway. It is as though something has winded him.

She comes closer, stepping carefully. When she is near he sees that the snow light has changed her eyes; they look not dark but almost silver.

'What are you doing?'

'He wanted to see the snow.'

There is a lightness between them, he feels it. It is something new, almost like friendship. It is the magic of the snow, the strangeness of it.

'It looks more as though you were both eating it.'

From somewhere in the folds of her cloak she produces a small package, wrapped in brown paper.

'I bought these for him.'

She hands it to him. He takes it; it is warm. For a moment he thinks it is the warmth of her, the warmth beneath her cloak. He feels something new go through him and looks hard at the package in case it is visible on his face.

'Chestnuts,' she says. 'The street sellers are roasting them on every corner. He likes them.' And then, an afterthought: 'And perhaps you will have some, too.'

'Thank you.'

There follows a reckoning silence. Neither of them seems quite certain of how to proceed. And then something rather unexpected happens: a shock of wet and cold hits him square in the face. He splutters, flummoxed and angered by the assault. For a confused moment he thinks that she has thrown it at him. Then he understands: one of the branches above has released its weight of snow onto him, a direct hit. The boy is laughing in delight. Even she has allowed herself a smile. As he sees the thing as they must have done, he begins to laugh too.

The Boy

He watches Nur *hanım*. She is different, somehow. She looks the same – apart from an extra layer of clothing against the cold, perhaps – but she wears the new thing on her like an invisible cloak that warms her in some secret way. He thinks he knows what has caused this change in her. It is the doctor. He realises that he has never thought of an adult needing a friend in the way a small boy might. He would never have thought it of Nur *hanım*, especially, because she has always seemed so strong. And she has never had a friend, as far as he can think, in her life. But now she is smiling, and her whole face looks different: less tired, less old.

She told him, all that time ago, that the doctor was not a friend: that he is the enemy. She seems to have forgotten this.

There is something else, too: that he is too young to interpret but not to notice. He can feel it, like a change in the atmosphere, like the scent of a new season. It is in glances, in words: but beneath the words. Something powerful, perhaps dangerous. Do they know it, too? He isn't certain. He knows, too, that he cannot speak of it to Nur. Not just because he does not know how to put it into words, but because he does not think she would like him asking.

The Prisoner

Acts of destabilisation. That is the phrase to remember. Do not let them become too comfortable.

'They have to live here like everyone else,' the officer says. 'If their existence becomes a little less secure, they will be that much less effective at the business of occupation.'

This is where they are powerful. Not in the way of an army – in an open show of might. Rather as agents of uncertainty and fear. However universal an occupation, it cannot be all-seeing.

He is involved in a number of smaller subversions. Some of these are raids on the artillery stores of the Allies, the weapons to be passed along a chain that will eventually see them in Ankara, with the rebel government. Some are caught in similar acts.

On his return from the coffeehouse, late at night, he happens across a British soldier drunk upon the quay. The man is bending down to vomit into the Bosphorus. The gold epaulettes upon his shoulders mark him out as an officer of high rank.

And these are the men to whom we are supposed to relinquish our city, who have made what was ours their own. The shame of it.

He acts almost before he has decided he is going to do it, the impulse of a moment: a hand shot out to catch the man in the small of his back. Only a tiny amount of force. But this is all it takes to send the officer toppling forward. The man enters the water with hardly a sound, as though he had never been there. The surface appears almost undisturbed.

Within: is there not a small ripple of disquiet at the deed? Yes, in spite of himself and all he has learned. Because this death must be nothing to him. After all, he has killed innocents and *those* deaths were necessary. He must believe that, or be destroyed. This man, on the other hand, was himself a killer. He must celebrate it for what it is: a triumph over his enemy.

But two days later, the news in the coffeehouse is that, by some miracle, the man survived. That they are searching for the perpetrator. There have been executions for much less. Is he afraid? He does not know what that means, any more. For a couple of days, he remains at the apartment – though he is almost certain that the man could not have seen him, and even if he had was too drunk to remember his features.

In the early morning a small band of British soldiers pound their way through the streets of the neighbourhood, making 'enquiries'. This, apparently, means ordering half-dressed, barefoot men into the cold street and humiliating them in front of the secret gaze of their neighbours, interrogating them as they shiver on the spot.

'Nur.' He goes to rouse her, but sees that she is already awake. 'They cannot know that I am here.'

He sees the suspicion in her expression; once it would have made an impression upon him, but now he is used to her looking at him like this. It is better, in fact, than the times he catches her watching him secretly, as though trying to work out whether it is really him.

At first he thinks that she is going to refuse. It was foolish – he sees this now – to commit the act so close to home. He would not have wanted to implicate Nur in it, no matter her disloyalty. But she nods her head.

From his position on the roof he hears how they talk to her, the degradation of it. According to the old way of things they should not even be able to demand an audience with the women of the house. He imagines that even if they are aware of this edict they probably take great pleasure in flouting it.

'No,' he hears her say, 'there is no one else here. My brother was lost in the war.' He hears the tell-tale give in her voice at the lie; but they do not know her like he does – or thought he did. It was not worth it for this, the humiliation of his sister, of the men in the street. The act was petty, ineffectual. In the hours afterward it had plagued him more than it should have done, a burr upon his conscience. He kept seeing it again in his mind, the defenceless – albeit shameful – state of the officer as he had made his move. It had been cowardly, beneath him. That was what had disquieted him, he tells himself, not so much the likely death of the man as the unheroic part he himself had played in it. And *then* to discover that the man had survived, that the debasing of himself had been for nothing.

So his next act must be significant. It should be meticulously planned in advance, orchestrated with bravery and conviction – not upon the whim of a moment, with all the grandeur of a pickpocket stealing a wallet. It must be something that will draw a line between the man all those years ago, and who he has become. Something that will prove as much to himself as to the enemy.

An idea occurs to him.

It would solve several problems at once.

At first his mind recoils from it.

Then he returns to it. Worries at it, as he might a bad dream that has terrified him.

Nur

Kerem is distracted these days, secretive. He comes home late at night; he has not mentioned the issue of the hospital again. She does not think that this means he has forgiven her: only that he has more pressing matters on his mind. There was this morning, when the British soldiers came. The army has had no presence in their uneventful streets since the very beginning of the occupation. Something of significance had drawn them here.

If it is what she suspects, it is not the cause she objects to, precisely. She is afraid for him – that is the heart of it.

There have been those murmurings of resistance since the beginning of the occupation. There are even rumours that there are women involved. If her situation had been different, if it had not been for her mother, the boy, she might have been tempted to join them herself.

She has no loyalty to the Allies: there is no doubt in that. She is under no illusion that the doctor proves the exception, not the rule – and even then she suspects that he may not be so open and blameless as he seems. She has seen how the nurses at the hospital look at her, his fellow doctor, too: as though she is an imposter. She thinks, too, of the British soldiers who chased her and the boy – a woman and a small child – on the night of the fireworks. She thinks of the things she heard from her rooftop lookout on the first days. Yes, even with her responsibilities at home she might once have been tempted to join the resistors in some small capacity. Before the boy's illness, before the inevitable compromise that had to be made with her conscience, before a personal tie had to be put before national duty. But even if she had joined them she knows that she would have kept some sense of proportion, of self-preservation. This is the thing that she fears her brother lacks. And she realises that her fear, when it comes to Kerem, is not one of *not* loving, after all. It is one of loving too much.

The Traveller

Bulgaria, Sofia, by morning; the last major stop before my destination. Here a fresh horde of passengers embark and now familiar faces in the carriage are replaced by new. I feel a strange sorrow at the loss. Though we have hardly spoken to one another, a silent accord had been established, as though we have been travelling along this route much longer together. We have all belonged to something.

The thing it took me some time to learn is this: belonging is not a fixed state. You can be told for many years that you belong; that you are a uniform part of a greater whole. That your identity is the same thing as the identity of a nation. Then, one day, you discover that the criteria for membership have changed. Differences are exposed; aspects of your life that you had never understood as different. Suddenly they have become radical, perverse, blasphemous. 'Look at the way you pray!' they say. 'Look at the food you eat, the tongue you speak in, the colour of your skin, the sort of bed you lay your head on . . . even the sound of your name. You are as different from us – we have only just realised it – as a cat is from a dog. You have been hiding among us, but now we see straight through your deception. Whoever told you that a cat may be friends with a dog? What nonsense! We are sworn, eternal enemies. We have found you out. We will tear you apart.'

I open the suitcase, and take out a small tobacco tin. There is a man in London who imports this variety of tobacco from the old place. For many years it has been delivered in a heavy, compact package smelling powerfully of burned toast, and then decanted into one of several small tins like this. My memories are scented with it, mingled with the chemical tang of a hospital ward.

The image on the lid depicts a reclining odalisque, flattering the Westerner's idea of the Ottoman woman, anachronistically flanked by two Egyptian sphinxes. 'MURAD TURKISH TOBACCO', the type proclaims proudly. Below a bold invitation: 'Judge it for yourself!', weathered to hesitance by the years. The colours on the tin are mere reminders of themselves, those once primary brights, the enamel paint disintegrating.

I discovered this particular tin in a drawer of the desk in the study. I remember how, sitting at his desk, I attempted to prise off the lid. Even though I put all my strength into it I could not find any give in the metal; it was welded shut by rust. This, naturally, only made me the more determined. Finally it gave – and suddenly, all at once.

It was not tobacco, inside, but sand. The discovery felt like a trick, a practical joke. Some of it had scattered onto the floor. I spent an hour collecting grains from where they had embedded themselves into the rug and excising them from between the floorboards. They were a pale colour; there were tiny shards of shell caught amongst them. The pink of fingernails, pinker, the inside of your lip. This was not the greyish sand of an English beach. I knew that this was the relic of a warm place, where the light got into things.

There isn't sand in here any more, though. Now it contains something altogether more precious.

Nur

'You have been to see the boy today as well.'

'It is important, *Büyükanne*. He is very unwell.'

'You have seen the English doctor too, then, I suppose. There must be some way in which he wants to gain from this. I cannot understand, otherwise, why he would help.'

'He is not English, he is Scottish. And . . .' quickly, realising the thing that she should have said first, 'he helped because I begged him. I believe he felt a certain duty.'

'I wonder.' Her grandmother closes her eyes, pantomiming deep thought. 'How many doctors do you think would travel across the Bosphorus in the middle of the night to an unknown neighbourhood to help a foreign woman? And then to take the child in, no doubt against orders . . .'

'I believe that he is not a bad man, despite everything.'

'But he is also one of the same men who incarcerated your brother, for four years. And you have seen what that has done to him, who he has become.'

'No, he is not the same. He was never involved in that: he was in Mesapotamia, and Persia.'

Her grandmother gives her a look.

'You have talked to him.'

'Only as much as I have had to, to appear civil.'

'You need to take care, *canım*.'

'What do you mean?'

'I know that life has been difficult for you these last few years. And I know that we do not always make it easy for you. And perhaps sometimes it is not clear that we see what you are doing for us. I do see it, though, my darling girl.'

The affection takes Nur unawares. She has to press the heels of her hands to her eyes to stop the tears that are suddenly fighting to appear.

'And I know that the loss of a husband . . . and of the little one.'

'Don't—' Her grandmother is the only one who knows of the second loss. Nur feels now that she is wielding it unfairly.

'I sometimes think it would have been better if you had not married at all. One more loss for you. And when one has lost a husband there goes with it a certain . . . variety of affection that cannot be replaced by family.'

Nur thinks that there is little point in explaining that she does not recall experiencing such a thing in the short time with Enver.

'And I only think—'

'Well,' Nur says, sharply, 'I think that if one spends too much time sitting, and thinking, and doing nothing else, one is liable to fantasise.'

She feels even as she says it that she has gone too far. She waits for her grandmother's wrath, known and feared since childhood. And yet to her surprise it does not come. Instead there is a strange noise, a small hitch of breath. Concerned, she looks at the old woman. And sees – miracle of miracles – that she is weeping.

'*Büyükanne* . . .'

'I do not say it because I am afraid of the shame. Though of course it would be great, if anything were suspected. I say it, little Nur, *canım*, because I am afraid for you.'

Spring

It carries with it all the wonder of the new season, the surprise of a magic trick – as though it did not come every year. The leaves upon the trees are the Platonic ideal of green, the original green, from which all other shades are imperfect iterations. On the ground beneath them, a memento mori, lie the desiccated skeletons of their predecessors.

The air smells of things growing. In the middle of the day the sun has the breath of summer in it. For some, this year, the breeze carries the scent of change. Mustafa Kemal's rebel government at Ankara is putting more pressure upon the Allied occupiers; the tail, some joke, has begun to wag the dog. The Turkish police take their orders from Ankara, now; there are petty squabbles over passports and customs. The Allied commanders receive a courteous note informing them that on April 23rd, parades celebrating the anniversary of the founding of the National Assembly will take place in the city. They agree, and the parades go ahead without incident, because they know the trouble that will result if they do not. In doing so they perhaps acknowledge that they are no longer quite in control.

The street sellers have moved on from chestnuts. Now they offer fresh mussels plucked this morning from the shores of the Black Sea, almonds on ice – *buzda badem* – so that one tastes all the hidden creamy sweetness of the flesh.

In barracks across town men yearn, as perhaps at no other time of year, for their own lands. For cherry blossom beside the Seine, for strolls across the Downs, for a riot of wild-flowers along the Ligurian coast.

For nowhere is the perfection of the season felt so power-fully as at home.

Nur

She and the boy have taken a short walk in the gardens of the house, he stumbling slightly on legs unused to the exercise. The doctor is nowhere to be seen; the nurse let her in to the boy with a sneer of disapproval. She felt this disapproval linger in the very air of the place, so she suggested they go outside. They have come to see the wisteria, newly in bloom, the scent of all her memories of the season. It is one hundred years old, her father told her once: maybe older. It can outlive generations. And yet it is a surprisingly fragile plant, too. Some shock will occur, perhaps even something beyond the gardener's understanding, and the end will come to it swiftly. It will wither and die and never blossom again. But this morning it is as beautiful as she has ever seen it.

'Hello.'

The doctor is sitting where she had not seen him, a book in his lap, hidden behind the fall of blossoms.

'Hello,' the boy says, and then looks up at her, a silent reprimand for her rudeness.

'Good morning,' she says, finally. It is strange. A few months ago there was a new accord forming between them, a lightening. And yet now when she sees him she feels a convulsion of fear behind her ribcage, a constriction in her throat. Everything they say to one another seems newly weighted, a thousand other possible meanings open to interpretation, misunderstanding.

She cannot fully understand this change. It is to do with her grandmother's warning, perhaps, and also her knowledge of her brother's new vocation, how it throws her own actions into unflattering, guilty contrast. And yet there is more to it too: an awareness that has nothing to do with anyone else; that is the exposure of some heretofore undiscovered aspect of herself.

'I wanted to tell you,' he says. 'I have the day off, and I've been doing some exploring. I discovered the boathouses beneath the house.'

She is suddenly struck by a memory. A story her father once told her.

'You're smiling.'

'Oh.' She rearranges her features. 'I was reminded of something.'

'What?' The boy is looking up at her. His English has improved, she notices. He will like the story, she thinks: this gives her licence to tell it – as would not be the case if the boy weren't here. So she tells them, stopping every so often to translate for the boy.

One night her father woke to what he thought was an earthquake. Fine streams of plaster were raining from the ceiling, her father said, the chandeliers were swinging. But it seemed somehow specific to the house, as though it were being shaken in the fist of a giant. So he wondered if a vessel had collided with the shore: only a couple of weeks ago a cargo ship had taken a bend in the channel too narrowly and sheared the entire facade from one of the *yalis*, leaving the rest intact, the rooms newly denuded. But beyond the windows the world was still and dark, no ship in sight.

It seemed to him that the epicentre of the thing was coming from somewhere underneath him, from the boathouses beneath the kitchen. With some trepidation he went below. There he saw a huge black shape, rising out of the water, thrashing itself about in agony or rage. He could make out the distinctive shape of the sheening body, the fin and tail. It must have followed a shoal of fish in through one of the arched entrances, he realised, and become trapped. As the water flashed from her, silver, she seemed made of moonlight, and her frantic motions appeared like a graceful dance.

Just as he began to formulate a plan she found her escape route, and plunged beneath, back out into the night. The water closed over her seamlessly, hardly a ripple. It was as though it had never happened.

'And perhaps it never was,' she says, remembering her father's love of a good story.

'A dolphin?' The boy is staring, wide-eyed. At first she thinks she has frightened him, then she realises it is excitement. She can see that from now on this idea will become an obsession.

'You must not go down there,' she says. 'One day, perhaps, I will show you.' She does not mean now, while it is a hospital. This is a reference – though she is not sure the doctor realises it – to an imagined future time, when by some miracle the house might be returned to her, and they might live in it once more, all of them. She turns to the doctor and finds that he, too, seems to have been transfixed by the story. His eyes do not leave her face.

'We will leave you,' she says, quickly, and turns to usher the boy back toward the house.

'Wait.' She stops: but only because it is a plea, not a command. 'I have this afternoon to myself, too,' he says.

For a terrible moment, Nur thinks he is about to suggest that they spend it in each other's company. He would not ask it, surely? But the English have different ways, different interpretations of propriety. She is suddenly aware of how little she knows, despite her command of the language. She is marshalling her excuses, when he says, 'Where should I go? Where would you suggest? Your favourite place in the city.'

She is relieved. At least, almost exclusively so. She wonders, incredulous, at that small part of herself that is not. Well, she reasons, she is old enough now to understand that there are some aspects of the self that one can understand no better than a stranger.

She thinks of the cemetery at Eyüp – but immediately dismisses it; she cannot send him there. She suspects that its melancholy, so oddly soothing to her, would not have a universal appeal. And it belongs to the people here; they walk within it, they lie beneath its soil. To share it with a foreigner would be a disloyalty.

Then she recalls a day from childhood. Her father, herself, her brother. The islands that to her until that point had been semi-mythical. Glimpsed far off in the Sea of Marmara, wreathed in mist, beyond the furthest reaches of the city. A small village of white shuttered houses. The rest of it a wild place. The scent of herbs and brine. At this time of year it will be perfect. She can give this to him.

'Do you want to be where there are people, or where there are none?'

'Oh,' the quick grace of his smile. 'None.'

George

He takes the ferry, an hour's journey.

When he has reached the point where the land starts curving away upon itself, he knows he has walked the length of the island. She told him that the best swimming spots were here, and this place seems to him as good as any. The vegetation is dense, with no clear opening; he will have to force his way through. He makes a shield of his arms, drives himself bodily into the thicket. Branches snap back against him, some catching his skin with thorns. He concentrates on the blue glimmer ahead, the promise of it.

At one point, forcing his way through a resistant patch, he plunges forward only to rock back on his heels in horror, finding himself perched above a twenty-foot drop. Even if he had survived the fall, he would have been too badly injured to climb back up. There is something horribly fascinating in the idea: would he be found before he perished? Probably not. To have survived it all: the Ottoman onslaught, malaria, sandfly fever, the perilous crossing of the Caspian – only to be extinguished here in this benign spot. He wonders for a moment if this could have been her motive in sending him here.

Ahead of him the path is still a mystery. He is aware of the danger now, the thought that he could have been plunging so recklessly forward seems incredible. He moves more gingerly, alarmed when the footing fails him, sending him skidding across loosened scree. Gradually, mercifully, the bush thins, and he knows how lucky he has been in his choice of route: sees the whole formidable face of the cliff above and to the right of him. Now, immediately below, he can see the thin swathe of sand.

He moves more quickly, surer now of his footing. He is released into sunlight, his feet sinking into softness. The full heat of the day returns. Only now does he realise that his shirt is torn in several places, blood beading from long scratches upon his arms. He takes off his shoes and socks, already filling uncomfortably with grains. But the first contact of the sand is blistering against the soles of his feet and he is forced to hop his way across the beach toward the water, laughing at himself as he does, at the spectacle he must create. The cold of the water is welcome balm. He knows that he is alone but, remembering Bill, makes doubly sure before he begins to remove the rest of his clothes. In the unforgiving light his body is revealed to him as spectacularly pale.

The scent of the herbs, the sound of the waves hitting the encircling arms of rock, the sheer size and radiance of the sky, the blue of a gas flame. He laughs and hears his voice echo back at him. In the reverberation it sounds uncertain, as though the sound is asking for the place to accept him, to allow him to become part of it.

In the early afternoon small iridescent jellyfish arrive in great numbers, massing along the waterline. He feels a vague squeamishness about them. He skirts the edge, looking for a clear patch. Every so often he thinks he has found it but as he peers down into the weeds and pebbles they emerge gradually from the depths like an optical illusion. He can almost imagine that they are just blots on the vision. But not quite. The heat has built to a crescendo, the water beyond the treachery of the jellyfish beckons him, navy blue. Finally he plunges, wades in through the mass of soft forms, chin up, gaze fixed straight out to sea. Waits for the first sting upon the exposed skin. It does not come. Something like real happiness passes through him, not just the giddy relief of escaping injury. It is something more; a feeling that this place has now sent its message of acceptance.

He swims until he is exhausted; later he lies on the sand. The fierceness of the heat has gone now, this is a golden warmth – amiable and attentive, drying the last of the seawater from his hair and skin. This is the first time he has been alone for such a long period of time. Not lonely: that emotion is a familiar friend. One of the things the last few years has taught him is how lonely it is possible to be while surrounded by an entire regiment of men. This, his own company, feels like a luxury by comparison. It is a gift that he does not deserve – and he knows this. It is a selfishness. But he will not think of that now.

He takes the last remaining pinch of tobacco from his tin, rolls himself a rather meagre cigarette, and lies propped upon his elbows. His feet burrow deep in the sand to discover a cooler layer, untouched by the sun. The sun is warm upon his shoulders. He feels the brief, guiltless happiness of an animal.

His last thought, before he drifts into sleep, is that this is the gift she has given him.

When he next opens his eyes he has forgotten where he is. The light has changed; dusk is on the approach. He realises he has forgotten the ferry timetable he looked at by the quay, and isn't absolutely certain when the last leaves. He will have to exert himself now, or risk spending the night here. As if to emphasise his predicament, he hears the inquisitive whine of a mosquito near his left ear. He swats it, but it or another returns within seconds. Soon there will be thousands. He has spent the whole of his war covering himself carefully from their attentions; the one time he did not he contracted malaria. He shrugs quickly into his clothes, wonders how he could have been so reckless. His tobacco tin lies open, empty upon the sand. He reaches for it and after a moment's hesitation he uses it as a scoop, filling it with white grains and shells. There is no one here to see him but he feels sheepish all the same about this strange act, so unlike him. It is a sentimental act. In it he is imagining a future self that might one day open the tin and be returned to this place of warmth.

On the ferry back he sits sun-dazzled, slightly burned, chafed with salt and sand. A few feet away a little boy stands and tosses crumbs of bread into the air for the seagulls. George has never much liked them, but now he sees the majesty of their construction: the poise with which they ride the air, matching the speed of the ferry exactly. Then, with precise, hinged motions of the neck, snatching the morsels with what looks like an arrogant ease. The boy is delighted by them, hopping on the balls of his feet. He must be six or so, and very slight. He looks as though a too-strong gust of wind might snatch him up. George is half-ready to pitch forward and catch him. The sight of him is a mingled pain and joy.

Then the mother appears from the lower deck, in parox-ysms of rage over the waste of the small crust of bread. George is somewhat relieved to be absolved from responsi-bility, to be able to look away.

As the ferry approaches the city a hush seems to descend over the passengers. Even those who have made this approach many, perhaps hundreds, of times seem awed by the sight. It does look particularly majestic at this hour, with the lights just beginning to come on. The final glow of the day seems to halo the skyline, surrounded by the encircling stain of dusk. He looks at it with eyes glutted with beauty.

The Prisoner

His thoughts have become fixated upon the boy. A pupil from his former days as a schoolteacher: an Armenian child, a figure who seems to have taken his own place in his sister's affections, who now occupies – along with the English doctor – the house that was once his home. The boy is a representation of all that he has lost, intimately connected with his own misfortune. In some rational part of his mind, he knows that it is absurd. Yet he cannot help what he feels; a deep, violent hatred of this child who is a manifestation, a mockery, of his own fracture.

This hate gives him a kind of power. It provides the focus that his other pitiful attempts have lacked.

Now he begins to feel excitement. The very violence – the audacity – of his idea begins to thrill him even as it frightens him. It is like something growing inside him. One thing that the years of imprisonment gave him: a peculiar focus, an intensity of thought. When a person's surroundings are so unvaryingly bleak, the inner world gains a new richness and texture in compensation. In certain circumstances it can become more real than that outside. At times he can summon the fact of it so vividly to himself that he believes it has already happened, that the power of his own thoughts has been enough to effect it. He wakes soaked in sweat, his heart hammering in triumph and fear.

This idea is shaped by his experience. In particular, by that cold that on so many occasions almost conquered him – no coincidence, then, that his thoughts should tend in this particular direction. An element in which things are fundamentally changed. An element in which, if one is to believe the myths, something – someone – may be made new.

That military cunning that deserted him in the face of the Russian advance now returns to him. He begins to plot. He needs a boat, and he needs the catalyst, the thing with which he will invoke his chosen element. It is beautifully simple. The craft will be easy; he has only to ask Erfan, whose father is in the boat-making business. The catalyst too: any schoolboy knows how. He is ready.

But the lives.

Necessary?

Necessary, yes. A sacrifice. An example. And part of something beautiful: part of this making new.

But Nur.

She is afraid of him now anyway, he can see it. And she is changed from who she was. She seems to have become hard, angry, fearless. His guilt is tied to the old version of her, the familiar version. She is gone.

But the past.

But what help has the past been to him? In fact, it must be annihilated. It can have no part in the man he is to become, or the country that is to rise out of these ruins.

The English occupiers. The boy, the Armenian boy. Everything that he has lost is the fault of these enemies. His house: colonised. His humanity: the things that were asked of him because of the Armenians' betrayal, those things that have made it impossible to return to the person he was in his old life. His sister: who now appears to be loyal to these enemies rather than to her own flesh and blood.

Here is the thing he has been searching for: the thing that will go some way to filling the void within. A purpose.

Nur

When Nur visits the hospital the next evening the boy asks the doctor. 'Have you shown Nur *hanım* the gramophone yet?'

In spite of herself she is intrigued. She has never seen one before, though her father had, and had described it to her.

And yet the object the doctor shows her is more strange than could ever have been conveyed in words. It has an almost submarine beauty, she thinks: the brass trumpet shaped like a shell. She walks around it, studying it from every angle. The doctor enumerates the parts for her with the precision of a medical man.

'It's yours?'

'I found it in a small village on the Caspian Sea, when we were passing through.'

'You took it?' She does not try to keep the censure from her tone.

'I bought it. Contrary to what you may have heard, the British army are not plunderers. Not as a rule.'

'How does it work?'

'I will show you.'

They gather nearer, the three of them. He winds the handle, gives a huff of exertion. Then, with great delicacy, he lifts the small brass arm that extends upwards out of the base.

'Look below,' he says.

She obeys.

'See it? The needle? That's what tracks the tune.'

'How?'

'It is all written, upon this disc.'

She looks hard, but cannot see anything other than concentric circles.

'I don't quite understand it either.'

She glances up, and sees his smile. She finds herself returning it.

Now, with infinite care, he moves the arm into place. She sees how elegant his hands are – like a musician or an artist's – the dextrous curve of the thumb, the tapered pale ovals of his nails; the hands of a doctor.

And then she steps back in shock. Sound is pouring from the thing. She had known that it would, and yet she had not expected it, at least not that it would be like this. The clarity of it – but not merely of one single tune, rather a whole orchestra. She can discern the separate parts, the strings, the wind. Can it be called music? It has all the discordancy of the jazz she has heard flooding out of Pera streets, but it is different again: violins, flutes, the high shrill voice of the piccolo. There is a violence to it. It speaks of things broken apart and reforming, forcing their way up through the old. It speaks of things growing, and things being pulled apart. The old torn asunder. The wonder and terror of the new. It does not try to be liked . . . it does not want to. It simply is: brave and vulnerable and fierce and strangely beautiful and hideous and, above all, new.

It is some time before she realises that she is weeping. The boy is looking between her and the needle, as though fascinated by both. Nur does not think the doctor has seen; his head is bowed, his eyes almost closed. A great relief. She turns away from him, and puts a hand to her face. Her glove comes away half-sodden; she is amazed.

After they have returned the boy to his room, and she has bid him good night, the doctor turns to her and says in a strange rush of words, 'I wondered if you would dance with me.'

There is a crackling silence, in which his words seem to echo. She is so surprised by his question that she has forgotten to immediately decline. She is reminded of that first day, when he asked her if she would join him for coffee. The shock at the transgression: as though no one had taught him the rules of how it should be, between Occupier and Occupied. But this time, of course, it is something different, so much more.

To his credit he seems almost as shocked by the question as her. He is first to recover his voice. 'I apologise,' he says, 'that was absolutely . . .' he is searching for a word, 'absolutely inappropriate.'

That gives her pause. Inappropriate. It is an interesting choice.

Because, really, what is appropriate about the situation? And by this she is thinking of the wider situation, not their own. This occupation is *inappropriate*. Unsanctioned. The requisition of homes across the city – some, unlike this one, in which families still live alongside the occupiers. Or the fact that there are some twenty half-clothed men lying in a room that used to be reserved exclusively for women. The colonisation of private, intimate spaces as ordained by states and governments. Or even the fact that a man like her brother – so gentle, a schoolteacher – should have been commanded to go to war and transform himself into a soldier.

All of these things, suddenly, seem so much more inappropriate than the simple act of moving in time to music with a person one has come to see – against the odds – almost as a friend. She thinks, too, of all the people so desperate to disapprove of her, simply because she goes out into the city to earn her living, because she does not cover her face. She remembers the shame of passing those French officers, the way they had seemed to view her presence in the street as a mark of promiscuity, of permissiveness.

It is this memory, most of all, that decides her. If there is one place in which she will not allow the concept of propriety – of inappropriateness – to dominate her actions it is here. Her home.

This is why she shakes her head, and says, 'No. You are mistaken. I would like to dance.'

The doctor is taken aback. It is as though he never thought she would accept his invitation or – more likely – never quite meant to make it in the first place. It was the music, perhaps, the strange magic of an entire invisible orchestra filling the empty space. The still air in the room now seems like a held breath. Does the house disapprove of her? This house is part of the former way of things, and that world, certainly, would disapprove. But the old world is gone. If, when, the occupation ends, there will be no resumption, no wholesale return to the old ways. That world has fractured. They must find a new way. They must re-inhabit it.

The doctor removes the Stravinsky, and chooses a new record.

'A waltz,' he says, and then flushes, as though he has said something indecent. He places the new disc upon the spindle.

She thinks she sees his hand tremble in the action. The mechanism itself: the elegant curvature, the burnish of the brass, the dark recess of the horn, seems newly to acquire an eroticism that embarrasses her – that seems so emphatic she cannot believe she had not seen it before. He must see it too.

That half-buried night with her dead husband. The fumbling darkness and then the surprise of a new sensation shameful, voluptuous, complex, insisting on itself through the discomfort. Not quite anything in itself but the shadow of something, the promise of it.

He takes her hand in one of his, places the other above her hip. His touch is so light that if she could not see her fingers in his, against her waist, she might think she had imagined it. And yet for a moment she is pinioned by shame. She thinks of her grandmother. She thinks of Kerem. All certainty has deserted her.

Then the music begins and she steps into it.

George

Ah. Now, here is a problem. He has managed to think of her in terms entirely unrelated to the physical. But now there is scent and warmth and breath, and her hand, in his. The soft indentation of a waist beneath the silky stuff of the dress. Now is the unarguable fact of her, human and . . . yes, beautiful, yes, desired.

Even if it had not been so long – and all of that fraught in memory with difficulty and guilt – even then he would desire her.

He is a coward. He has ignored this aspect of himself, concealed those other motivations even from his own sight. He is a coward because he asked her to dance, when it should never have happened, and because he will not put a stop to it now, though he should do so immediately and perhaps salvage something from this intact.

He is a coward because he has allowed her to think him good, and noble, and not like others. He has hidden the truth of himself from her.

The Boy

They think that he is asleep. But he knows how to be quiet, as quiet as a cat. He has slunk so silently from his own room and into this one that he might be just another one of the evening shadows gathering in the corners. The music is pouring from the wonderful machine. Nur *hanım* and the doctor stand very close together and her hand is in his. The two of them move together with the same kind of magic that holds a formation of birds in perfect synchronicity. It is pleasing to watch them, as it is pleasing to watch anything graceful, but he senses that there is also something dangerous in it. He is reminded of that day when Nur *hanım* had suddenly seemed so small to him, surrounded by the other people in the street, and he had been afraid for her. He is afraid for her now – though, again, he would not be able to explain why.

Nur

That night she wakes from strange dreams. The unconscious world of them so lucid that the real one seems thin by comparison. But as with so many dreams they are elusive. She cannot summon them to herself logically, or in any complete form. She is left only with a feeling. She would rather forget this too.

She presses a hand to her face and finds it hot. As she does she feels, more vividly than she does her own, the sensation of another's fingers. As she rises from beneath the sheet she remembers the weight of a body. Not a suffocation, a longed-for weight. No, she reminds herself: longed-for only within the realm of the dream. And more: the warmth and tenderness of skin. Of breath, of blood beneath the skin, of lips, of hair. There is a rhythm to these images, they seem to chase one another through her memory without end, a serpent swallowing its own tail.

The bedroom, of course, is empty. And yet at the same time it is strange to find herself alone.

She knows that these are not real memories. They are not of the husband she hardly knew, and lost.

Nur sits, and waits for the shame. It is something of a surprise when it does not come.

Now, in this unguarded hour, her mind feints toward the impossible: plays with it, turns it over, teases it out. And in doing so there are brief inversions by which it ceases to appear impossible. It is madness to think like this. There has been no spoken understanding between them. Yet at times it feels as though there has been something both less and more than that.

In the early morning she takes a ferry to her secret place. Amidst the cemetery at Eyüp, among the figs and cypresses – life and death – time seems to stand still. The city is very far away here. There is a melancholy, as there must be in such a place. But also peace. In the avenues among the tombs the light is green and ancient. The old white marble is tinged by it.

Some of the graves are hundreds of years old, the stones seem to sag with the effort of such a long stretch standing upright. Names now are obscured by time; all those who once remembered them are long gone, too. This is the real death, perhaps, when one is gone entirely from living memory.

But here one is close to the past. Sometimes, here, she feels if she reached out her hand she might brush away the thin veil that separates the now from the then.

The fig leaves, as she moves past them, release their scent. It is her favourite smell. She takes a folded leaf and crushes it to her wrist to release the meagre sap, just to keep the fragrance with her a little longer.

A grey cat follows her out from behind a tombstone, mewling. He has a white smear across one eye, comic, as though he has rubbed his face in paint. She bends down to him. His coat is surprisingly silken for a stray: there is a pride, she thinks, in the way he cleans himself, meticulous, with that rough pink tongue. Only his once-white paws, now permanently grey, are a testament to a life spent trotting about the refuse and dust of the city's streets.

Now he stops, delicate nose aloft, and goes absolutely still. She wonders what has spooked him. Another cat, probably.

They have terrible fights at night, the city's cats. Fights that sound as though they go almost to the death, so loud and anguished are the cries. But she has never seen any of them with anything much worse than a scratch. They are wise animals, they know how to keep themselves alive. A bad wound would fester, could prove fatal. The important thing is not to invite the danger in the first place. Everyone could learn from them. She could learn from them.

She bends and he allows her to caress his ears, the delicate bones in the side of his face. His eyes close in brief bliss, he presses his skull with surprising force into her hand. Then he pulls away, stretches first front- then hindquarters, watches a leaf skitter across the ground, momentarily alert, settles himself on the patch of dirt immediately before him, closes his eyes. To be an animal, she thinks: to go about one's business as always and eat and sleep and be content. Nur takes another step. It must be just the wrong movement, she yelps with pain. The cat opens one quick amber eye, searching the ground for the small prey that might have made the sound. Disappointed, he shuts it again.

She bends and massages the ankle bone. The pain reminds her of another stumble. A dropped book, an English soldier. Scottish, she reminds herself. A Scottish doctor. That was what started it all, of course. Most unhelpful of him to make himself agreeable – firstly by his act of gallantry in picking up her book, and second by not embarrassing her on the jetty. It was so much simpler when she could hate them all universally, absolutely.

She pulls a fig from the branch above her, and knows because of the force with which she has to tug that it is not ready. It is far too early. A sticky sap spills itself onto her forearm. She bites into it, and the taste is as bland as she deserves, the unripe sourness puckering her lips. But the promise of what could be is there, in the fragrance of it. She casts it away.

She takes the long ferry home to Tophane. Rounding the nub of the headland she can just make out the white shape of Maiden's Tower. Kız Kulesi, a small, lonely edifice rising from the sea two hundred yards or so from the Asian shore. The story is one of those fables so well known to Nur that it might almost be part of her own family history. And yet she still remembers the first time she heard it. They had been passing by in the *kayık*, on their way home, and her grandmother had pointed it out to her.

'Can you see it?'

'Yes,' Nur had replied. 'But it isn't a very big tower.' Not like the one in Galata, built by the Italians who had once been here. From which you could see the whole city laid out before you, right to the ancient walls. And beyond: the distant dark humps of the Princes' Islands, the vertebrae of a sea-serpent's spine, slumbering in their blanket of mist. She doubted that one could see much at all from this small, squat edifice, and surely that was the very purpose of the tower?

'Ah,' her grandmother said. 'But that is because it was only made to fit one person, you see. And it wasn't so much about looking out as keeping in. I think you are old enough to hear it.'

A sultan built it for his daughter, the legend had it, to protect her from the fate he had dreamed befalling her: the deathly bite of a snake. By forcing her to live in the tower, protected from harm by the water and the guardianship of her ladies, he believed he could keep her from this terrible destiny. But she was foolish, in the way young women are apt to be, and she had longings, to which young women are also susceptible. The tower kept her safe, but it also provided a perfect vantage point from which to see all she was missing out on. The lights of the great city, in which thousands loved and lived, following out their destinies in happy ignorance, without fear. The boats coming and going, laden with exotic cargo and lucky passengers bound for places she would never see. And above, the great blue reach of the sky, where birds wheeled free.

One day, a little craft passed laden with fruits. The girl could have asked for anything she wanted and it would have been delivered to her: the sultan was determined that his daughter would want for nothing. All he asked was that anything entering the tower was thoroughly checked first. But that, naturally, removed much of the pleasure from things. The sultan's daughter would watch as loaves of bread were pulled into pieces small enough that there could be no chance of anything remaining concealed within, as oranges were peeled and pitted and split into segments presented on a white plate and then given first to one of the ladies to test, as dates were de-stoned and quartered and mashed to a pulp. Everything reduced to less than the sum of its parts. Nothing completely hers, because of the fingers that would have touched it and searched it and taken all the magic from it.

When this fruit-laden boat passed almost silently beneath the window, the girl watched it with longing. She saw the jewel-red pomegranates, the piles of ripe yellow pears, flushed with the sun's kiss, the dusky spillage of purple grapes. And then she saw the boatman, and he was yet more beautiful than any of his wares. So when, seeing her half-hanging out of her window, he called to her, and asked her – did she want anything? – how could she not answer him? (Speech with strangers was also forbidden by her father, as though the words themselves might drip poison into her ears.)

'The grapes,' she said, because suddenly she could almost taste them: the bitter skin splitting to yield untold sweetness. Each would be a substitute, she thought, for a boatman's kiss.

'How will I get them to you, *effendi?*' the boatman called.

She thought. She had to be quick, or one of her women would come and she would be found out. She found a long silk scarf, and lowered this to him.

'Tie them in there,' she said. 'And you may keep the scarf afterward, as payment.'

Of course – because this is how things work in fairy tales – the sultan's daughter didn't have the chance to enjoy her grapes, or to fall in love with the boatman. As she lifted the fragrant bunch to her mouth a snake uncoiled itself and delivered the deathly bite. It was her fate, waiting for her. There was nothing that she could have done.

It is impossible, Nur knows this. She would be cast out. In another place, time, perhaps. If it had been before the war, or a century after its passing. If there had been no war. But then such thoughts have no meaning; and no succour.

Her cousin Hüseyin has transcended a boundary – but it is a very different thing for him. He is a man, living abroad. She is a woman who has lived in an occupied city, who lost her husband and her own unborn child at the hands of the enemy. She has lived here while they have insulted Ottoman men and women, arrested and even killed them; whilst they have made the city their playground. She would not merely be cast out from her home, from her people, she would be cast out from herself.

Not for the first time she wishes she had never set eyes upon the man.

Acts of Destabilisation

The darkest hour of the night. There is still faint noise from the city. But here there is almost absolute quiet broken only by tiny musical disturbances in the water, the secret movements of fish.

A figure detaches itself from the shadows, like something cut from the fabric of the night itself, moving with incredible speed across the grass. Then a small catch of sound, a tiny plume of light.

The fire begins with surprising hesitance, for something of such latent power. The wood is old, loose-grained, friable, which should help with the burning. But it is also damp from the sea air: the accumulated moisture of two centuries. If anything were to save it now, this might be it.

More alcohol.

With something almost like a concentrated effort of will, the fire gathers itself. Pale flames begin to lick at the wood, with some discernment, like a chef tasting a new dish for the *carte*. They move languorously at first – in no particular hurry now that the decision has been made, the balance tipped.

Then something changes. A gust of wind from exactly the right direction, perhaps. Now the flames become voracious, insatiable, and faster, faster, snickering up the old beams, gathering strength from nothing – from the very air. Now it is growing loud. There are great exhalations of heat, smaller gasps and cackles, a low, snickering sound that is, perhaps, most terrible of all.

The night is lit up with it.

The still black waters reflect the spectacle, so that they, too, seem to have caught light like oil. And he sees himself in the reflection too, a faceless figure surrounded by flame, the agent of all the destruction.

It is terrible, magnificent. A shame, really, that none is here to appreciate it. Save for he who soaked the wood, in preparations that were almost tenderly attentive, in alcohol. He who lit the match, and watched it catch, and willed it on, trembling a little with fear and excitement and then the new sense of his own impotence, because it has so quickly gone beyond the limits of his control.

Before, wielding the starter, he had held all the power. Now it has been taken from him, has grown far larger than him.

He could not stop it even if he wanted to. Does he want to? No. No, he doesn't.

Not even now, confronted by the reality of it – far more magnificent and terrible than he ever imagined when it lit up his dreams?

He could still help them. He could warn them. It would still be a fantastic act of rebellion, a symbol. But life would not be sacrificed.

No, too late, impossible. But he could try.

George

It is a scent from earliest memory. It carries upon it a season. George is ready for it, tired of the heat, ready for the softness of it, the richer colours. Wood, dried by summer sun, wood and resin, burning up. A scent of sweetness and warmth. How strange, though, he cannot remember how he came to be here, in the English countryside, in autumn.

How did he return? No . . . he cannot remember.

Constantinople, the Bosphorus, a swim in turquoise waters, a sick little boy, a woman named Nur – these are the things he remembers.

He opens his eyes. A dream. No, not entirely a dream: the woodsmoke remains. The dark is thick as soup. But at the furthest reaches of his vision there is a strange illumination, an inconsistent flickering. He cannot think what it could be, beyond the idea that too much of his dream has bled into life – that he has been left with some retinal imprint of it. The scent of it, too, in his nostrils. The taste of it, filling his mouth with bitterness.

His thoughts are full of sleep, he has to struggle toward

clarity like a man wading through a bog. It has to be the dream, because there is no other explanation. It is far too dark, far too late, for someone to be having a bonfire.

It is another minute before he heeds the animal part of his mind, that centre of pure instinct, that is sounding the alarm.

By now he can feel the heat of it, pressing in, forcing the cold air of the room into retreat. Still, he clutches at the hope that he is mistaken. The alternative is too terrible.

He stumbles outside. The building is on fire. He stands for a moment blinking before the billowing sail of heat, his vision blurring, disbelieving.

As he looks, he sees one of the shadows detach itself from the mass of dark, running. At first he thinks it is someone come to help, is about to beckon them, and ask them to join the line. Then he realises that the figure is not running toward him; is making instead for the cover of the trees behind the house.

'Hey,' he shouts. 'You! Stop there!'

The man falters, and turns. George is certain that he did not mean to do this, that the reaction was an involuntary one. He will castigate himself for it later, no doubt. In turning he has allowed George a full look at him. Lit by flames, the pale oval of his face – young, dark-featured – is as clearly visible as it would be in daylight. George is certain that he has not seen him before. At the same time, though, there is a certain familiarity. In this moment he does not have the space within his thoughts to begin to explain it. Perhaps it will come. He is certain now that the fire was no accident; that here is its cause. Too late, he remembers to make chase. His legs are clumsy; the other moved with an animal agility. The ground seems purposefully to obstruct him, twice his ankle turns over almost upon itself, sending a raw pain up his leg. Still, he keeps going, plunges into the dark thicket. Only now does he see that it is utterly useless. The arsonist could be crouched behind some tree, above him in the branches, or far gone from here. He could even be lying quietly a few feet away on the earth, shrouded in dark – and George would never know. There is no purpose in running, now.

It is still some way from the ward. But it seems to be blossoming at an incredible speed. He stumbles back inside. Three figures, white-clad, seem to shimmer out of the darkness of the rest of the house: Bill and two of the Sisters, in their nightclothes. They gape at him, still half-asleep, mirroring his own disbelief.

'The patients,' he says to them. 'We have to move them out onto the grass.' His voice is calmer than it should be. 'We need to make them safe. Then stop the fire.'

They nod at him. He would like to shake them – they seem stupefied by the horror of it – forgetting that he had been exactly the same; has had those crucial few moments more with the reality of it. Finally they seem to light into action.

The patients are awake – those who are sensible to the catastrophe, at least – and alarmed. Some of those who are able have already fled outside and are now returning, rather shame-faced, to help with the transport of the bedridden.

It is the boy that George sees, goes to, first. He has shrunk himself into a foetal curl, his hands covering his head, his legs drawn up. When George goes to him, calls his name, he is insensible with fear.

He does the only thing he can: lifts him and the bedclothes in an awkward bundle into his arms – the small cargo within the sheets unyielding, rigid – and carries him outside. He is remembering the boy's parents.

'I am carrying you to safety,' he says. 'It isn't a big fire, but we need to make sure that everyone is far away from it.'

Even as he says it he hears the roar of it, and feels the heat lick the back of his neck like the breath of a dragon.

He places the child, in his bedclothes, on the dew-wet grass. 'It will be all right,' he says. 'It will all be all right.' No answer comes. With a sudden thrill of fear he bends close to the covered face. He is breathing: shallowly, very fast. He would like more time to comfort the child, but there may not be enough time for all of it as it is.

One of the yellow fever patients is so deeply in the depths of the fever that he seems not to know what is happening: he asks for an iced water, very politely. George almost envies him his state of ignorance. The patients who are most far gone are the hardest to manoeuvre; they are dead weights, impossibly heavy, limbs lolling unhelpfully from the stretcher. But this is not the first time George and Bill have had to do it; memories surface from the time before. Of course, some of those were, in fact, dead.

They are lacking in the fitness they once had, the endurance born of hard marching, but they remember the right holds, the way to use the weight rather than fight it, the strange staggering dance of the feet over rough ground.

How could he not have foreseen this? That being across the water, in this lonely place, would cut them off absolutely from the help of the fire brigades. No, he knows why. Precisely because he somehow could not have imagined such a thing happening, in an isolated building beside the city's greatest source of water. It flashes across his mind – the strangeness of it. He cannot imagine what could have caused it. But there is no time to think about it, not now. It has reached the ward.

The last patient has been dragged onto the lawn, far enough – for now – from harm. Life has been preserved; this is the most important thing. But the equipment: the precious, carefully guarded supplies of quinine and morphine, these are all now at risk. They must work now to kill the fire, before it can do more damage.

The smoke swallows him, it fills his mouth and nose, steals all the breath from him. He backs away, retching and coughing. It is impossible. But gradually he remembers what he knows of fire. He presses the front of his nightshirt over his mouth, hunkers down upon his hands and knees, and crawls into it, beneath it, like an animal. In the fierce hot dark he gropes for the bottles and vials. Some have broken in the heat already, his fingers find jagged edges. But several are intact, and he thrusts them into the front of his nightshirt. Then there is an explosion right before his face: the violence of it stuns him. The skin of his face and ear feels as though it is consuming itself. He staggers back, hunkered on all fours, gasping with pain. He needs water, but he does not have water. He does not have time to do anything other than attempt to save himself. With a great effort he begins to crawl. His lungs feel as though they have been filled with incandescent coals, and it feels as though someone is forcing the same coals against his cheek and ear. He realises, dimly, that he may not make the distance. Now sensation is fragmenting: he is beginning to be confused, confused by the pain and the smoke as to which direction he should be moving in – it begins to seem that it might as easily be up or down as forward or backward, left or right. In the lucid part of his mind he enumerates his symptoms, almost calmly. The confusion, the agony of his face, the burning airlessness in his chest, the gradual disintegration of his faculties.

The Prisoner

He climbs into the *kayık*, fumbles for the oars. They are
somehow more unwieldy than before – he cannot seem to
make them obey him. He knows what the main obstacle is,
that his hands are trembling almost too much to grip them
properly.

The man saw him. He knows it. Will not do to think
about that. It is done. It cannot be helped, now. Ah – but
what possessed him to turn back? To have thought for a
second that he might be able to reverse the thing he had
done, or try to warn those inside. The shame is not in the
act, he tells himself now, the shame is in that moment of
doubt. It is only a problem if he gets caught. The man has
never seen him before, and if he never sees him again, there
will be no crisis. Stay hidden, out of sight, it will be easy
enough.

He begins to row. Perhaps it is some aspect of the current,
heretofore unknown to him, but there seems to be more
resistance against the bow. The oars make more noise – before
all had seemed silent, effortless. Everything is slower, clumsier.

He reminds himself that it is only a little way. The difficult part of it is done.

He tries not to imagine Nur's face. She will know, as soon as she hears about the fire. His mother and grandmother are too blinded by their love for him to suspect him of any such thing. But Nur is different – her love is exactly the thing that will make her see.

'Who goes there?'

He stops rowing, hunkers low. Goes as still as he is able, though it is impossible to stop himself from trembling. He tries to think himself into the blackness, to dissolve into it, but the surface of his skin seems almost to shimmer with his guilt. Then the wobbling beam of a torch. When he feels the light enter his eyes, he knows that the game is up.

George

Just as he has decided to close his eyes, to rest a while, he feels himself seized, dragged bodily, into cooler air. His face is drenched in water.

Bill hunkers down above him. 'I thought you were a dead man. You bloody fool. You and your quinine. I can tell you now, before you look in a mirror, you've paid quite a price for it.'

For several minutes he lies, half-insensible, before returning to himself. Then he looks up, sees the blaze. The sight terrifies him. There are six of them against this, and he, getting shakily to his feet, is as weak as a cat.

No: there are a few more, the more able-bodied of the patients are offering their help. And then a strange sight. New figures are emerging. Ten perhaps, in total. Some of them women, wearing veils that catch and snicker in the warm air sent up from the flames. Several men, most of them elderly. A few youths – even a couple of children. All carry receptacles.

A line is formed, stretching from the blaze to the Bosphorus.

The containers – saucepans, buckets, even a large coffee pot – travel between them, filled with water. Each individual dousing seems a pitiful effort, doomed to failure. But after the first couple of efforts he does not stop to regard the effect, or even to catch his breath, because the next full bucket is always waiting for him.

He works without thought. Even the agony of his face and lungs is a faintly realised thing. He has become a machine, no, a part of a machine.

At some indiscernible point, the balance shifts. A stemming, a diminishing, has occurred. The fact of it spurs them on. Then comes the moment when he reaches for the bucket, and finds that it isn't there.

'Look.' He turns, finds that it has been Bill beside him all along; he hadn't even realised. 'I think we've done it.'

He does look. The wing of the house is a blackened, sodden mess, as though a giant hand had scooped a great cavity out of the property. The few timbers that remain, forlornly intact, look like the ribs of some giant, charred animal corpse. A desultory steam rises from it. There is a strange illumination now, and he turns and realises that this is because dawn is now upon them: the sky above them looming pink and gold, as though it, now, is aflame. He looks about, to thank their Turkish helpers. He finds that they have all gone, almost as though they never were.

She stares about her, white-faced, at the wreckage of the ward. When she looks at him she glances quickly away again, but then this is hardly a surprise. Half of his face is covered in white gauze, which does not quite conceal all the ragged edges of the burn. Pure acetic acid, that had been kept in a vial beside the quinine, and used for the treatment of infection. It ate into the soft flesh of the cheek, and he will bear the scar of it forever. He was lucky to keep the eye. Finally, his first war wound.

'I am sorry,' he says. 'I forget what it must be to see it like this, your home.'

For several minutes she is silent. She circles the detritus, as one appalled but unable to look away.

'I imagine you will want to take the boy home. As I am sure you are aware, the fire impressed itself upon him deeply. I do not think he is quite himself.'

She had gone to the boy, and held him. No words had been exchanged. There had been such tenderness that he had felt he must look away, even leave the room. It had been a tenderness of a very particular, almost sacred nature. He had thought, before, that it could only be found between a mother and her child.

She looks up back at him with the blank eyes of a sleep-walker. Gradually her gaze seems to find focus. 'All of them survived? Your patients?'

'Yes.'

She seems to sag a little with relief. Her face contorts. She seems to be working herself up to something.

'What is it?'

'The man. The one they found this morning—'

'The arsonist? Yes. They caught him as he was trying to escape, though of course he will no doubt claim otherwise.'

'He is my brother.'

'Your—' He stops, confused. Because he cannot think of anything else he says, 'I thought – forgive me – that your brother was thought dead.'

She opens her mouth as though to speak, and closes it again, as though thinking better of it. Finally, she says, 'We did not know until recently. He was held in a Russian camp. He returned to us several months ago.'

He feels betrayed. All this time, when she has been coming here, she has not trusted him enough to tell him. Then he catches himself. But of course she had not trusted him; how could he have expected more?

Her brother. Thoughts chase themselves around his mind. There is one that is almost too terrible to approach, but it must be said. 'Did you know that he planned to do this?'

At this she steps forward. For a second he actually thinks she might be about to strike him. 'You think I would have known,' she says, caught somewhere between entreaty and outrage, 'and not tried to stop him, or warn you? With the boy there? How could you even ask such a question of me?'

'I do not know.' Everything seems different, now, nothing certain. Because there has been a deception, or at least a concealment. She never spoke of the return of her brother, and suddenly this seems to him like an odd omission.

'You cannot think that of me. I have been afraid of him. Perhaps I should have seen . . . but I could not have imagined this. It is . . . as though we did not get the same person back. The war did something to him. He went to it when he was so young. He had not had the chance to become himself—' She stops, then begins again. 'If my mother lost him again . . . if we lost him again – for her, for all of us, it would be . . .' The language fails her; she seems unable to find a word bleak enough. Her posture is rigid, like a soldier standing to attention. He sees that her eyes are dry. There is something honest and naked in the appeal.

And yet. An incident of this nature only serves to remind one that there are clear sides, that there are still enemies. She is not on the same side as he: does it not stand to reason that she is on the other?

He draws himself up. 'He attempted to burn down a hospital,' he says. 'With twenty-six men in it, most too weak to escape on their own. With a child in it. They could all have died.'

'I know. I cannot believe it. But I do not believe he could have meant it,' she goes on, in a rush, not allowing him time to refute her words. 'I know him. He loves . . . symbols. I think he wanted to do something symbolic. I do not believe he would actually have wanted all of them to die.'

She cannot see it, he thinks. She is blinded by the all-powerful subjectivity of her love. Perhaps she should be allowed to protect this illusion, if nothing else. But he cannot stop himself from saying, 'If it were to be a symbol, why a hospital? Why not a military barracks? Because he was certain of those inside not being able to save themselves? To fight back?'

'Because it was our house. I imagine he thought it was . . . not his right, but something almost like a duty.'

He remembers the figure glimpsed in the furious light cast by the flames, blank-eyed, still as a fox. He meant it.

He summons his resolve. 'I do not think I understand. What exactly is it that you are trying to suggest I do?'

'No one was killed.' Does she really believe that it is this that makes the difference?

'They were not spared on his account. He left it to burn. If he had had his way, every person in that building would have been burned too.'

'I am sure, now – seeing what he could have done – that he feels remorse.'

'How can you be so certain?'

'Because this is not the man he is. He is a good person, a kind man, a schoolteacher' – he scoffs at this – 'and because I know him.'

'Because you know him, or because you cannot see past your love for him?'

'I am asking you to give him a second chance.'

'Even if I wanted to, there is nothing I can do for him now. His fate is not my decision. They have him.' His own use of 'They' gives him pause. It creates a distance – one that seems to him vaguely unpatriotic, and which he is not sure whether or not he intended.

'There will be a trial?'

'Yes.'

'You will be there as a witness.'

He sees now, clearly, what it is that she is asking of him. He had suspected it, but to hear it aloud is another matter. That she has the nerve to suggest it, to him, standing here maimed by her brother's crime, astounds him. And, knowing the little of her that he does, it shows him how desperate she must be.

'You cannot think . . .' he lowers his voice, 'you cannot ask me to lie about what I saw.'

'I am not asking you to lie,' she says, quickly. 'I am asking – I suppose I wanted to know – how certain you can be of what you saw.'

He thinks back to the night. Already it has about it the surreal atmosphere of something dreamed. Or, rather, a story told to him rather than something he experienced firsthand. He finds the figure, within this memory, and he is perhaps the only clear point in it, the one element without blurred edges. And yet there is something uncanny about it, the closer he looks. The pale face, the blank eyes, the animal poise of him. The figure now appears not quite human – too poised, too clear: more like the idea of a perpetrator than anything real. He had seemed almost like part of the fire itself, an agent of chaos. He cannot imagine how an ordinary man, in the light of day, in the banality of a courtroom, will match up to him.

He shakes his head, to clear it. 'I have to be honest about what I saw,' he says. 'Surely you understand that?'

She remains silent, expressionless. Somehow, despite everything, he feels that she has retained the high ground in the exchange.

'You should not have come. You should not have asked this of me.'

He sees movement beneath the mask she has made of her features, some spasm of pain. He sees, briefly, the control she must be exerting upon herself. He closes his mind against the thought.

The Prisoner

He is afraid.

How?

He is afraid of himself.

When he had lit that match it had ceased to become his, like a giant beast escaping the leash. But all of the death, that was his.

He has tried to close his mind to it. But the images come, still, as he lies in his temporary cell. He wakes half-suffocated by the smoke that seeps from his dreams.

He tries to weep. For those who must have been killed. For himself. And for the others, the ones before, the faces that visit him in dreams.

But his eyes are dry. All tears have been scorched from him.

George

The temporary court is convened in an empty school building. The room in which proceedings will take place, presumably, was once where assemblies of the children took place. He thinks, inevitably, of her.

She took the boy that morning. Whatever understanding, whatever tentative accord there has been between the three of them has been severed. It might have always been so, when the boy was no longer his patient, but the fire has made it irrevocable. The building has been very quiet without the child, without her visits, as though something more than what the fire took has been burned away. But in every book upon the shelf, in the coffee pot upon the stove, in the fall of blossoming wisteria which somehow escaped the conflagration – for God's sake, even in his own gramophone – he sees them. He is trying not to consider the fact that he may never see either of them again.

Without looking, he knows when the prisoner has been brought in; a hush falls over the company. Somewhere behind him is the agent of that night of chaos and he is suddenly fearful. Because that figure had not been quite real to him and now he is about to be confronted by what felt to him as much a projection of his own mind, an inner darkness, as a human being. He is passing within a few feet of George now, and George watches his back – surprisingly slender, shoulders narrow as a boy's – as he is led toward the make-shift dock.

George looks at the young man in the dock. It is him, of course. There is no doubt in his mind. And yet at the same time it is not him; the resemblance seems physical only. On the evening of the fire there had been a particular energy and intensity to him. All of this now is gone. He is diminished. He looks extremely young – how old can he be? Twenty at most? His shoulders are thrown back in a posture of defiance, but this somehow draws attention only to their narrowness, makes him look more like a child defying its elders. He refuses to make eye contact with any person in the room, his gaze fixed upon some point on the wall. The makeshift dock is become an island. The condemnation of the courthouse, silent, seems to surround him like a sea.

George reminds himself that this man wanted to kill him; to murder his patients. Pity here would be misplaced. And yet he thinks perhaps he has never seen a less threatening figure.

There is something in the expression that he recognises. He has seen it in the faces of other men. It is born of war. For a medical man it is a frustratingly intangible condition, and yet it is immediately recognisable.

He understands his strengths as a medic well enough; they are the same that revealed themselves at St Bart's some eight years previously. He has a particular talent for identifying the early stages of disease, and even for recognising the subtleties of hybrids, or entirely new pestilences. One might say that it is an art as much as a science: there is a certain amount of intuition required, brave leaps of judgement.

He has never been such a good surgeon: his hands simply do not have the requisite dexterity. One can be taught, to an extent, but there is only so much that practice can achieve. It is equally impossible, as one of his tutors told him, for a poor sculptor to ever become a great one. There is something missing: the evasive magic of talent.

At the front one had to be something of a jack of all trades. One morning might present fifty cases of cholera, or a man losing his lifeblood through the stump of his severed leg. Perhaps a badly infected boil, ready to release its poison into the bloodstream, or a blight of dysentery that could fell a whole squadron. Though at least these afflictions were tangible, visible, and could be treated practically. If one did everything according to an established set of criteria – and the patient was not beyond help – there were fair odds on saving a man. What George found more difficult were the invisible, internal afflictions; those that took up residence in the mind. It did something to all of them, but it did something more to some.

The first time he came across it was in 1915, at the aid post at Anzac. Scores of wounded had been lying upon stretchers awaiting treatment. He had been kneeling in one corner attending to an injured man when a shell had exploded in the midst of the station. Many of those on the stretchers were killed instantly, where they lay. But the man he had been attending had been relatively unharmed, beyond the injuries he had already sustained. And yet . . . George would think later that it was like something had broken inside him, some hidden part of the mechanism. A tiny but essential cog, already loosened, rattled out of place. Everything on the surface remained intact, so that one could not see the fault until the thing tried to work. His mouth had opened and closed as though he were trying to talk, but no sound had come out. There was nothing physically wrong with the throat as far as George could ascertain: only seconds before, the man had been talking.

It had been more unnerving, somehow, than the grisliest injury. George had slapped him, hard, across the cheek in an effort to shock sense into him; it had had no effect. There was no process for such an injury – that was the thing. He had grown frustrated with the man, had shouted at him. 'Don't be a bloody fool, old man. Come on. Talk.' Later he had been given up as a bad job.

Later than that, in a moment of singularly lucid calculation, the chap had put a pistol to his head and blown his brains out.

There is only one symptom, and it is in the eyes. Oh yes, he sees it now.

At first the prisoner is silent, as though stunned – or perhaps it is an attitude of defiance. But beneath the repeated, violent questioning something in him seems to collapse.

Finally, through the translator, he begins to talk. He denies everything. But the fact of his talking is in itself a weakness, a yielding, one step nearer to a confession. The crowd feel this, George senses them scenting blood.

— What had he been doing that evening, at that hour, if not up to no good?

He had been attempting a night-fish, the translator explains for him, with a lantern. He has a household to feed; they must understand.

A pause is left, just long enough for the absurdity of this answer to sink in.

— But of course it would make sense that you should have to go fishing at night. As you are so busy during your days meeting members of the Karakol at the coffeehouse?

— I meet with my friends. Can a man not have friends?

The pugnaciousness only seems to delight his interrogator.

— You must admit that you have an interesting, and rather specific, choice in friends.

It goes on like this, and George feels the sympathies of the room harden further against the defendant. There is something like excitement in it, too, he feels – several times an order for quiet has to be barked. If they had their way he senses there would be jeering, heckling. He wonders what these upstanding gentlemen would say if one told them how much they have in common with a group of Russian peasants observing a bear-baiting.

He can find no entertainment in it. He alone, save perhaps the arsonist himself, knows exactly what is at stake. He only wants it all to be over.

Nur

It would have to be now, of all mornings, that her mother should decide to regain some of her lucidity.

'Where is Kerem?' she asks her daughter, as Nur combs the thin skein of hair before the mirror. 'I wanted him to accompany me for a drive to the city walls.'

Not quite lucid, then, Nur thinks. Enough, though, that Nur has to lie to her, which she had not been prepared for.

'He has gone out early,' she says. 'And he came back late last night – after you were asleep.'

She sees a shiver of suspicion in her mother's gaze, before her eyes lose their clarity.

'Well. We must make sure to have something nice for him to eat when he returns. Tell Fatima to go to Mahmut Paşa.'

Her grandmother is silent, as though the roles have been reversed. She may have heard what was said when the Turkish police came to the apartment and informed Nur – some intimating sympathies with the prisoner – of what had transpired. If not, she suspects something. For the first time, Nur thinks, she looks truly old.

George

'It is not him.'

There is a collective intake of breath. George does not blame them: he is surprised even at himself. He did not know until a second before he spoke that this was going to be his answer.

Until then he had believed exactly what he had told her; that he could not do it, because of all that was at stake.

— I suppose you mean that you do not recognise him.

He can hear the relief. Ah yes. Not the same thing at all as a total rebuttal. It can be overcome.

— Considering the circumstances, the danger in which you found yourself, it is hardly surprising.

The way back is offered up to him. And perhaps he could now retreat, and allow them this possibility. He has not gone so far yet that the decision cannot be reversed. It isn't really a decision after all, when one considers it, only the impulse of a moment. But he knows within his own mind that there is no turning back; it is done now.

'No,' he says, and clears his throat, so that there can be

no mistaking his next words. 'This is not the man I saw that night. I do not recognise him because it was not him.'

There is a long silence.

His questioner goes to speak, makes a small noise like a hiccough, and seems to think better of it.

He does not look once at the man in the dock. He has not done this for him.

That evening he has a visitor.

'You saved him. He told me what you said.'

'I do not want to talk about it.'

This seems to throw her. 'I can understand that,' she says, regaining her poise. 'What you did for him – it was extremely brave.'

'Was it?'

'I believe it to be so.'

'I am not certain that it was, though.'

'What do you mean?'

'I think, in fact, it might have been a kind of cowardice.'

'I do not see how it could have been that.'

'You don't?'

'No.'

'Well. What if I told you that in the end I did not do it because of my sense of good and bad, but for you?'

She does not answer.

He does not know what makes him do it. Perhaps it is the whisky; more of it than he would normally drink, and earlier. It makes things seem possible. He raises his hand – she is only a couple of feet away – and places it against her warm cheek.

She is very still.

Neither of them speak.

Where his fingertips brush her neck he can feel the rhythm of the pulse beneath the skin.

He wants her to look at him.

She clears her throat. She keeps her eyes trained upon some unknown spot on the floor. 'I understand that there is a great debt. First the boy, and now my brother. I see this. I know it. It is not accepted lightly. I understand how much I owe to you. I do not know how I could ever repay you. But I understand that you have been a long time from home. . . without a woman's company.' She swallows. 'If—'

He withdraws his hand as quickly as if she had burned him.

'What are you saying?'

'I – I am not sure.'

'There is no debt.' He wants to take her by the shoulders and say it, but he will not risk touching her again. 'I am not that sort of man. Do you see?'

She is silent.

'Please. Tell me that you understand that.'

She nods. For a long time after she has left he sits as though stunned.

That night he lies awake. For perhaps the first time, he loathes the silence of this place. He would like to be back in Pera, with the clamour of the streets after dark, full of Rabelaisian scenes, comic and sordid and anonymous. Men go to forget themselves in those streets, whether from all that they have seen and known in the last few years, or from responsibilities at home. He has been there, and for both reasons. It would not work now, anyhow. Not unless he got extremely drunk. And he can get drunk here just as well as there. He climbs from his bed, and walks to the study. The treasured bottle of whisky is there upon the desk, as though waiting for him. He holds it up to the light. A third remains. Not quite enough to get so drunk as he would like, but it will do. He would like very much to forget the expression on her face when she had offered herself to him. He would also like to forget the thing he did, when he had no right. Her offer had been repugnant to him in the extreme, but she is not the one to blame for it. In making that gesture, in that moment of gratitude, he had forced it from her.

Nur

On the ferry back to the European shore she sat absolutely still, her gaze unmoving. To the casual observer she would have looked like one stunned by a new grief. It is such a common expression, has been for so many years now, that it is not worthy of special notice. Those passengers embarking and disembarking at the stops before her own stepped over and around her.

Something has broken, and it is her fault. The knowledge of it sits inside her. She cannot quite bring herself to recall the details of the exchange in the study – her mind can only feint toward it, then retreat, scorched. And yet she cannot leave it alone.

The expression he had worn when she had made her offer. The thing that shames her most is not the impropriety of it, though that is bad enough. It is the lack of truth in it. She knows that she would have given herself to him willingly.

Nur

'He has been here every day, Nur *canım*. Asking to speak with you. I cannot imagine what the rest of the building thinks of us. An English soldier. It is not seemly.'

'I know, *Büyükanne*.'

The old woman sits a little straighter in her chair, and fixes Nur with a gimlet eye. 'I never thought that I would say this to you. I disapprove, heartily. But I think you should see him – if only to prevent him from destroying the door downstairs with his knocking. The humiliation of it!'

'I cannot see him.'

'Whatever there has been between you – and I know that it can be nothing, because you are a clever girl, and a widow, and of good family, and my granddaughter, and only imagine the shame of it – I think that you must. You owe it to him. He saved Kerem.'

'I know, but—'

'They are leaving, all of them. The British, the French, the Italians. It was announced this morning. I would not say this to you if it were not the case. But if you do not see him now it will remain with you forever, whatever it is. You will never be free of it. Do you understand?'

Together

She has come to see him. He should have known that it would be thus; on her terms.

There is so much to explain, and so little time in which to do so. The Allied scramble to leave now is something hasty, rather indecorous. They came into this city as conquerors, asserting their right to rule, seizing property, instruments of law, determined to remake it in their image. Now they are party guests fearful of overstaying the welcome of the host.

'When do you leave?'

'In the next couple of weeks. I have to arrange transport for the patients, first, make sure that they are properly accommodated.'

She tries to imagine the journey for the sick men – by rail, perhaps, or in the listing hold of a ship. But the distances of that journey are unfathomable, in her ignorance they dissolve into abstraction. He knows those distances well. He has conquered them – he has travelled their vastness to be here.

Then she realises that she is wrong: that perhaps she does know them. Not in the way he does, not by the memory-ache of muscles, the blistering of tired feet, the blur of landscapes seen and hazily retained. But she does know. Those distances are between them now, encompassed by only three feet of air. The gap in understanding. The spaces, unnavigable, between culture, history, religion, sex.

This, then, was why they can never fully understand one another – the thing that separates them just as efficiently as any geography. Hoping for anything else must be a kind of pitiful vanity.

He will take mementos with him, perhaps, like all the others. Trinkets bought in the Grand Bazaar. A few grainy memories in which the city may remain unchanged, eternal, stamped with permanence, but in which the faces will become blurred by time as the memory fades. Features will dissolve into confusion, and they will mean nothing to him.

George

He steels himself to begin.

'That evening, when you came to me—'

'I do not want to discuss it.' She will not look at him. He can see her thinking: how can he shame her like this? Can he not understand her humiliation?

He has to explain. 'I did not refuse you because I did not want to accept what you offered. It is difficult to express how much I wanted to. But I had a reason. Not just because I did not want you to think that was why I acted as I did in court. And not just because I did not want you to demean yourself – though I think you should know that you could never do that, in my eyes. I think you are, quite simply, a better person than any I have known.'

Such clumsy, faltering words. All of them inadequate. All that he would like to say – and these words are not helping him but thwarting him from truth, sincerity.

The unwieldiness of language. Of all of them, perhaps English is the most unwieldy, the stiffest. No little thanks to the Victorians with their fondness for machines, efficiency.

His tongue, perhaps his whole education, is the product of a mechanical design: a design for conquering, for Empire-building. Over a century it has been tempered, cauterised of finer sentiment.

Perhaps there exists another tongue in which he might express himself better. Ancient Greek: the Greeks with their subtle, unembarrassed understanding of the ways of the heart. But he must make use of the poor tools at his disposal.

'I refused because I have not been honest with you, because there is so much that I have not told. I have been a coward. I am not quite sure how to begin.'

Before he can, there is a knock upon the door. Sister Agnes, or Bill, perhaps. For the coward in him it is something of a relief – a little more time in which to think of how to do it.

'Have you heard the news, old fellow?' It is Calvert. His relief at the interruption ebbs from him.

'Just a moment, Lieutenant, if you wouldn't mind.'

He knows in an instant that it is the wrong thing to have done, pulling rank. Calvert's face goes very taut. The tell-tale colour appears upon his cheekbones.

'The thing is, *Captain*, it's rather important. I was asked specifically to come and inform you.'

He turns to Nur. With his look, he tries to say, *I'm sorry.* She gives a small nod.

He turns back to Calvert. 'What is it?'

Calvert looks scandalised. 'I cannot say it in front of this woman.'

'Ah, but I'm sure that you can. I have no concern whatsoever that we are to be betrayed. Either that, you see, or it will have to wait.' He is almost enjoying himself now, common sense be damned. He cannot understand why he ever tolerated Calvert's company, even allowing for the fact that at such a time as this beggars cannot be choosers.

'So be it,' Calvert says. 'I suppose it doesn't signify greatly now, anyway.' He rocks a little upon his heels. And George feels a sudden trepidation. 'Well. Our regiment's got its marching orders – *finally*, considering some of the chaps went home weeks ago. Time to go home, old chap. Back to our loved ones.' He leaves a delicate pause, just long enough for George to hear the sound of impending disaster. 'Back to our wives.'

Of course, it is not the thing he says so much as the way he says it. George sits, stunned, feeling the fact of it pass over him. He looks toward Nur and sees that she knows it too.

Then

He had two weeks' leave. London was at once miraculously the same and irrevocably changed – the latter, perhaps, because of the change in him. Norton, one of his fellow medical officers, had invited him to a supper in Bloomsbury. It was a revelation. People like this had existed before the war, no doubt, but he had never encountered them then. The women in particular seemed to have come from another planet; the future. They wore clothes that looked foreign – loose, printed fabrics, silk headscarves, gold jewellery that defied any preconceived notions of taste. A couple of the men were conscientious objectors. They gently ribbed Norton, who was their friend, for his 'damned patriotism', and spoke of the struggle between classes rather than states. George tried very hard not to appear surprised or offended by any of this. He realised that he had already grown used to the idea of himself as a hero. In the streets he had felt the silent approbation of passersby. Here he felt like a curiosity, rather quaint, even a freak.

He drank more than he ought to have done – it was

difficult not to, after the months of relative abstinence – and more than he really wanted to, considering the only drink on offer seemed to be sweet vermouth.

He tried to remind himself that these characters, here, were the exception. He went out onto the small, wrought-iron balcony that looked out over a square of green, diminishing in the dusk to blue.

'A pipe? How quaint. My father smokes one.'

He turned toward the drawl, and felt something inside him give. 'Excuse me, madam, but what would you prefer I smoke? An opium pipe might be more to your taste?'

'Goodness.' She took a step back. He had seen her inside, holding forth. He saw now that she had a curiously compelling face. The nose a little too long. It lent her a rather aristocratic appearance. Her lips were full, almost bruised-looking. It was the sort of face at which the longer one looks, the longer one needs to look.

'My apologies,' she said, silkily. 'But one has to find an opener, you understand. You looked so stern, scowling out at the world. I had to find a way in.'

Her name was Grace – it didn't quite fit her. There was something too compliant, too soft. She lived a *bohemian* life, she told him, proudly, but as she spoke it became clear that her lifestyle, with its freedoms, came from privilege – not the sort of want that one might associate with the word. On closer enquiry a great deal about her seemed similarly counterfeit. Yet where this might have, should have, been a deterrent, he only found her the more intriguing for it.

'It is so seldom,' she told him, 'that one meets a man of good heart, and conscience. One who does what he does out of a real conviction of doing good. So many of them just want to play the warrior, to beat the drum.'

He had felt the words like a kiss.

'And the conchies here . . . I'm not so sure that they are any better. One shouldn't say that of one's friends, of course, but one can love a friend dearly and also understand that he is a frightful coward. Goodness,' she put a small white hand – wink of gems – to her mouth. 'I have become a little too honest. I think that vermouth must be cut with gin.'

She had put a hand on his forearm. It felt like another kiss. More.

A little while later she had stretched herself against a chair like a cat, arms above her head, and he could not help but notice the free movement of the uncorseted breasts beneath the silky stuff of her dress. Everything became very simple. He wanted to take her to bed very much – perhaps never had he felt so strong and uncomplicated a desire in his life. And she seemed to feel the same.

She had made it as plain as could be that she wanted him, too. She had an apartment in town, she told him: her father had bought it for her.

He had vaguely seen Rawlings raise his eyebrows as they left, but had felt no shame. He, too, had become a being driven by self-interest: specifically his desire.

The apartment was a reflection of her person: she had been unable to disguise the fabulous privilege that under-pinned it with any trappings of bohemianism.

He could hardly hold himself back; he knew from the beginning that it would be a struggle of will. She tasted of cigarettes and vermouth and rouge. Her mouth became a smear of plum-purple. In the crook of her neck, perfume and sweat. She bit his shoulder, her sharp nails found the skin of his back.

Afterward, she laughed. His head hurt with the force of it: he felt as though he had smoked from an opium pipe. Within a couple of hours he had become obsessed with her.

In the morning, as they lay in her great white bed, he had said: 'I think we should get married.'

She had laughed at him, climbed out of his embrace, and gone to the washstand by the window where she cleansed herself with a sponge – nude, unselfconscious, quite possibly visible from the building opposite or from the street.

'Darling,' she said. 'You cannot ask someone to marry you before breakfast. Besides that, it is ridiculous. I am far too good for you.'

'I think I might be in love with her.'

Norton had laughed. 'Not with that one, I hope, for your sake. She's as mad as a March hare.'

'I can't stop thinking about her.'

'It's been three days, my friend. There are other sorts of fascination, you know.'

'I asked her to marry me.'

Norton spat out a mouthful of beer. 'She didn't say yes?'

'No.'

'Well, thank goodness for that. Thank goodness one of you has some sense.' He seemed genuinely frustrated, even angry. 'Go and visit a whore, for God's sake, like a normal man. I had you down as an intelligent sort, someone who knows what's what. I hope for your sake that she does the decent thing and continues to refuse you.'

He looks across at Nur. How can he begin to explain any of it to her? Her face is turned from him; he is powerless in the face of her coolness, her performance of indifference. Because it must be a performance, mustn't it? He knows that he has no right to want it, but he wants her to care.

He could kill Calvert – he really feels it – in this moment. His hatred for the man is enough that he could do it and not care, would feel only the satisfaction of the act.

It would change nothing. Whatever blame can be laid at the other man's feet it is only the revelation of the fault, the greater guilt that is his. Now, looking at how he has behaved he is repelled, as he would be by the actions of another man, a stranger. He has always had an idea of himself as somehow inherently good. But if one is to judge the man by the deeds, he does not come out well in this. He wonders now quite how it all came about, almost as though he is not the one who has lived it, who has acted and chosen, and concealed. If he were inclined to pardon himself – which he is not – it might be seen as a series of accidents.

He had spent most of his next leave in Scotland and came to London for the final part, staying in a small hotel in Pimlico. A couple of days spent exploring his old haunts, amazed that both he and the world were so different while they had remained unchanged. There had been a card for him at the hotel when he returned. As soon as he picked up the envelope he had a premonition that it was from her; the flamboyance of the hand, perhaps.

Darling G. Something has come up. We must meet. Take me for supper?

When she arrived she looked better than ever. The new fullness suited her, he thought, especially as a contrast to these pinched times. It was as though she were immune to the war, as though it had been unable to touch her. Irritated though he was with her, her power over him seemed undiminished.

She had two glasses of champagne, and came to the point. 'Do you know, I rather think we should get married, after all.'

He almost choked on his glass of beer. He assumed she

was having her little joke with him – he smiled to show that he wasn't a fool. But she did not return the smile.

'After our *affaire*,' she managed to pronounce it with the French inflection, which somehow made it a thing of romance and tragedy, 'I realised I was in a spot of trouble. I did not want to bother you about it, until I could discover whether or not certain measures had been successful.' She indicated the new fullness of her figure. 'I think perhaps I do not need to say more. No doubt you guessed at my condition as soon as I entered the room, and you saw how fat I have become.'

'No,' George said, and heard the strangeness in his voice. 'No, I did not.'

They were married in a matter of days, with only a friend of hers as a witness, who seemed to look at him with a mixture of humour, contempt and pity. But it wasn't terrible, he reasoned. True, they did not know one another well. He could not be absolutely certain that they would like one another better if they knew one another more. But he did admire her. And there was the – for want of a better word – sexual bond between them. There were marriages agreed on less. Besides, he might be killed at the front. In which case it could not matter greatly anyway.

In the two weeks before he was posted home for good she lost the child. He returned to find a woman who bore no resemblance to the one he had married. She was desperate with grief, transformed by it. He saw suddenly someone who was not all poise and seduction, someone who needed love.

He was extremely sorry for her, and for himself – though he had not even been sure before that he welcomed the news of the child, the responsibility that would be his when he returned home. As a man of medicine he was able to understand the critical changes that had taken place, how they had caused her to lose the child and why it was that she would most likely never conceive again. What all of his learning could not teach him was how he might help her. He tried taking her out to dinner, to the theatre, to a holiday beside the sea. He tried merely sitting with her, talking to her. But none of it seemed to have any effect. She was unreachable; catatonic with her loss. Something in her had been broken, but it was beyond his reach – beyond the understanding of his science. He saw as never before how little they knew one another; that really, despite the intimacy they had shared and the vows they had made, they were complete strangers. He became almost obsessed by the idea that if he only knew her better, he might have held the key to her recovery. And then there was his suspicion that what she really needed was love; and this was the one thing he was fairly certain he could not give her.

Then her parents visited, and insisted that she came to live with them for a time; he did not object. There had been 'problems' before, he understood from them; episodes of hysteria in her youth. They had not wanted to worry him before now. He did not object, either, when they suggested that she might be better looked after in one of the kinder institutions available for women like her, who had apparently gone beyond the reach of their family.

When he learned a week later of an opportunity back in the Near East, a hospital in the newly occupied Ottoman city, he approximately convinced himself that it was his duty to go.

So he volunteered, yes: but could anyone say that his presence here has not been valuable, even essential?

No one questioned his motives for return, that was the thing. No one knew of it, here – save for a discreet few.

So here he has been seen as a good man, even a heroic man. Never a coward, or a scoundrel. Only he has known the truth.

Nur

Nur looks down the Bosphorus toward the Black Sea, from which an early autumn mist is approaching, thick as smoke.

He has turned to her; she can see the pale shape of his face at the edge of her vision. She thinks there might be something pleading in his expression.

Finally, with some effort, she turns, rising to an awareness of the sound of his voice like a swimmer surfacing from underwater.

'It does not matter,' she says. There is a coldness in her head, it has entered her words. She knows what it is: it is an anaesthetic, against the pain. She is grateful for it. It allows her to speak in a tone of someone discussing some regrettable – but slight – *faux pas*. 'There has been nothing to be ashamed of.'

She will not think of the warmth of a palm against her cheek. Of the contract of it, the promise in flesh.

'Nur,' he says, 'I have to explain.'

George

'I do not love her.'

'You married her.'

'Yes. But—'

'You made a promise to her.'

'Yes—'

'Then you must go back.'

He realises what this is, with a new, terrifying clarity. This is the moment upon which a whole life turns. He will return to it, time and again, over the years. It will be with him until the end of his days. He must get it right. He has a vision of himself as a drowning man with his hands tied, unable to save himself.

'"I mistook it – with Grace, for something else . . . something more. I did not have this to compare it with.'

She says nothing.

'There is something, isn't there? Tell me that you know there is something.' And by something, of course, he means: everything.

What *would* he say to her if he could throw off the strictures and conditioning of a lifetime?

He would say so much. He would say just this: love.

She does not agree, or refute it. Now there is only a kind of pity in her expression: for him, for herself.

'This has not been real,' she says. 'None of this. It is that which has made it seem possible, if only for a short time. Even before you told me, I knew it. It is absurd to pretend otherwise.'

'I do not believe that.'

It is true that he has thought of this place as an escape. His time here has existed in provisional, fantastic space – cloaked in a semblance of duty but free from real responsibility. It has been circumscribed by the knowledge of the inevitable return. But what he feels for her might be the only real thing he has felt in his life.

'We could not live here: I could not live with the shame. You would never be accepted. We could not live in your country, because I cannot leave.'

'We would find some way.'

'Your guilt would be with you, always. And my shame. I do not know much of your country, but I know enough to be certain that people would not forgive you for what you had done. I do not think you could forgive yourself. It is important for you to know that you are a good man.'

'Not as important as other things.'

'You would become a monster. To others, but more importantly to yourself.' The force of her logic is suffocating, devastating. She is not finished. 'We would come to hate each other.'

His vision is blurred. 'I will come back.'

'Do not say that.'

'Why not?'

'Do not say it, unless you can mean it. I do not think you can. There has been nothing between us of which we should be ashamed. You can go freely, without guilt. You have made no promise to me. So do not do so now.'

'I mean it. I say it, because I mean it.'

He takes her hand; she does not resist. With one finger he traces a semi-circle in the soft skin on the inside of her wrist.

'I will come back.'

The Prisoner

Mustafa Kemal and his army are coming for the city, a nation's pride will be restored, a new state born from the ashes of the old. The Eyüp coffeehouse plotters will have their triumph over the occupiers. The occupation – a broken promise, a humiliation – will come to an end.

Despite everything, he has his freedom. But he is still a prisoner. He is not really here, in this city, nor in the prison camp in Egypt. He is back in the desert, seeing the faces that haunt his sleep every night. He has returned to hell. In truth, he has never really left.

He finishes his letter. It is short, but it has taken him most of the night. The apartment is quiet, sleeping.

He leaves it tucked beneath her latest work of embroidery. She will find it: but not too soon. He has not attempted to acquit himself. He has merely tried to get it all down, everything, even those things that should be too horrible to put into words. She has to know the extent of it; the danger. The things that he has done with his own hand – worse even than the fire. He wrote of the things that have happened to innocent, simple, country-living people. To children. In the name of a state growing strong.

This will not end because the war has ended. This is something older and deeper than that. There are those – I have spoken with them, called them my friends – who believe that if we are to move forward, to discover a new identity for ourselves, we must get rid of the elements that make us weak. Sameness is seen as strength: a unity of culture, belief, ethnicity. Anything that goes against sameness, therefore, is a threat.

He briefly considered telling her all of it, in person. He imagined asking for her forgiveness. Then he realised that whether she could give it or not was immaterial because he cannot forgive himself.

But perhaps there will be some venture toward understanding. Some comprehension of what a young man – not really a soldier at all . . . a schoolteacher – might, in the name of his state, in the name of honour and glory and victory and strength, be asked to do. How much he might be asked to give: an ever-increasing tally that ended with his humanity. Perhaps she will see that everything that has happened since has in some sense been an inevitable consequence of that.

It is also – thinking of the boy now – a warning.

You must find some way to make him safe – from people like me.

A quiet crossing, very early morning. There are no passengers upon the ferry to witness the strange sight of a young man clambering from the deck and lowering himself into the Sea of Marmara – entering the water with hardly a splash. To watch him striking out purposefully toward the island where the dogs had been banished, long ago, because the city no longer had any place for them.

The *çay* seller wonders, briefly, what has happened to the fare he was sure had embarked for Tophane and for whom he has now come looking, optimistically bearing his samovar, his tea glasses. The ticket collector wonders it too, but later, only when they have made a full circuit of the various stops and no one has disembarked. But by then there are new passengers climbing aboard, noise and chaos, change to be found and small children to be avoided on the perilous gangplank. And besides, it was very early – he rubs the sleep from his eyes – so he might have imagined it after all. He also considers the rather unsettling possibility that it could have been the brief corporeal appearance of a *djinn*, a bad spirit. He isn't a superstitious man, but stranger things have been known to occur in a city as old as this.

So there is no one to witness the final voyage of the young man, striking out manfully at first toward the distant islands (an impossible distance, even for a good swimmer). And then the pace beginning to slacken as his limbs grow tired, his head held a little lower in the water. The movements growing slower . . . slower, almost as though the swimmer has given up, as though it has all been planned, as though he had known he would never reach his destination. And unseen: the great, powerful current readying itself to sweep the body out to sea.

No one to witness that involuntary struggle for air, the brief violence of it. Before the struggle subsides and the lungs are flooded and the eyes close and peace comes, perhaps, at long last.

The Traveller

After days of travelling – after interminable hours of unvarying countryside, of tedium and pains and longings for the journey to end, and fearing the end – the city itself comes as a surprise. I am not ready for it. I do not think I would have come back, of my own choosing. But I made a promise. We come first to the Sea of Marmara. Great rusty-hulled freighters in primary colours, either stilled at anchor or too huge and lumbering for one to see their movement. Shoals of smaller craft, sails scimitar-sharp. The light reflecting off the water is too bright – I have to turn away from it every few seconds. But then back to looking, waiting for the first glimpse, blind spots dancing in my vision.

In this sea are the islands. There, somewhere, is the beach from which the sand came. And which I will not visit, I think, for fear of it having been discovered, peopled, littered, transfigured.

Perhaps he would have gone back.

But I am not him. The Scottish doctor who was so unlike

me, who no one would ever have mistaken for my father, yet who I learned to love like one.

Nur

In the weeks following the departure of the enemy, the liberation of the city, she has a great deal of time for thought.

There are celebrations. The city is liberated. A new, modern state will be born from the ruins of the old.

But she is not thinking of this.

She is not thinking of the other thing, either. She has known loss before. She understands the way in which it will work. It will be absorbed into the self, it will become a part of the self. A change will occur; mysterious, intangible, but definite. The person will be altered forever by it. But she will not think of that yet.

She is thinking of her brother's letter. The evil of the deeds described there. Perhaps she would not have believed in it, not really, until then.

She would have ignored them, those other clues: Hüseyin's warning, the sight George described in the desert, the children who disappeared from her classroom. Two fires. What was it that Hüseyin had said? That one could be too close to the thing to see it clearly. The idea – that she might have simply continued to overlook these signs, these portents – frightens her.

But reading Kerem's confession, written by a man who had no reason to lie, destroyed by what he had done, she finally understands. She sees the full horror of it; she sees the danger. She sees that she does not have a choice.

Her skills as a correspondent do not match her abilities as a conversationalist. This is not the chief issue. There is also the fact that there is a great deal that cannot be said. They must be consigned to the realm of the impossible.

There is also the fact that her hand is shaking so violently that she cannot seem to make her fingers grip the pen properly. At times she has to press so hard, to control the shaking, that the pen makes small rips in the paper.

A first attempt has to be sacrificed, because the ink has run so badly it can no longer be read. The second time, she remembers to press her veil to her face so that she can protect the paper from her grief.

She finishes thus: *I understand that this is a very great and difficult thing I ask of you. I would not ask it unless I believed it to be absolutely necessary. I would not want to ask it. I do so in the knowledge of my own very great personal loss.*

She looks at this last sentence. Thankfully, it begins a new page. She discards it, and begins afresh. *I understand that it is undoubtedly impossible. Nevertheless, I await your reply.*

She signs her name.

This is how one story ends. But where another, possibly, begins.

The Traveller

We are nearing Sirkeci station.

I remember a small boy. The snow falling, transforming the city into the most beautiful, least real, version of itself. The echoing space of the terminus, others milling about, buying tickets. They walk to a small kiosk with a couple of tables, the two of them. A small, domestic scene.

They might have been mistaken for mother and son.

Beyond the station entrance the snow continues to fall. Blanketing the city, perfecting it. This is how it appears to a small boy who presses his hot face against the glass as the train departs the station. Already like somewhere not quite real. A place from a dream.

I open the old suitcase. It was old, this case, back then – when a small boy carried it beneath his arm, its weight unbalancing his stride.

I find the book, draw it out. It is so fragile that I have had to encase it between two wooden boards. The spine is broken so that some of the pages, of their own accord, would otherwise attempt to come loose.

It is of vital importance to my understanding of myself, and of my past. The contents have been my holy book, my way of belonging. And yet, though I have looked at it often, I have no real need to read the words upon the page. Since I was a very tiny boy I have had all of them committed to memory.

Every single dish at my restaurant has its origins in these pages. It felt absolutely necessary that this was the case.

Aubergine, rendered into smoke-flavoured velvet, studded with bright seeds of pomegranate.

Courgette flowers, evanescently light, with white cheese and honey.

A salad of chopped herbs, lemon, oil, which is the precise taste of the colour green.

Pastry so fine it melts into nothing upon the tongue, leaving a delicate sheen of butter and sugar upon the fingers.

'Grandmama's stuffed cabbages'.

Chicken simmered with molten, dissolving figs.

My restaurant is called Stambol. Because that is what we called it, those of us who lived there, those of us to whom it belonged, who belonged to it. Constantinople was for the enemy, who could only understand it by the name that had been given to it by another Western conquerer.

Sometimes I feel a fraud. I am considered, through Stambol, to be a kind of expert on a place: or at least one specific element of its culture. The truth is that the version of the place as I knew it is now long out of date, a version preserved as though within a glass dome – utterly false. I am about to be confronted with the reality of this.

Food, for me, has always been a way of belonging. I know

that this was what I was really trying to do when I opened the restaurant. It was more than the indulgence of passion and ambition, it was the creation of a place and time, somewhere in which I had once belonged. A resurrection. One critic wrote that he had travelled via the senses to somewhere he had never visited in life. 'Each forkful,' he wrote, 'transported me, bodily, to a place of warmth and light, history and colour.' This was a coup, especially from a man who tends to prefer starched tablecloths and French precision. But I was envious of him, too. Because try as I might – the most faithful interpretations, the most authentic, best-quality ingredients – I could never quite seem to make that journey myself.

A very *English* school. The dismay of greyish meat, boiled to stubborn tastelessness; khaki-coloured vegetables spouting lukewarm water. A lumpish beige-coloured rice pudding with an optimistic exclamation of raspberry jam. What I wouldn't have done then for a little bag filled with spices and salt; a concoction that made anything palatable. This sorry fare tasted as bad as a clod of earth taken from the rain-sluiced sports field beyond the refectory window. But when you have known hunger – not the schoolboy meaning of 'starving' but the real thing – you do not refuse a single bite of anything. And there was also one small, embarrassing hope. Perhaps if I ate this food for long enough I would become like the other boys around me. My difference from them would be less visible.

But I could remember fresh almonds piled atop a cake of ice, the white flesh creamy and sweet. Figs, eaten straight from the trees, the nectar beading through the skin and sticky against the palms.

This book arrived on my eighteenth birthday. I told him I did not want it: that life, the old country, was part of the past now, a past from which I wanted to separate myself.

'I understand your anger, but it is ill-placed. It was never her fault.'

'She gave me up.'

'She believed that she was saving your life. She may well have done so, for all we know.' He smiled, then. 'And her loss was my gain.'

'She did not love me enough.'

'She loved you too much.'

I must have looked unconvinced by this argument. He went away, and returned with a sheaf of old newspapers. 'Part of me wishes that you never had to read these,' he said. 'But if it helps you to understand, then I think it may be necessary.'

I could not see how some miserable articles could help me do this. But then I began to read. About the Armenians: my people, though I had never thought of them as such. I learned of women and children forced to leave their homes carrying their worldly goods upon their backs to walk across a desert on their bare feet. I learned of villages and neighbourhoods set alight. Of unimaginable sights. A hillside of discarded, broken bodies, denuded and pitiful. Bloated corpses in a stream. Thousands of bones discovered beneath a thin layer of sand. I learned of the attempted annihilation of a people, a way of life: what had once been my people, my way of life. I learned that the little boy found in a burned building, who travelled alone across the entire breadth of Europe in a railway carriage – from one who loved him, to another who would love him – was one of the luckiest ones.

And he showed me a letter. I recognised the hand, because it was like my own. Its sender, after all, was the one who taught me to write in the first place.

I looked at him.

'I show you all of this,' he said, 'not to cause more anger, or upset. It is because I want you to see that there were many sides in that war: not just two. There were elements that cannot be understood or explained even now, even knowing that in war terrible things happen, that people act in ways that cannot be understood.

'She did it because she loved you. Can you see it now? If she had loved you a little less, and herself a little more, she would not have let you go.'

At the time, I was too caught up in my own distress and confusion – and also far too young – to consider what it must have been like for him. To get that letter, with its entreaty. To have to decide how he would answer it, this plea from the woman who had been so much to him. It must have changed his life. He was still a fairly young man, with a sick wife and now a small, traumatised boy to look after.

The loss was something he wore upon his person. Even if you had not known his story, I think, you would have seen it on him. You would have thought: here is a man grieving for something. But then of course in those days, that was nothing out of the ordinary. Everyone was grieving for something.

I could at least see that he was a different man to the one I had known in the old place. There he had been more vivid: ruddied by the sun, full of humour. The man who met me on the platform seemed diminished. I assumed this was England at first. I felt myself shrinking as I got off that train and stepped into the yawning greyness of that vast old English station, the grey English day beyond, the cold tight about me as though it were trying to press me into the shape of its choosing. But I don't think it was that, looking back. It wasn't because of what he had returned to. It was because of all that he had left behind.

415

Later, something else would occur to me. If it were not for me, the promise he made to keep me safe, he might yet have gone back to her.

I have wandered the streets of this city so many times in my mind that it is hard to believe they are quite real, that this is not all merely the work of my imagination. But there are changes: cars, more people . . . more speed. In the distance a bristle of skyscrapers that dwarf the minarets of the Blue Mosque, and yet are somehow held in thrall by it. The future still has a long way to go here to match up with the past.

Halfway across the wide and tranquil channel of water, on the juddering passenger ferry, I realise that my hand has found the tobacco tin within my bag and is holding it tight. It provides a strange comfort.

I see, with a shock, a dark-haired woman on the terrace: a young woman, reading. I feel a powerful sense of trespass. As I approach, picking my way along the path that leads to the front of the house, I see her look up, put away her book, stand up.

I tell her who I am looking for. The old language is sticky and unwieldy in my mouth. My adopted tongue has almost suffocated it. But she seems to understand.

'She's inside.'

'Oh.' I feel a thrill of something almost like fear. 'You are her daughter?'

She laughs. 'Hopefully I do not seem quite that old.'

I realise my mistake. She can only be thirty years old. But for the first time I realise, really understand, what this means. The person I have really been expecting to see is the woman I remember, exactly as I last saw her, who would have been a similar age, I suppose, to this stranger.

'I was a pupil of hers,' she says. 'A long time ago. Now I work as a translator, for a publisher here. But when I heard that she was ill I came to look after her. I owe her a great deal.'

'So was I: a pupil. Even longer ago. I think I may owe her even more.'

She gives me a long, appraising look. 'I think I know who you are.'

We step inside. My first thought is that it is smaller than I remembered. Not a palace, after all. It seems very empty, too: the long room that had once been filled with beds, prone forms, the bustle of nurses. But this is a house in which memory is. In which they – all of them, all who have been here – seem only to be in the next room. Not ghosts so much as echoes, ancient reverberations of the stone.

'I should warn you. She is no longer quite herself.'

The room is the one in which he lay for all those months: that boy who both is and isn't myself. One of the smallest in this large house, perhaps, but with the best view of the Bosphorus.

The figure upon the divan is unrecognisable to me. I do not know what I had expected: the same eyes, perhaps, or the same quick, clever hands – even if the rest had changed. But the eyes are closed, and the hands folded upon the bedspread are unfathomably aged, clawed and spotted. I could far more easily believe that this is the old woman I knew all those years ago. So grand and proud, who terrified me into ruining a dish of stuffed cabbages; such a memory haunts a chef forever. But logic tells me that of course she is long departed. These, then, are the changes that time has wrought. I should not be surprised. For what resemblance do I bear, plump and grey, slightly balding, to the small quick boy who lay here not so long ago?

I know that it is her; that must be enough. But she looks so still: a saint upon a bier. I have to watch, carefully, for the gentle rise and fall of the sheet.

If I had only come a little earlier . . .

But it would never have happened. I would never have done so of my own accord. It had to be him; with his undeniable request. His command. And there is no purpose in dwelling upon such things. Life is not symmetry, or pattern, however much we try to see these within it, in the stories we tell of it. It is ragged, misshapen, endlessly frustrating. But perhaps there is beauty in that too.

They loved me. This I know.

I reach for her hand, then pause. I feel an imposter, an uninvited guest. But then these are the hands that I reached for stumbling along cobbled streets, that felt for the fever upon my brow, that smoothed a sheet, that rumpled hair. That carried me from a burned house, into a new life.

I take her hand.

It is surprisingly warm, though I cannot tell if this is the blood beneath the skin, or simply borrowed from the diamond of winter sunlight that has fallen from the open window. Just through the window I see the pomegranate tree. It is bare-boughed, dead-looking. But I know this winter deception. In spring miniature brown-green leaves will appear from the dry branches, as startling as if they had grown from stone. Then the fruits: small as an English rosehip first, then green as apples. Finally, they will burgeon into ripe red globes, fall to the ground with a muted explosion that no one hears. Except, perhaps, the birds. Then it will seem that all the birds in the city – indeed, the whole of Turkey – have gathered here to feast. The garden will become a carnival of sound, a chaos of wings.

There is a kind of sanctity in the silence in the room that

I am fearful to shatter. Then from the water comes the loud, rude sound of a ship's horn, shattering it. It is like the starting klaxon: the permission that I have unknowingly sought.

I tell her of the boy's journey. The train, the strangers, the mountains. The terrifying crossing of the grey sea. The arrival in the great old English city. The enemy city: now home. The man waiting to greet him. Smaller, somehow, without his military khaki. I tell her of the school in the English country-side – the teachers who could have learned from her. I tell her of the restaurant. I do not tell her of the woman, the invalid wife, who even a small boy could see had something broken inside her.

I cannot tell whether I cause pleasure, or pain, or indeed whether I am heard at all.

'I understand,' I say, 'what you did.'

I look out again, through the trees toward the water, a silver irradiation.

What can never be known for certain is how much danger I would have been in if I had stayed. By most accounts, the genocide – the name they found for it – ended around the time the new state rose from the ashes of the Empire. I might have been one of the lucky few. But that was not a risk, in her love for me, that she was willing to take.

Nearer at hand a flock of tiny birds moves as one, like blown leaves. I wonder what it is I am trying to gain from this. I feel a movement, faint but unmistakable, beneath my fingers. And one of the small, gnarled hands – lifted slowly, as though it is a very great weight – comes to rest over my own. The warmth is from the skin, after all.

I have come back here for him, at his behest. He left no room for dissent. He knew that if he did not ask me to make this journey, did not make it impossible for me to refuse, I would not have had the courage on my own.

I want to tell her about him. I want to tell her about the relics, the things he kept from that time: our shared inheritance. The hours he would spend in his study in silent contemplation of that photograph, this house, with the attitude of a man at prayer. But I do not want to cause her pain.

'Nur,' I say, instead: her name at once foreign and familiar. 'I have brought him back.'

I leave her, now. I step through the doors that lead outside, I step down onto the stone jetty. I take the painted tin from my pocket.

It had to be love.

A man, and especially a man like him, the man who became my father, does not ask for his final remains to be delivered to a place he knew so long ago upon the basis of a whim, a fond memory.

I raise my hand. The Bosphorus waits beneath me. Patient, eternal, curious. It has come from the Black Sea. It will find its way, now, out to the Sea of Marmara, to those mysterious islands where once he swam in water clear as air.

I let go.

A Note on Names

If you know a little about Istanbul's history, you might be aware that at the time of this novel's setting, the city was, in Western European parlance and in *some* official Ottoman usage, known as Constantinople. You'll see the British characters in the book refer to it as such. Istanbul was its official designation after the foundation of the Republic of Turkey in 1923, and other countries were exhorted to refer to it as such. The name, however, was not by any means new. It had been used in common parlance before and during the Ottoman Empire. In fact, etymologically, the name 'İstanbul' can be translated to literally mean 'the city' or 'in the city' from the Greek phrase, στην Πόλη.

This perhaps gives you an idea of its huge importance as a metropolis throughout the ages: it was *the* city – no need to refer to it as anything else! Nur and her family would almost undoubtedly have referred to it as İstanbul.

Acknowledgements

Thank you to editor extraordinaire Kim Young, Charlotte Brabbin, Ann Bissell, Hannah O'Brien, Isabel Coburn, Emma Pickard, Rebecca McNamara, Rhian McKay, Charlotte Webb, Niccolò de Bianchi and the wider team at HarperCollins for the great passion and skill you have shown in the publication of all my books. An exciting few years await!

To Cath Summerhayes, my fabulous agent (and Cath's wonderful mum – one of this book's first readers!), Katie McGowan, Irene Magrelli and all at Curtis Brown.

To my darling mum, for accompanying me on my research trip, clambering through ruined buildings with me in forty-degree heat and drinking cocktails on a rooftop above the city into the small hours!

To my beloved dad, who read this book very early on and proclaimed it his favourite yet!

To my family and friends, for your incredible ongoing support – for buying copies, reading them (!) and sharing the love.

To the Imperial War Museum, for its excellent archives,

wherein I discovered diaries and letters from men billeted to the city during the occupation and glimpsed the human stories behind official accounts.

To Gül Hürgel, for showing me *your* Istanbul – including a magical nighttime picnic in Maçka Park!